SUFFRAGETTE

THE GUARDIANS OF TIME • BOOK FOUR

SUFFRAGETTE

THE GUARDIANS OF TIME ⊙ BOOK FOUR

VIVIENNE LEE FRASER

www.viviennelfraser.com.au

Vivienne Lee Fraser
www.viviennelfraser.com.au

Cataloguing-in-Publication details are available
from the National Library of Australia
www.trove.nla.gov.au
ISBN: 978-0-6455157-6-3

Formatting and cover design by KILA Designs
www.kiladesigns.com.au

For the Williamson women in my life. It has been a privilege to be related to so many strong, independent, powerful women—aroha nui.

A special shout out to my sister, Lauretta. This was a four book series until you said I couldn't finish there. Your voice kept popping into my head as I wrote. Hope you can see how much you influenced this story.

PROLOGUE
TIME FIXER HEADQUARTERS
– JUST TO THE LEFT OF TIME

Sunlight falls across the bed. Beta squeezes his eyes closed, trying to block it out, but finally the light forces his eyes open. Drowsily rolling away from the offending brightness, he snuggles into Cynthia's sleeping form. His lips curl into a smile. He had forgotten what a pleasure it was inhabiting a body, but over the past week, Cynthia had made it her mission to help him remember.

As if sensing his gaze, Cynthia's lids flicker open, and she smiles sleepily. 'Harold, how come you're awake so early?'

'I guess it's this new body. I was a Time Guardian for so long, and without a corporeal form, we didn't sleep. Now I'm out of the habit.' He sighs. 'Besides, I'm so used

1

to Sigma contacting me at odd hours, I expect him to call at any moment.'

'After having been lauded by the Time Guardians and Time Fixers for preventing the end of the world, isn't he taking a well-earned sabbatical?'

'He is, and I fear it might be a long one. That last mission.... Well... let's just say he has much to think about.'

'Then he won't be calling, and you can relax.' Cynthia cups his face, leans in as if to kiss him, then pauses. 'What is it?'

'Sigma's never taken leave before, and I fear he will find some trouble to get himself into even while he's on a break.'

Chuckling, Cynthia raises herself onto an elbow, and waves of unruly red hair tumble across her shoulders. 'You know, Isolde is a real pain in the butt, but I miss dealing with her little rebellions. Funny, but I think they might actually keep me from becoming complacent.'

Beta reaches out and tucks a stray strand of hair behind Cynthia's ear as he muses, 'That's an interesting spin on a difficult situation.'

Cynthia touches his hand in thanks. 'I find myself hoping that her little jaunt back to her own time will renew her commitment to the Time Fixers.'

Beta scratches his chin, surprise stilling his hand when his fingers rake across stubble. Yes, it's definitely odd being back in a body.

'Just out of interest, what period is Isolde actually from?'

'The turn of the twentieth century,' Cynthia says, then chuckles in amusement. 'Not a great time for women, especially not independent, thinking ones like Isolde.'

'I can imagine. I assume she was part of the suffragette movement,' Beta says, rolling onto his back and linking his fingers behind his head.

'She was, until she became disillusioned,' Cynthia confirms.

'Because of the lack of progress? Or because of the violence?' Beta closes his eyes, and scenes of women being manhandled by constables play in his mind from the one time he had been in England during that period.

He rolls a little as Cynthia pushes herself up and leans against the headboard. 'Both, actually. Back then Isolde could not quite come to terms with the idea of using, shall we say, more militant tactics to change people's minds about giving women the vote. After the supposed suicide of one of her mentors, Emily Davidson, she lost heart.'

Beta opens his eyes, and his brows draw into a frown as he struggles to remember his history. At the time, the newspapers had been scathing of the suffragette who had thrown herself in front of the prince's racehorse. Years later historians theorised that Miss Davidson might not have launched herself forward but could have actually tripped.

'I thought later investigations found Miss Davidson's death was as likely to have been a tragic accident as a suicide.'

A sad smile pulls at Cynthia's lips. 'True, but that came much later. At the time, Isolde was torn. Even with such a great sacrifice, the position of women in society seemed unlikely to change in her lifetime. And if they couldn't even get voting rights for women passed in Parliament, how would they ever change society's view on what really mattered to her?'

It takes a moment for Beta to catch on to what Cynthia alluded to. 'Ah, you mean changing how society thought about marriage so she and Jo could be together? I thought things were loosening up after Queen Victoria's death.'

'They were, a little. Perhaps in London among the bohemian set, they would have been able to be together and be accepted.' Cynthia's shoulders rise in a shrug. 'In the rest of the country, though, things had changed very little.' She sighs. 'Without the love and support of her soulmate, Izzy was cast adrift and was looking for some direction. It's such a tragic love story.'

Beta rolls over towards Cynthia. 'So, she became disgruntled and joined the Time Fixers?' he prompts.

'We offered her a place, and she didn't have many options at the time. She was living in London, and her only friends were in the movement.'

He places a hand on her thigh and gives a gentle rub of support. She reaches down and wraps his fingers with hers. Her grip tightens, and her green eyes shimmer with unshed tears as she says, 'She couldn't bear to return to her home in Hampshire because Jo was about to marry another.'

He gives her a moment to wipe the tears from her eyes. She sniffs and releases his hand. 'That's why Basia could not have chosen a better guide to take her back in time.'

Unable to make the connection between Izzy's love life and the girl from their last mission in a dystopian future going back in time, he asks, 'How so?'

Cynthia runs a hand through her hair, but it drops back over her face. Irritated, she reaches over and grabs

SUFFRAGETTE

a hair-tie from the bedside table. As she pulls her tresses back into a loose ponytail, she says, 'They have both lost their loves, although obviously Basia's Allan was shot, and he died. Then there's the way both of them are searching for a way to move forward and build meaningful lives in the wake of their loss.'

Silence falls heavy in the room as Beta's thoughts turn to Basia. Within the space of a week, the young woman had met the love of her life and followed him halfway across Hampshire, only to have him literally die in her arms like something out of an old movie. Suddenly a thought creeps into his head, and he sits up, turning to face Cynthia.

'I thought Izzy said something about seeing if she could make a life with her Jo, and that was why she wanted to rejoin her timeline. Did she change her mind?'

Cynthia shakes her head. 'No. She decided to spend a little time in London with Basia first. The idea was, when Basia returns to her timeline, Izzy will go down to Winchester and see if she can pull together the threads of her life.'

'Oh, so she's a Hampshire lass. That explains why Sigma kept running into her on his missions down there.'

'She has always had a soft spot for that area, and, well, I guess she had a certain person she wanted to keep tabs on throughout her reincarnations.'

'Jo?' Beta asks.

'Jo, John, Johan, Josephine—it's all the same to her. Still, it was Josephine she lost her heart to, and Josephine she wants to be with.'

Beta's eyes widen as the full weight of Izzy's plight

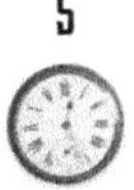

hits him. 'Now I understand her a little better. Her desire to shake up the world has its roots in her love for a woman she could never have.'

Cynthia nods again. Then she covers his hand with hers as if the touch gives her strength. 'Unfortunately, when she time travelled with us, she found out that even once women had the vote, it would still be a long time before love between two women would be accepted by society.' Cynthia smiles wanly and sighs. 'As I said, a sad story, but not one we can do much about.' She squeezes his hand. 'So, enough of this maudlin talk—what is on your agenda for today?'

'More meetings to sort out communication protocols for joint missions. And you?'

A grimace settles on Cynthia's face as she says, 'I have an appointment with Jason and his parents. I hope to persuade them to take him home and keep an eye on him while he undergoes retraining for a head office role.'

'You want him working in mission control?' As he speaks Beta is sure his expression mirrors Cynthia's grimace. To him, Jason is a bad egg, and the Time Fixer should be thrown in jail for what he did—fatally shooting a key player on the first ever Time Fixer/Guardian mission, a person who was instrumental in saving humankind from annihilation. And if they threw away the key, well... he'd be okay with that as well.

A finger pokes him in the ribs. 'Hey, are you listening?'

'Sorry, I was miles away.' Beta smiles and pats her hand.

'I was saying I don't really want Jason out and about at all, but at least if he's in head office, we can keep an eye on him.'

It's Beta's turn to laugh. 'I guess that's one way of looking at it, but wouldn't you prefer him out of the Time Fixers altogether?'

Cynthia snorts. 'Of course I would—'

'Hey, they won't foist him on us, will they? I mean, it's difficult enough to set up this joint unit as it is....' Noticing Cynthia's furrowed brow, he stops. They wouldn't do that... couldn't do that... could they?

'Unfortunately his family have built up a lot of influence in the Time Fixers over the years, so I really can't say. What I do know is no other team leader wants the man who killed Basia's Allan and nearly brought about the end of history on their team.'

Cynthia picks at the duvet cover with her other hand, a sure sign she is bothered about something.

Wanting to ease her burden, he quickly glances at the clock before snuggling back down in bed. He half rolls over and pulls Cynthia into his arms. 'Enough work talk. We still have some time before we're required elsewhere, don't we?'

She leans close to him and whispers, 'We most certainly do,' before covering his lips with hers.

CHAPTER ONE
WELCOME TO LONDON

Basia's nose wrinkles with distaste as the smell of London hits her in all its decaying glory. She had been so excited about travelling back to a period in history she adores in books that she hadn't considered her imagination might be holding on to a sanitised version of reality.

The next assault to her senses is the noise. The loud, bustling background sounds of people moving in the underground city of Portsdown had been a surprise for someone growing up on a farm. Here, in early twentieth-century London, her ears are assaulted with the clamour of goodness knows how many people going about their daily business. The calls of street vendors, the din of machinery, and the sounds of moving vehicles have merged into an ear-splitting racket.

Isolde pulls her from the alleyway they appeared in

and into the hustle and bustle of a main thoroughfare, giving her eyes a view of what her ears have been telling her. There are people everywhere, and the street is full of motorised buses, horse-drawn carriages, and a handful of cars. Her jaw drops at the sight of the vintage cars— only they aren't considered vintage here. Isolde yanks on her arm, pulling her out of the way of a car turning down the alley they had just left, and her jaw snaps shut.

Izzy drags Basia back onto the footpath. 'You're not in Kansas now, Dorothy.'

'Huh?'

'I guess that's a little before your time,' Izzy says as she leads the way through the throng of humanity crowding the street.

Basia has never seen so many people in one place before, not even when she had been in Portsdown, and they are all staring at her and Izzy.

'We have to go home and get changed,' Izzy says, scanning the street, her lips pursing as her gaze falls on a couple men who are watching them. 'We're attracting too much attention dressed like this, and with recent suffragette activity on the rise, there are some who would not think twice about attacking us for dressing in male attire.'

'You're joking, right?' Basia asks. Izzy turns and directs a frown her way. 'All right, you're serious, but surely we're not in any real danger.'

'We could be. Look, let's just go home, and I will explain there,' Izzy says, tugging urgently at her arm.

Suddenly this little trip back to London's past seems less like an adventure and more like risking her life again. This is meant to be a fact-finding mission for Basia to learn how the suffragettes led a social change movement, not a dance with death.

Okay, it's also a chance for her to recuperate and mend her heart after a life-changing week—a chance to take stock of her life and to decide where she wants to go from here. It's hard to believe that it was only a few days ago she was a farm girl. Her daily routine in a post-apocalyptic Hampshire had been boring, her days taken up with learning to be a medic, reading, and bemoaning just how boring her life was.

In a single week, she had helped a team of time travellers save the world from ending. She had promised the man she had hoped to spend the rest of her life with that she would carry on his work uniting the different factions of survivors, therefore ensuring the continuation of human-kind. It's been a lot to process.

Leadership isn't a mantle she wears easily, which is why Isolde—or Izzy, as she prefers to be called—had agreed to take her back to the turn of the twentieth century. She wanted to introduce Basia to some of the people working in the women's movement so she might learn how even the most mild-mannered person might change the world.

'Harlots! Think you can replace us men, do ya?'

Basia's head whips round as if pulled by the anger in the words, and her eyes focus on a group of about five boys around her age peeling away from the horse-drawn cart they're loading. As they stride towards Izzy and herself, they emanate such menace that everyone clears out of their way.

SUFFRAGETTE

Izzy tightens her grip until Basia's fingers complain. 'Run!' she commands, and Basia has no choice but to follow.

Her feet thud against the hard, uneven stones of the London streets as they dodge through the mass of people. Some move out of their way, but many attempt to hinder them, perhaps hoping their pursuers will catch them up and teach them a lesson.

As the boys gain on them, Izzy turns down an alley, and Basia gasps in panic. It's a dead end. She stops, pulling Izzy to a halt in front of her. 'We can't go down there. We'll be trapped.'

'Come on,' Izzy urges, tugging at her hand again. When Basia doesn't move, she lets go and says, 'Your being here isn't going to work unless you trust me.'

Glancing over her shoulder, Basia sees the shadows of their pursuers as they enter the alley. Something hits her shoulder. 'Ouch.'

'We have you now,' one of their attackers brays, his voice echoing off the buildings, adding to the menace.

All right, trust Izzy it is, then. Basia takes off, following her friend as she streaks between the towering alley walls. *I hope she has a way out of this.* They're almost at the end when Izzy pulls her into an opening.

Pushing Basia in front of her, Izzy turns and slams the wooden gate closed before ramming an enormous lock across. Leaning against the brick fence, Basia's chest rises and falls at a rapid pace as she tries to catch her breath. Fists pound the wooden planks in frustration, but the bolt holds. *We made it. We're safe.*

'C'mon, youse can't stay in there forever,' a voice shouts in frustration.

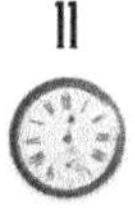

Basia looks at Izzy, her eyes sharp with amusement as her mouth pulls up in a smile, and the girls burst into laughter.

'Hey, this ain't no joke. You get out here and face up to what's coming to you.'

The new command sets them off again and results in more banging of fists against wood. Drawing in great gulps of air, Basia quells her laughter, then pushes herself off the wall and turns in a circle, checking out her surroundings.

They are within a gated yard at the back of a dwelling. The brick walls on either side are taller than she could easily reach, and in front of them is a three-storeyed brick house. Directly opposite the gate that had saved them is a stout wooden door—and it's firmly shut. They may have avoided a beating, but there's no way out.

Their only option is to hope the boys tire of waiting and leave. Hopefully that happens before the owner of the house finds them camped out in the yard.

'We're trapped,' Basia groans, giving voice to her fear.

'No we're not.' Izzy grins. 'Have a little faith.' She reaches up to dislodge a brick near the gate. Her fingers disappear and return holding a key.

'We're breaking in?' *Great, my first day in London, and I'm already a criminal.*

Izzy chuckles. 'Not exactly. This is where I live. I leave this key here for emergencies.' The wooden gates rattle as the thumping grows more vigorous. 'And I would say this is an emergency, wouldn't you?'

Izzy turns the key in the lock before letting Basia into an empty kitchen. A fire crackles in a coal range, but the room is otherwise silent. After closing and locking the door, Izzy joins her.

'This room doesn't look much different to our kitchen on the farm back home,' Basia says, allowing her amazement at the similarities to show.

'Mrs Gardiner is thinking about getting a gas oven, but it will be a while before we get any running water inside round this area,' Izzy responds as she pushes Basia into a dark, narrow corridor.

The inside of the house smells of boiled cabbage and something else... something greasy. Basia wrinkles her nose in distaste. She can't see where she's going and takes tentative steps along the carpeted floor.

Izzy pushes past her impatiently, leading them up three flights of narrow stairs. It's all so odd and unfamiliar, and it has Basia questioning her decision to leave her own time to come to this dismal place.

I should go back.

As soon as the words enter her head, her stomach knots.

No I shouldn't. Ooh, I hate this uncertainty.

Although she had agreed to become part of the rebellion when the boy she fell in love with was killed, she has never been certain she's the right person to reunite their war-ravaged world. Before she commits to such an important role, she needs time to adjust to the changes in her life—and time to mend her broken heart.

Unable to bear the constant sympathy of her family and friends, Basia had jumped at the chance to travel back in time to learn a little of how the politically savvy females in the early twentieth century had developed as they fought for women to get the vote.

Running away now would not solve her problems, and it won't bring Allan back. Squaring her shoulders, Basia lifts her chin and whispers to herself, 'I will find a way to help heal our world, and in the process, I might heal myself.'

'What was that?'

'Nothing,' Basia pants, concentrating on placing one foot after another as she follows Izzy up the narrow stairs. 'Just wondering how much further.'

'We're here,' Izzy says, stopping on a small landing.

Basia joins her, trying to catch her breath while Izzy searches for her key.

'Isolde, is that you? I did not expect you back so soon. Did you get what you needed for the story?'

Izzy leans over the banister, and Basia follows suit. 'Hello, Mrs Gardiner. Yes, I did. I am just here for a quick change of clothes before taking my notes to the paper to see what they can do with it.'

'I see you have a friend with you.' The tall, black-clad woman peers upwards, trying for a better look at Basia, who takes a step in behind Izzy so the woman won't notice her strange clothes.

Izzy half turns, a questioning look on her face. Shrugging, Basia thinks, *Don't ask me. I have no idea how best to explain why I'm here.*

'Ah yes, this is… um… my friend Barbara from school. I bumped into her on the train back.'

'Ah, another of you girls taking up a new life in London.' The woman catches Basia's eye. 'I am afraid I have no spare rooms—'

'It is all right, Mrs G. She can stay with me for a few days until she finds her feet.'

Mrs Gardiner frowns, shakes her head, then says, 'Mmm, just for a few days, mind, and you will pay extra if she joins us for meals.'

'Of course.' Izzy turns and bundles Basia back into the shadows before opening the door behind them.

Basia is surprised to find herself in a well-lit attic room. It's clean and tidy, if sparsely furnished. In one corner is an old cast-iron double bed with a faded quilt on top. Under the dormer is a desk covered in a shocking explosion of books and papers. Behind the door is a large wardrobe with drawers at the bottom. The only thing in the room that isn't strictly essential is the large multicoloured rag rug on the floor.

Once the door is firmly closed, Basia turns and asks, 'Barbara? Is she made up or a—'

Izzy places a finger over her lips to silence her, opens the door a smidgen, and listens at the gap before closing it again. 'Mrs Gardiner is a great landlady, but she does like to snoop.'

She strides to the wardrobe, opens it, and starts rifling through clothes. 'Basia is a name that would raise questions, and we don't want to draw attention to you. I had a friend at school called Barbara. The name is close enough to yours, and your accent is pretty generic English, so it should work.'

'Okay, that makes sense.'

Izzy isn't finished. 'Also, you need to not talk too much. You know far more about many things than is right for a girl in this day and age, so your saying little is our best option. Also, speech in this time period is a little more formal than you're used to.'

'I've read lots of books, so I think I can wing it,' Basia says, more than a little put out.

Izzy barks a laugh. 'Only lower-class people use contractions like "I've", and "wing it" is not a concept people will know. Fortunately, Barbara was a fairly shy, quiet girl, and I commented on this a little to my friends in London, so no one will be surprised if you don't say much.'

'Am I to be invisible?' Basia's brows draw down into a frown. 'How am I supposed to learn anything if I'm in the background?'

Izzy's shoulders rise in a shrug. 'You're asking the wrong person. It's a shame Bruno—I mean Sigma isn't with us. He maintains that a Time Guardian taking animal form can learn more than one appearing as a human because they can listen and observe without anyone noticing them. I can't change you into an animal, but we're fortunate that I came from a time when it is not unusual for a girl to be shy and retiring.'

'All I can do is try.' Basia sighs, not in the least certain she will be able melt into the background.

Izzy drops some clothing onto the bed, and Basia picks through it, shaking her head as she imagines trying to wear such strange things. Finally, she asks, 'What are these?'

'Underthings.'

As she holds one piece up, Basia's eyes go wide. 'Is this a corset? Do I have to be tortured into it?'

'Of course not. It's laced to support you like a bra. It doesn't need to be tight.' Izzy adds shirts and a skirt to the pile, then rummages around for boots.

Glancing sceptically at Basia's foot, she hauls out a

pair of black boots right from the back of the closet. 'These belonged to the girl who had the room before me. She forgot them when she packed up. I don't know why I kept them, but now I'm pleased I did.'

The next half-hour is spent helping each other into appropriate clothing, and then Izzy finishes by styling their hair into loose buns. As Basia pulls on the surprisingly comfortable and not too badly fitting boots, Izzy retrieves two short jackets out of the wardrobe, handing one to Basia.

'Right, we're ready,' Izzy says.

'For what?'

'I have some savings, but we need some more money if we are to eat while you're here. I seem to remember having left some articles behind that I had written. If the newspaper will take them, that should tide us over for a while.'

'The newspaper,' Basia repeats. 'You work for a newspaper? How exciting.'

Izzy shoves some pages from the mess on the desk into a leather satchel. 'No. No newspaper would ever employ a woman. I work for the NUWSS, writing pamphlets.'

At Basia's blank expression, she expands, 'The National Union of Women's Suffrage Societies.'

'Ahh.' Basia nods. 'If you work for them, why are we going to the newspaper?'

'Because the NUWSS doesn't pay enough for a soul to live on, what with prices in London being so high. I do some

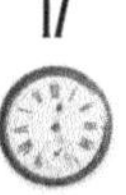

ghost writing for a journalist friend to make ends meet.'

Basia tilts her head to the side. 'So you *do* work for a newspaper?'

Before Izzy can answer, Basia stands, takes a step, then wobbles precariously.

'Are your boots too big?' Izzy asks, pausing for a moment as she surveys the footwear.

'No, they fit okay. I'm just not used to the heel.'

'Here, let me look.' Izzy drops to her knees and checks Basia's shoes before tightening the laces. 'Try again.'

Basia takes another couple of steps and manages to move a little more gracefully. 'Better, but I prefer my hiking boots.' She looks mournfully at her footwear abandoned by the bed.

Izzy nods. 'Me, too, but we would stand out too much.' She returns to the papers, searching through them for something in particular.

'So, you didn't answer properly… about the newspaper work.'

'Ah. Got it.' Izzy shoves the new page into the satchel with the others. 'I have a friend who oversees freelancers writing for a couple of newspapers. He throws some stories my way sometimes and will also take some of the pieces I write about the suffrage movement. Of course, he prints them under his name. With two of us to feed, I'm going to need a little more work from him.'

'I can do something to help,' Basia offers. Having fought for her independence these last couple of weeks, she isn't keen to give that up.

Izzy raises an eyebrow, and Basia's cheeks heat up. 'All right, I probably can't do much, but I could help write a couple of articles, or maybe check your work. Or I could clean up that desk for you.' She sends Izzy a cheeky grin.

A smile twitches Izzy's lips as she holds Basia's gaze for a second, then nods. 'Actually, you probably could write things up from my notes, but you would need to be careful not to include any spoilers from the future. If you did that, it would free me up to take on some more work and cover any additional costs.'

Feeling a little less like a burden, Basia folds their clothes and leaves them in a pile on the bed while Izzy shoves their boots into the back of the wardrobe. 'Put those clothes in there too,' she tells Basia. 'It wouldn't do to have anyone walk in and see them while we're out.'

While Basia hurries to hide their modern-day clothes in the back of the wardrobe, Izzy lifts the mattress on the bed and takes out a coin purse. She shakes it, making it jingle.

'For emergencies,' she says. 'Room and board are included with the job, but I'll need to pay extra for food for you. Also, if we're to be here for any length of time, you'll need your own clothes. But before we spend, let's go and see if we can make some money.'

After slipping the purse into her bag, Izzy ducks her head through the satchel strap and leads the way out of the room, making sure to lock the door behind her.

As they descend the stairway, Izzy tries to remember how much money she has in her stash. Enough for maybe a few items of clothing and a week of food—then things will get desperate. With the Time Fixers providing everything she needed for so long, she had forgotten how hand-to-mouth her existence in London had been. Now, with an extra mouth to feed and clothe, they would have to be careful with their coins.

The front door opens directly onto the street. The two girls pause for a moment before exiting, making sure the coast is clear. Checking the busy street, they find no sign of the boys who'd followed them. With their change of clothes and hair, Izzy and Basia will blend in with the rest of the Londoners and will be unlikely to draw additional attention to themselves.

As they step out, Basia stumbles, bumping into a gentleman walking by.

'Sorry. I—' she starts to say but is silenced by the glare he directs down his nose at her.

Izzy slips her arm through the other girl's. 'Best we walk together until you get used to your new footwear.'

'And this cursed long skirt. The corset may not be tight, but I feel like I'm walking with a rod up my back,' Basia complains. 'How did people wear this all the time?'

Izzy strides past the alleyway and is surprised to see a couple of their pursuers camped out by the gate. One of the boys catches her eye, but he doesn't make a move towards them or show any signs of recognition. Izzy relaxes and answers, 'They do not know any better.'

As they stroll through Spitalfields towards Fleet Street, Basia starts to lag behind. At first Izzy thinks it's because of her boots but soon realises it's actually because she's gawping at everything that moves. Her face shows every reaction to the bustling early twentieth-century London street, and people are beginning to notice.

'Basia,' Izzy whispers. When the other girl doesn't respond, she jerks her arm, and Basia slowly turns her head. 'Basia, get a grip. You look like you just landed in London from outer space.'

'I feel like I have,' Basia whispers back, unable to stop herself from turning to follow every new sight. 'This is not at all like I expected it to be. It's so... dirty... and run-down. Not at all grand like in my novels. And the women—they look so tired, not glamorous at all.'

Izzy chokes out a bitter laugh. 'Most women alone in London can not afford to live the high life. Spitalfields is not, shall we say, the best part of London. It's all I can afford, given it comes with the job. And in spite of how the area might look, Mrs Gardiner runs a respectable house.'

It's Basia's turn to chuckle. 'I knew the books I read showed a more upper-class way of life, but I had no idea so many people lived like this.'

'This is not as bad as some areas. And there are some great things about living around here, like the local teahouse,' Izzy reassures her. 'But you must try to blend in. A woman who looks lost in London is a target for all kinds of bad people.'

'Oh, yes, sorry. It's just....'

'I understand. Your first few hours in a new time period can be overwhelming. And I guess London is not the easiest place to drop into.' Izzy pats her hand reassuringly before leading them onwards.

Basia manages to keep up this time, and, without the need to check on her friend, Izzy imagines what it would be like to see London through Basia's eyes. The sheer number of people must be scary and, at the same time, quite exciting. Then her eyes latch onto the things that had made her discontented when she had lived here before: a man striking his wife and no one bats an eye; the gaunt woman selling flowers, wearing a dress more patches than fabric, her eyes lowered to the ground so no one sees her shame.

Then there are the less obvious things. The fact that there are more men than women out and about because men have business to take care of and women should be at home, the way men walk the streets as if they own them, and the way women move out of their way as if in acknowledgement of the fact. Her chest tightens with anger, but experience has shown her there is little she can do to change any of this.

As they draw closer to Fleet Street, the number of women decreases, and those they see are dressed substantially more elegantly. Their dresses swish in the way only expensive fabrics do, and their heads tilt with confidence, showing off their ornately decorated hats. Izzy tries to ignore them, but she remembers that not so long ago she walked like that, assured of her superior place in society.

Fleet Street itself is a little quieter, but the air is vibrant with activity, and for a moment, Izzy allows herself to dream about what it would be like to actually work here. To go into the newspaper office, receive her assignments, then head down to the cafes or pubs with the other journalists when her work was done.

She sighs. It will be years before women are admitted to respectable newspapers as reporters, and many more before they'll be allowed to report on anything more than society events or bake-offs. She should be grateful her work is published, even if it is under someone else's name.

SUFFRAGETTE

Stopping outside the door of a particular establishment, she waits until she catches the eye of the porter. He recognises her and calls to one of the runners lazing on a bench just inside the door. 'Go find Mr French for the lady, and be quick about it.'

The porter turns back to her. 'Shall I tell him you will be in the usual place, miss?'

Izzy nods, and the porter smirks. He believes their liaison is of a romantic nature, and he's happy to help them sneak about. Perhaps he even believes she's married and is meeting Lionel on the sly.

She wonders briefly if he would be so quick to get Lionel for her if he knew theirs was mostly a business relationship, and that a love affair with a woman was the furthest thing from her childhood friend's mind.

Her grey mood lifts at the look of sheer delight on Basia's face as she leads her into a teahouse a little further along the street.

'Izzy, this is delightful. This is exactly what I imagined London to be like. I feel like a heroine from one of my books.'

Basia's eyes sparkle as she scans the cake display, and a smile pulls at her mouth as she studies the women and a smattering of men seated at the tables. Izzy doesn't have the heart to tell her this isn't even one of the better places to take tea.

Gently pulling Basia behind her, she finds an empty

table, and they are already seated with tea and cakes ordered when Lionel enters.

'Lee?' Basia whispers quizzically as Izzy stands to accept Lionel's kiss on her cheek.

'Lionel, this is my friend Barbara, from school. Barbara, this is my oldest friend and benefactor, Lionel.'

'I guess from that introduction that your father still has you cut off and I am paying for tea,' Lionel says as he takes Basia's hand and raises it to his lips. 'I am delighted to meet you, Barbara. Isolde has told me absolutely nothing about you, but then, she never tells anyone anything. However, I am not going to let that stop us from becoming the best of friends.'

He takes a seat as Basia continues to stare at him. Izzy kicks her under the table.

'Ah, yes. Isolde has mentioned you, and I am pleased to finally put a face to the name.'

Lionel's eyebrows rise. 'She told you about me? I wonder why.'

Disaster is averted when their tea arrives, and the trio busy themselves with drinks and food. When the waiting staff departs, Lionel appears to have forgotten his chagrin over having been discussed. 'I am afraid I am unable to stay for long. I only came because I have the perfect assignment for you, and I need you to start on it today.'

'First things first,' Izzy says. 'I need to know if you can use any of these.' She reaches into her satchel and draws out some pages.

Lionel briefly reads through the pile. He holds on to one and gives the others back to her. 'This one on the conditions of women pieceworkers I can use alongside another I have on the tailor's guild complaining their income is being reduced by the increase in clothing factories.'

'Lionel!' Izzy's tone is threatening. 'No. It will take away the focus from women doing piecework for pennies.'

'Trust me, Isolde, I will not show the women in a bad light. I simply wish to better highlight how changes in the garment industry are affecting a number of the working poor.'

Izzy relaxes and asks, 'The usual rate?'

Lionel nods, and she takes a sip of tea before pulling out a final piece of paper from her bag. 'I have this. It is an exclusive.'

As Lionel reads it, he turns white. 'Isolde... I... you know I....'

'I was there, Lionel. This is a true eyewitness account.'

Lionel sighs, runs a hand through his hair, then pushes the page back towards Izzy.

'If you had come to me a week ago, before other papers printed the official version, I might have had a chance of convincing my editor. If this is really the truth—that Emily Davidson tripped and was trampled to death—then this is a great tragedy.'

'It is the truth. I swear it. The version the papers are running—that she threw herself in front of the prince's horse during the Derby—is a lie. It is propaganda designed to malign the masses against us.'

Lionel reaches for the paper, then draws his hand back. 'If it were up to me, I would publish it. But you know the editor will never let it through. Perhaps you could rewrite it. Make it lean more towards a... more of a "what if she had tripped"....'

Izzy's lips purse, and she opens her mouth to argue.

Lionel reaches out again, and this time he takes Izzy's hand in his. 'You and I both know we need to pick our battles, and I am telling you, there is no point in fighting this one.'

'But—'

'Besides, the new piece I want your help with is really important. So much so in fact, the paper is prepared to pay expenses as well as a modest fee for your work.'

Her disappointment at her inability to alter the narrative about Emily Davidson's tragic death is overwhelming, but Izzy forces herself to ask, 'What is it?'

'The Women's Pilgrimage is due in Hampshire this week, and my editor would like someone to write about it—and he chose me.'

'How does that affect me?' Izzy asks automatically, still working on how she might convince Lionel to take her Emily Davidson story.

'I have some things to tidy up here before I can move on to this, so I need someone to do some background research for me on the local suffragette movement. I thought perhaps... you might be ready to... go home.' Lionel changes his face to appear beseeching.

Izzy freezes. 'Lionel, you know I cannot go back. I cannot face.... You know what I left.'

Before Lionel can respond, Basia sits forward and says, 'But, Isolde, I thought you wanted to see if you could fix things.'

Izzy catches her bottom lip between her teeth. Basia is right. She'd asked the Time Fixers if she could go back to her own time to see if she could remake her life here, and part of that had been to see if she could repair her relationship with her family... and maybe Jo too. Still, this was all happening too quickly.

Her disappointment over the treatment of Emily Davidson's death combined with the mess of her own life had led her to join the Time Fixers in the hopes she could nudge civilisation towards a better world. When she realised her work had done little to change history, she thought perhaps she could take up the reins of her old life. And, yes, that would mean facing her family in Winchester sooner or later, but she had hoped for later.

Lionel takes her silence as agreement. 'Good, that is settled, then.' He reaches into his pocket and produces an envelope. 'Here are your expenses for the trip and a little something extra just in case. As you will not have time to let me know what hotel you are staying in, I will call in at your aunt's the day after tomorrow for the first draft. Now I must be off. I will settle up on the way out. Nice to meet you, Barbara.'

Seconds later he is gone, and Izzy is still frozen in shock, staring at the spot Lionel just vacated, when she feels a gentle hand on her arm.

'Izzy, are you okay?'

It takes a moment for the words to penetrate the fog of her thoughts. 'Um, yes. I... um, guess we should get going, too, if we are to travel to Winchester today.'

Out in front of the teashop, Izzy hails a cab. The journey back to her lodgings passes in a blur. She only fully comes out of her head when they're back inside her room.

'Was that Lee?' Basia asks, taking a seat on the bed.

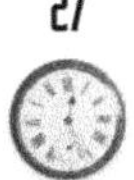

'I mean, like I was the reincarnation of Lee's sister, is Lionel someone who becomes Lee in the future?'

'What? Um, yes, I guess. I had never really thought of Lionel in that way, but he might be. Though, he and his cousin Stanley are very similar, so I am not sure.... Perhaps Stanley becomes Lee.'

Basia frowns. 'So there's someone in this time who will become me?'

Izzy kneels, pulls a valise out from under the bed, and begins packing clothes inside.

'Izzy?'

'Mmm.'

'Pay attention. Will I run into an earlier version of myself? And won't that cause some sort of... anomaly?'

Izzy pauses. 'Possibly.' She stops what she's doing for a moment. 'Actually, to be honest, I've never seen two versions of the same person together in all my five years of time travel. So I guess time or history must do something to keep the different versions apart.'

Basia swings her feet as Izzy finishes packing. 'You talk about time as if it's a living thing.'

'What? Yes... it sort of is. I know it isn't alive as such, but it does sometimes act as though it's a sentient being. There are rules to time travel, and if you don't follow them, you will find yourself kicked back to your own time.'

Basia falls silent, and Izzy senses she wants to ask something else. When she finally does, Izzy is prepared for it.

'So, we'll see your version of Johan, my brother, in Winchester?' she asks.

'Most likely.'

'And are you intending to make things up with him?'

With her, Izzy says in her head, but she answers with a noncommittal 'Maybe.'

'What's he like, this Jo?' Basia presses.

'Josephine is serious and committed to her family, kind of like your brother,' Izzy says as she closes the travel bag.

'Your Johan, Jo, is a she? Oh.' Basia's legs stop swinging, hesitating for a moment. 'And that's not good, is it? Not in this time period. And not for some time into the future.'

'Can we talk about this later?' Izzy asks, the clasp of her bag clicking to accentuate her request. 'The last train to Winchester leaves in just over an hour, and we still need to buy you some clothes.'

Basia is aching to ask more questions, but she appreciates now is not the time for a heart-to-heart. They've only been back in Izzy's timeline a few hours, and her friend must be overwhelmed with everything happening so quickly.

'Have we enough money for clothes?' she asks instead.

Izzy opens the envelope Lionel gave her and counts the money inside. She closes her eyes, and her mouth moves as if she's calculating. She sucks in a breath and opens her eyes. 'We will be fine if we can stay with my aunt rather than at a hotel... and if we just buy the basics. You can borrow something of mine for evenings.... Yes, we should have enough.'

'Evening dress? Surely we won't need anything like that.'

Izzy's mind was somewhere else, and she didn't respond. 'Come on. If we hurry, we'll have time to go to a second-hand clothing stall I use in the Petticoat Lane Market.'

Before Basia can object, Izzy grabs her arm, pulls her off the bed, and almost drags her to the door. She keeps up her frantic pace as she takes them through a maze of back streets until they finally reach the market.

Izzy slows as she wanders along the street lined with stalls. She ignores the vendors' calls, clearly searching for a particular one. While Izzy takes the lead, Basia is overwhelmed by the crush of people and the array of goods on display. Izzy comes to an abrupt stop halfway down the street, and Basia almost bangs into her back.

She pushes Basia forward towards a mass of clothes piled up on a table. The stall is decorated with still more pieces hanging from ropes strung around the sides.

'I need a day dress and some skirts and blouses. Oh, and shoes for the dress, and boots. And that valise will do nicely.' Izzy points to an old brown leather bag.

The stall holder looks Basia up and down, then shows Izzy some garments. Izzy shakes her head or nods, and Basia stands there saying nothing, feeling as though she is some doll to be dressed up. The two haggle over price, Izzy adds some undergarments and another skirt and blouse, and the deal is done.

The now stuffed valise is shoved at Basia, and Izzy hauls her back through the crowd and searches for a cab. Once inside one, Basia slumps into the seat. 'I hate pink,' she says.

'That day dress will be very becoming on you. Besides,

it was the only dress that went with the shoes.'

Basia humphs, unable to argue because Izzy's right. At least the light blue skirt and white blouses are more to her liking, and they'll mix and match with the clothing she's wearing. Perhaps she'll never need to wear the day dress.

Basia leans her head back to rest on the seat, wishing she could slide back into her jeans and T-shirt and get out of these layers of clothing that threaten to stifle her.

The cab pulls up outside a station near the river. Not just any river, *the Thames.* Basia sits up in her seat and stares out the window, doing her best not to gawp and fails. The bustle of people, actual steam trains billowing smoke, the Thames right there—it's easy to believe she's in a dream. Only Izzy's hand on the small of her back guiding her out of the cab and into the station keeps her on track.

'Quick now,' Izzy says as she exits the ticket queue. 'The train leaves in ten minutes, and it is the last one today.'

'That's plenty of time to make it to the platform, isn't it?' Basia quickly realises her mistake as they struggle through the crowds to the barrier. She clutches her satchel close to her chest as they push between bodies and bags.

A tall, suited man rushes past, catching Basia's shoulder and turning her around. When she's righted herself, she can't see Izzy anywhere. Panic tightens her throat until she catches sight of Izzy's frantically waving hand over by a barrier.

Taking a deep breath, she pushes her way through the crowd, determined not to get waylaid again. Blowing out a breath, she relaxes as Izzy takes her hand and leads her through the turnstile and onto the platform.

As the clock strikes three, a guard checks their tickets and assists them onto the back of the train with only moments to spare. If he had not helped them inside and passed them their bags, they wouldn't have made it.

Izzy leads them through the carpeted first-class section, and Basia glimpses plush seats and well-dressed gentlemen inside the cubicles. 'I could only afford second-class tickets,' Izzy says, opening the door to another carriage.

The corridor is wooden, and Basia struggles to stay on her feet. As the train curves out of Waterloo Station, she slips and grabs for anything to right herself, which happens to be a door handle. Her weight causes the door to slide open, propelling Basia into a compartment occupied by a young woman. Basia straightens herself, smiles, and makes out that she is exactly where she's meant to be before saying, 'Excuse me, do you mind if we join you?'

The woman raises her eyes from a book and looks over the top of her glasses as Izzy joins them. She shakes her head before returning to her reading.

Izzy slides the door shut, and they stow their bags in the overhead racks before taking a seat opposite their travelling companion. Basia sits by the window and cannot take her eyes from the sight of Edwardian London as they pass through it.

'How long until Winchester?' she asks Izzy without shifting her gaze.

'About two and a half hours.'

More than two hours. Basia sighs and glances over to their travelling companion, wishing she could sink into a good book too. The woman is reading a battered edition of *The Return of Sherlock Holmes.*

A first edition! Her eyes widen with the realisation. She turns to Izzy, who is leaning back against the seat, eyes closed.

'Izzy?'

'Isolde,' Izzy corrects. 'It is best if you use my proper name while we are in Winchester.'

'All right, Isolde, then.' Basia tries to keep the frustration out of her voice. She has followed Izzy around for hours, and she wants to know more about where they're going and what they're doing, not another reminder that her speech is not what it should be. 'What is this Women's Pilgrimage thing you are going to Winchester for?'

Before Izzy can answer, the woman across from them says, 'My goodness, girl, where have you been living, darkest Africa? The march is almost all anyone is talking about.'

Placing her book in her lap, their travelling companion then reaches into a carpetbag on the seat beside her and produces a newspaper. She opens it and points to a section before handing the publication to Basia.

Scanning the print, Basia reads the advertisement calling for women to join a nationwide march to Hyde Park from all corners of Great Britain.

'I thought suffragettes were all about courting attention with violent displays and hunger strikes,' Basia says as she hands the paper back.

The woman frowns at her and snorts with disdain. 'That is why this march is so important. After what happened at the Derby, many moderates have turned away from advocating votes for women.'

Izzy inhales sharply before she snarls, 'Emily Davidson's

death was a tragic accident.

'I am sorry, was she a friend of yours? I did not mean to offend, merely to state a fact. The newspapers have blown her death out of proportion and used the event to stoke the fears of moderates.'

Izzy relaxes a little, and the woman across from them sits up a little straighter in her seat. 'Look, this march is a chance for us women to explain why we want the vote. Newspapers love to paint us as radicals, but we are not. For the most part, we are ordinary women who just want a say in how our country is run.'

'Are you a part of the Women's Pilgrimage?' Izzy asks, a glimmer of excitement twinkling in her eye.

The woman smiles for the first time since they entered the carriage. 'Why yes, I am. The lady I work for has been giving speeches along the way. She wanted her father to go through the address she is giving in Hampshire in a couple of days, so I took it to him in London. I am to meet her in Winchester in two days' time to go over the final version.'

Izzy leans forward on her chair and studies the other woman. 'I think I have seen you before. You are Miss Fielden's secretary, are you not?'

The woman blushes. 'I am, yes. Maisie, Maisie Ottaway.'

She holds out a hand, and Izzy shakes it. 'I am Isolde Fielding, and this is my friend, Barbara Trelawney. A pleasure to meet you. I am doing some background research on an article for the *Sunday Times*, and I would love to interview you about the march.'

Maisie withdraws her hand and shrinks back into the corner. 'In spite of having a female chief editor, the *Sunday*

Times has not always been friendly to our cause.'

Izzy grimaces. 'No, it has not been. Like most papers it has tended of late to focus on the activities of the suffragettes—after all, sensation does sell papers. However, my friend is writing the article, and he promises me he will be sympathetic and will tell the suffragists' side of the story. Besides, I always write a second article for our pamphlets just to be sure.'

Maisie's eyes widen. 'Oh my, you are *that* Fielding—I have admired your work and own some of your pamphlets. Of course I will answer questions, but I must remain anonymous. Miss Fielden's father is in a precarious position with regards to the Pilgrimage... what with being a member of Parliament and all.'

Izzy takes the woman's hand in hers. 'You know you can trust me. I will not pass anything on that could hurt anyone who supports the movement.'

Maisie's shoulders relax, but before Izzy can pull out her notebook, the rattle of the tea trolley interrupts them. Izzy buys them all tea and cake, and then they chat, getting to know one another before the detailed questioning begins.

CHAPTER TWO
WINCHESTER

With the tea things cleared away, Izzy rests her notebook on her satchel and asks her first question. 'Why are you supporting the Women's Pilgrimage?'

Maisie's fingers twist in her lap, and the only sound in the carriage is the chug of the train as she appears to search for an answer.

Izzy waits patiently, then tries again. 'Let me put that another way—can you tell us why the women's movement is important to you?'

Maisie's fingers slow, and she tentatively says, 'It has been difficult for us moderates since the incident at the Derby, then the attack on Parliament. Those harridans—' Her hand rises to her mouth, and her eyes widen in shock. 'I am so sorry. I realise some of the women involved must be your friends.'

And they pay for my lodgings, Izzy adds but keeps it to herself because to get her story, she must keep Maisie talking. Instead she says, 'I think we can all agree the sentiments on the street have turned against all women in recent weeks—suffragettes and more moderate suffragists alike.'

'Well, yes, it has not been easy for any of us,' Maisie says primly as she smooths her skirt. 'Only the other day, my mother had rotten potatoes thrown at her by stallholders she had worked beside for years simply because she mentioned I was on this march.'

Beside her, Basia gasps.

'Oh, Miss Trelawney, not to worry. Some of the other stallholders stood up for her, and things are back to normal in Covent Garden Market now.'

'Of course, the march through England has been advertised in all the main papers and talked about at many meetings as well as in many homes for some time now,' Izzy says, trying to bring the conversation back to the topic at hand. 'Supporters of suffrage for women on equal terms to men are heading to London from six starting points around the country, and they plan to converge on Hyde Park for a rally. Is that so?' she prompts Maisie.

'Yes, we have been advertising in the main papers for months, trying to encourage people to walk at least part of the route with us. We aim to educate people along the way that most of us do not want a radical transformation of society—all we want is a voice in making the laws of the land.'

Izzy nods in encouragement, but Maisie doesn't elaborate any further. 'So, how did you become involved with the suffragists?'

Maisie beams, and her voice rings with pride as she answers. 'I am involved because I work for Miss Fielden. I started with her family as a maid. Much to my surprise, we became friends when Miss Fielden taught me to read better with her suffragist pamphlets.'

'That is an unusual thing for an employer to do,' Izzy says.

Maisie frowns, as if sensing some sort of trap. 'She did not brainwash me, if that is what you are thinking. She found me trying to read one of her pamphlets one day. Instead of reprimanding me for touching her personal things, she sat down and helped me read it. After that, every time she had a new pamphlet, she would lend it to me and told me to come to her if there was anything I could not understand.'

'Sorry, I meant no offence,' Izzy reassures her, silently applauding Miss Fielden for her philanthropy.

Somewhat mollified, Maisie continues. 'Some months later her work with the Women's Social and Political Union became too much for her, so she asked her father if she may employ me as a secretary, and here I am. She is a great woman whom history will remember as a staunch fighter for women's rights,' Maisie finishes up proudly.

Basia catches Izzy's eye and raises a questioning eyebrow. With her work in the future, Izzy well knows that Miss Fielden, in spite of the inspiring speech she would give in Haslemere in a few days' time, will end up a footnote in history, not one of the shining stars.

It's a fate many of the suffragists will suffer. Even Basia, who is relatively well read, had no idea the more moderate suffragists existed. Her sole insight into those who worked tirelessly for women's suffrage had been of the more radical suffragettes—who actually only make up a small part of those advocating for a women's right to vote.

Maisie turns to Basia. 'Are you a reporter, too, Miss Trelawney?'

'No, I've no job at the moment,' Basia responds. 'I'm taking a bit of a holiday with Izzy.'

As she spoke, Maisie's brow drew down into a frown, and Basia's mouth forms an "O" as she realises her mistake. This was why Izzy had asked the woman from the future not to speak.

'You will have to excuse Barbara. She has been volunteering in the slums up north and... well, her speech has become somewhat common, and she has picked up some unusual habits,' Izzy says, directing a pointed stare at Basia. 'I hope she will have fixed this by the time we meet my aunt.'

Chuckling nervously, Maisie pats Basia on the hand. 'I know how easy it can be to fall into bad habits when people around you speak differently. It always takes me a couple of days to adjust after I have visited my parents.'

'Barbara will not have that luxury,' Izzy says, and Basia squirms in her seat, clearly getting the message.

'Perhaps it is best not to say too much to people first off,' Maisie tells her. 'That is how I do it.'

Basia smiles her response, and Izzy relaxes a little.

'To answer your question, Barbara came to London from Manchester to decide her future. I had to come to Hampshire and cover the march, so she decided to travel with me.'

'Have you any idea what you want to do in London?' Maisie presses. 'There are so many opportunities for the modern woman.'

Beside her, Basia tenses. Izzy takes her hand. 'Is it all right if I tell Miss Ottaway?'

Basia nods, her shoulders relaxing with relief.

'I am sorry if I have made you self-conscious about speaking,' Maisie says to Basia. 'I really do not mind if you sound a little… common.'

Izzy squeezes Basia's hand. 'It is not that, Miss Ottaway, but more that Barbara still cannot believe she is here and not at home with her parents. You see, she risked a lot by not going back to her family after the charity work she did in Manchester.'

As if sensing a drama, Maisie inches forward on her seat. 'Oh, Miss Trelawney, how very brave of you.'

'And she probably would not have had the courage to do it if she had not believed it is her future to do good works. When we return to London, she will apply to join the Nightingale Home and Training School for Nurses at St Thomas's Hospital.' The cover story rolls off Izzy's tongue with ease, and Basia sends her an appreciative glance.

'Oh my goodness,' Maisie gasps. 'I do so admire the Nightingale Nurses. I hope you do apply and get accepted. It is such a noble calling.'

'I am sure she will,' Izzy says. 'She has already had some training at home, working with a local nurse.'

'It must be difficult taking such a step when your family would no doubt rather you stayed at home and married instead of studying nursing in London. I dream of the day when having a career will be commonplace for us women.'

Basia draws her bottom lip between her teeth as a mix of emotions flashes in her eyes. Izzy can only guess at what she's thinking—that Maisie had inadvertently described her life.

Before the Time Fixers and Time Guardians' joint mission to save humanity from extinction, Basia's family had indeed wanted to keep her close to home, if not actually married off, for her own protection. It wasn't a surprise to Izzy that someone in that situation would choose to leave her home and run away on an adventure with Allan, an escapee from an underground city. He had been passionate about returning home to tell his people it was safe to live above ground.

Unfortunately Allan's actions had brought factions in post-apocalyptic Hampshire to the brink of a war that could have ended humanity. Before his death, Allan not only managed to get a commitment from Basia to carry on trying to bring above- and below-ground people together, but he also sacrificed his freedom on the promise that the two sides would hold peace talks

Appreciating her friend's discomfort, and knowing the complexity of the situation she was in, Izzy changes the subject. 'What are you able to tell us of the contents of Miss Fielden's speech?'

Maisie stiffens and starts plucking at the seam of her skirt. 'Oh, Miss Fielding, I cannot tell anyone anything about it, not even someone as respected as you.'

She hadn't expected an answer, but it had been worth a try if only to take the heat off Basia for a bit.

'That should be enough for my article. Thank you for

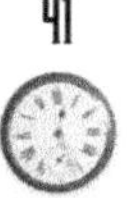

talking to me,' Izzy says as she returns her notebook to her bag.

With the interview over, the three women relax into a comfortable silence, retreating into their own thoughts. Basia leans her forehead against the window, watching the scenery pass by. Izzy allows herself to be lulled by the chugging of the carriage wheels and battles the urge to sleep.

Obviously tired from days of travelling, Maisie's eyelids begin to droop, and she is soon snoring gently. The charlady returns for their cups, and when they're alone, Izzy whispers, 'Are you all right?'

Basia nods, resting her head against the seat, but doesn't take her eyes off the scenery rushing by.

'Sorry about the slip-up,' she whispers. 'I will try to speak more like a heroine from a Jane Austen novel in future.'

'Or not speak at all.'

Basia chuckles.

Izzy leans in and, in a low voice, says, 'I am sorry about springing the background story on you. I tried to keep it as close to the truth as possible—that is essential for a good cover story.'

'No, you did well. It's just, it *was* quite close to the truth, and it reminded me why I came.'

Izzy smiles. 'There is nothing to say you cannot enjoy yourself a little while you are here—indulge your passions, perhaps.' She's referring to Basia's penchant for reading novels from the eighteenth and nineteenth centuries, and her country-manor view of the times. She's excited to see Basia's reaction when they reach her aunt's house.

Instead of a hand-to-mouth existence in London, her friend would be thrown into her idealised view of early twentieth-century England.

'My aunt Augusta is part of the set in Winchester, and there is no reason you should not enjoy yourself with her while I work on the story for Lionel. Goodness knows she would probably enjoy the company.'

She doesn't add that it will take the pressure off her to spend time with her aunt. 'Once we are done here and are back in London, there will be time enough for you to be introduced to some of the WSPU leaders. Then we should be able to find a way for you to move things forward in your time without upsetting the balance and starting a war.'

'I'm not 100 percent sure I want to be one of the ones leading the change at home,' Basia whispers so quietly, Izzy almost doesn't catch what she says, but she does hear the sadness lacing her words.

Turning her head, she sees unshed tears in the other woman's eyes. They remind Izzy that in the space of a week or so, Basia found her soulmate, then lost him to the cause she was now expected to champion for him. She herself knows how hard it is to lose the love of your life, and how easy it is to channel that heartbreak into a movement for social change. Well, she thinks she knows.

'Are you having second thoughts about carrying on Allan's work?' she asks, keeping her voice low so as not to wake Maisie.

Basia shrugs. 'I promised to help in the heat of the moment. Now... I am not sure it is what is best for me, or for the people in both communities.'

'You should not take anything on until you are sure you can commit,' Izzy advises, drawing from her own experience.

When she first joined the WSPU, she'd been able to immerse herself in the cause. However, when their actions became increasingly violent, and people began turning against them, she had no longer been sure she was doing the right thing.

She'd been spiralling into despair when the Time Fixers approached her to join their team. With them, she had hoped to find a different way to make society better. Both ventures had altered very little for Izzy, or for women in general, if Basia's post-apocalyptic future was anything to go by.

'Still, I want to help our world heal—I can't leave it hurtling towards a war,' Basia says.

No, but can you actually do anything to prevent it? Izzy wonders.

She had gone to Basia's home on a mission to prevent humanity from wiping itself out. In the post-apocalyptic world, she found that the small above-ground settlements mostly valued women for their ability to breed and men for their skill in defending them. Hard-won equalities were stripped bare in the face of limited resources and a human population close to extinction.

Below ground, things were even worse. Women may have had equal status with men, but the totalitarian state had become corrupt in a way that reminded Izzy of twentieth-century communist Russia.

If being in Basia's time had taught her anything, it was that history really does repeat itself. She was now

so disillusioned, she was back in her own timeline, trying to squeeze some happiness and meaning from the life she had been born into.

'Do you think one person can make a difference?' she asks Basia.

'Allan made a difference, I believe. So, yes, I think one person can make a big difference, but perhaps not everyone can. I think most people will end up just doing the best they can to live what they believe to be a good life.'

Basia's words are wise. Once this jaunt to Hampshire is over, Izzy hopes she can return to London, forge a writing career that might make a slight difference, and perhaps find a small measure of happiness.

Before that can happen, though, events have conspired to force her into returning to Winchester and facing the demons of her past head-on—this was most decidedly not what she had planned when she'd decided to go home.

Basia wriggles beside her, and then an arm drapes over Izzy's shoulder. 'I guess we both have a lot to sort through, but perhaps we both can have some fun along the way.'

As the train pulls into Winchester Station, Basia catches sight of the clock. It is just after five thirty in the afternoon. Bathed in late-afternoon sunshine, the Victorian brick building is postcard picturesque.

The train shudders to a stop, waking Maisie. Still half

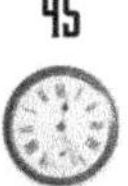

asleep, she hastily shoves her belongings back into her carpetbag, dropping her newspaper on the floor as she does so.

Izzy is already on her feet and passing down their valises. 'Can I get your travel bag down for you, Miss Ottaway?'

The woman in question pauses and looks up from grabbing the newspaper. 'Yes, please.'

Moments later, a guard opens the carriage door to the platform, and Basia is the first to step into an English countryside she has only read about in books. Her heart beats faster, and she turns to Izzy with an enormous grin on her face. 'This is just perfect.'

'If you react this way at the station, what will you be like when we get into the city proper?' Izzy winks, taking the sting from her words.

'Oh my,' Maisie says at the number of passengers disembarking. 'I did not expect it to be so busy. How will I ever find a porter... and a taxi?'

'Follow me,' Izzy instructs, then takes off in the opposite direction from the crowd.

Maisie and Basia share a quick glance before following. Izzy stops at a wrought-iron gate at the end of the building, and when they catch her, they find she's talking to a man on the other side.

'Are you sure I canna be getting one for you, too, Miss Isolde?' the man asks.

'Thank you, Thomas, no. It is only a short walk to Augusta's place, and it is a lovely evening for a stroll.'

'Right you are.' The man's wrinkled face breaks into a grin, compressing the multitude of folds and revealing

46

a gap-toothed smile. He opens the gate and allows the three girls through.

'Miss Ottaway, this is Thomas. He will help you find a cabbie to take you to wherever you are going.'

'Oh, thank you, Miss Fielding. I am ever so obliged. I am told the lady I am staying with has a house not far from the station, but I have never been to Winchester....'

'It is no bother, really. My aunt has an arrangement with Thomas.' She leans into Maisie and says, 'Just tip him a few pennies for his time. He is cheaper than a porter, and he will find you a trustworthy cabbie, so it is well worth every penny.'

Thomas already has Maisie's travel bag in hand, and she throws her thanks over her shoulder as she scurries after him.

'I hope you are up for a short walk,' Izzy says as she leads them past the front of the station.

'No,' Basia mutters under her breath as she totters behind in the unfamiliar heels. It appears the comment was rhetorical and that Izzy, in her determination to walk to her aunt's house, has forgotten Basia's inability to walk in the borrowed footwear.

Fortunately for Basia, it appears Izzy's aunt's place is truly not far from the station. Or at least she hopes that's why they've stopped outside the military college on Southgate Street and are staring at the houses on the other side.

When there's a break in traffic, Izzy grabs her arm and hauls her across the busy main road. She halts again at the bottom of some steps leading up to the porticoed entrance of a four-storeyed house.

'Here we are,' Izzy announces. 'Home.'

Basia's jaw drops. 'Oh my god, Izzy. This is a mansion.' She turns a suspicious gaze to her friend. 'Who the hell *are* you?'

Izzy laughs. 'I am a nobody, but one of my cousins is a duke—the Lord of Denbigh. My branch of the family has wealth and land but no title. Aunt Augusta, my father's sister, married a Northern industrialist. When he died she retired to Winchester and has been spending his money on charitable works ever since.'

'Does she have children?'

'Goodness no. Aunt Augusta never wanted to be bothered with kids. She's much happier bestowing her largesse on orphans and the oppressed than she would be spending it on ungrateful offspring—well, at least that is what she says.'

'Izzy!' Basia reprimands, shocked at her assessment of their potential hostess.

'It's the truth. I can't complain, though. She's always been good to me until…. Well, let's just hope she's forgiven me for the argument we had when I left for London.'

Suddenly Basia's stomach drops. 'Izzy, are you telling me we spent most of your expense money on clothes for me when you weren't sure we'd be able to stay with your aunt?'

Izzy had the good grace to appear a little apologetic. 'I was trying not to think too much about it. You see, before I left, my aunt found out I had been writing some pamphlets for the NUWSS, and to say she was angry is an understatement. She believes the militant suffragettes are actually preventing moderates from supporting votes for women, and she issued me an ultimatum—leave the NUWSS or leave home.'

'Clearly you chose to leave home,' Basia says dryly.

Izzy shrugs. 'It wasn't quite that simple. I'm a member of both the NUWSS and the WSPU—the Women's Social and Political Union, which is the NUWSS's more well-behaved cousin. To be honest, I'm not a great fan of some of the violent acts members of the NUWSS have carried out, but I didn't like being told what to do.'

'Izzy, this is not sounding good.'

'It gets worse.'

Basia cringes.

'I had just learned that I had lost Jo to another, and I was emotionally drained. I may have overreacted. I stormed out, telling her I would not have anyone telling me how to live my life—not my father and not her.'

'That was a bit melodramatic,' Basia laughs.

Izzy grins. 'It was, I guess. In all honesty, though, I left for London to hide away and lick my wounds.' Her smile falls away.

Basia places her hand on Izzy's arm. 'I'm sorry you didn't find love with your Jo here, but you can always come back with me, and I'm sure you and Johan... would that be allowed?'

Izzy takes a deep breath, and the tension leaves her shoulders. 'Let's worry about all of that after we find out if we have somewhere to stay tonight.'

With that, she marches up the steps and knocks firmly on the door. Basia joins her as a tall, pasty-faced man with slicked-back hair wearing a formal suit appears in the crack of the doorway.

'Ah, Miss Isolde,' he says, not moving to let them in.

'Hello, Jensen. Is Aunt Augusta receiving?'

He peers down his nose at them, as if deciding whether he'll allow them to enter. Finally, he pulls the door wider. 'Come in. She is taking tea in the drawing room. Please remain here while I enquire as to her availability.'

Basia follows Izzy into the wood-panelled, checkerboard-floored hallway to find Jensen is still there and is staring pointedly at her.

'My friend is Miss Barbara Trelawney of the Northampton Trelawneys,' Izzy says as they place their bags on the floor by the coatroom.

'Very good, Miss Isolde.'

Jensen turns on his heel and disappears through the door to his right.

Basia half turns to Izzy. 'What was that about?'

'Jensen will announce both of us, and he needs your family connections in case Aunt Augusta questions him about you.'

Basia has read about the strictures of upper-class English society, but seeing them in action is a little odd. It's difficult to comprehend that, although she's Izzy's friend, that might not be enough to gain her admittance here—she has to be the right kind of friend.

She doesn't have long to dwell on this, though, as Jensen re-emerges through the door and opens it for the two girls to enter.

Basia has to control her excitement at being shown into an honest-to-god drawing room. She drinks in the Persian rug, the green-papered walls, and the William Morris print curtains before settling on the chairs grouped around the fire opposite them.

The red settee in front of the windows is empty, but one of the two matching chairs by the fireplace is occupied by a woman.

As she turns to face them, Basia almost stumbles. There is no doubt this woman with her dark violet eyes and greying black hair is related to Izzy. In fact, seeing her, Basia knows exactly how Izzy will look in twenty-odd years' time.

'Jensen, could you please arrange another pot of tea and two more settings, and perhaps some more cakes and sandwiches.'

'As you wish, ma'am.'

The door snicks shut behind him, leaving Basia and Izzy standing on the carpet in front of Izzy's aunt. Her stern demeanour causes butterflies to flutter in Basia's stomach. She feels like she's done something wrong and is about to answer for it, but for the life of her, she can't think what it could be. Basia tries not to fidget as Izzy's aunt stares at them with a haughty scowl.

'So, Isolde, you have spread your wings, found life wanting, and have finally returned home where you belong,' the woman states, her piercing blue eyes raking over Izzy. Basia should be offended at being ignored, but, in truth, she just feels grateful the woman hasn't acknowledged her presence.

Beside her, Izzy squares her shoulders. 'No, Aunt Augusta. I have work to do in Winchester and have called to pay my respects.'

'Work?' Augusta snorts the question.

'Yes. I am writing a piece for the *Sunday Times* with

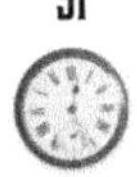

Lionel.' Izzy tilts her chin as if daring her aunt to challenge her assertion. 'My friend, Barbara, has travelled with me to see some of the country before she begins nursing school in a few weeks. Miss Barbara Trelawney, my aunt, Mrs Augusta Hartfield.'

'Pleased to meet you.' Basia manages to force the words out through trembling lips, not keen to draw the attention of their hostess.

The room falls silent, only the crackle of the fire offering some respite. The butterflies in Basia's stomach began to dance—has she said something wrong again?

Finally, Augusta gestures towards the sofa. 'Please, girls, take a seat.'

Basia lets out a breath, happy to follow their hostess's direction. She's making herself comfortable on the settee when there's a knock, and then the butler follows a tray-carrying maid into the room. Jensen removes the tray from the table, and the maid places the new one down. It's all done so effortlessly and with such grace, it's like watching a dance.

When they're alone again, Augusta pours their drinks, and Basia waits for Izzy to move and show her how this all goes. Izzy's eyes flick to Basia, and leaning forward, she places a sandwich and a cake on a plate, then begins taking dainty bites. Basia follows suit as Augusta picks up her cup and sips thoughtfully.

'So you have found work in London, then?' Augusta asks, half turning in her chair so she can better see Izzy.

Izzy's chin tilts upwards a little. 'Yes, Aunt. I told you I could take care of myself.'

A grimace passes over Augusta's face before she

schools herself back into mild interest. 'And you have found lodgings?'

Izzy pauses, her sandwich halfway to her mouth. She places the food back on her plate before answering. 'Yes, in a boarding house in Spitalfields. I do some secretarial work and write pamphlets for room and board.'

This time Augusta's face clearly transmits her distaste. 'If you had not been so obstinate, you could have stayed in your father's townhouse. Am I correct in assuming all this is being provided by the NUWSS?'

Izzy's eye flash defiance as she says, 'Yes.'

Augusta's face is thunderous. 'I told you when you left that I will not have a lawbreaker in my house. If you are a part of their violent protests, I will not have you here now. Not only is what you are doing illegal, but you are making it harder for us women to get the vote.'

Izzy's knuckles whiten as she grips her plate, and Basia wonders how much force the delicate china can take before breaking.

'I told you then, and I am telling you now, that while I do not condemn their actions as you do, I do not take any part in them either.'

Aunt and niece hold each other's gaze, as if they're each waiting for the other to back down. Finally, Izzy says, 'I want to focus on becoming a journalist, not getting myself arrested.'

Her aunt's face loses some of its hauteur as she accepts the olive branch. 'What story are you down here to write?'

'I am covering the Pilgrimage,' Izzy tells her.

Augusta relaxes. 'Now that is something I can support. Many of my friends are going to join the march when it

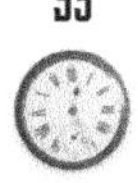

reaches Portsmouth.' She turns to Basia, as if she's seeing her for the first time. 'My apologies for our rudeness, Miss Trelawney, but as you possibly know, my niece and I did not part on the best of terms.'

'Please, you do not need to apologise. We dropped in on you unannounced, after all,' Basia reassures her hostess before reaching for her tea, hoping Augusta will forget her presence again.

Turning back to Izzy, Augusta says, 'You have just missed your father. He only left for home yesterday. He kept hoping you would come back and agree to meet with Lord Rathrune's son to discuss your future.'

Beside Basia, Izzy stiffens. 'Lord Rathrune's son and I meet all the time, and we never discuss marriage. What is more, I have told Father I am not interested in marriage or in becoming someone's wife. I will marry for love or not at all. In the meantime, I will forge my own life on my own terms.'

For the first time since they arrived, Augusta's mask slips and her face softens. 'Ah, your mother still has a hold over you even in death. I know her marriage to your father was not a good one, but not all marriages are like that.'

'So many are, though, and times are changing. Not all people of our class are prepared to accept an arranged marriage. That is why I take my mother's advice—not to settle for anything less than a love match.'

Augusta slowly shakes her head. 'I know it is difficult, Isolde, but sometimes the best we women can do is find a man who allows us to have our own life. I thought you and the lad could have come to an arrangement, especially as you are such good friends.'

Izzy's eyes drift down to the teacup in her hand. 'Lionel and I grew up together, and I am sure we could come to an arrangement... but....'

Basia stares in shock as she realises Lionel is the person Izzy has refused to marry.

Augusta sighs, places her cup back on the table, and reaches for Izzy's hand. 'You wonder why you should have to?'

Izzy nods, her face a mask of determination. In contrast to her niece, Augusta's face is a study in sorrow. 'Given where both your hearts lie, it would have been a good match, though your father suggested it for other reasons.'

Basia shifts uncomfortably in her seat, aware she's witnessing something rather personal.

'You know Josephine is to be married in two weeks,' Augusta says, and Izzy blanches, withdrawing her hand.

Izzy's cup clinks, her hand is shaking so much. Augusta takes it from her and places it on the table.

'So soon?' Izzy's words sound strangled.

'They saw no point in a prolonged engagement,' Augusta says. 'There are some pressing matters in Australia that Stanley needs to deal with, so they moved the wedding date forward.'

The room falls silent. Izzy's first day back in her own life is turning out to be quite eventful. Basia places her hand over Izzy's in a gesture of solidarity, telling her she's there if Izzy needs her.

Blood pounds in Izzy's ears. The wedding is in two weeks. Does that mean she's too late to change Jo's mind, or just in time? No, she didn't come back to force Jo to change but to find a way to… to… be in her life. Still, a part of her must have hoped Jo would change her mind—otherwise, why had the news devastated her like this?

Her heartbeat is so loud, Izzy doesn't catch what her aunt is saying. Shaking her head, she tries to focus.

'Isolde, are you all right?' Basia's voice is close to her ear.

'Um, yes, I am fine.' The words sound hollow, even to her own ears.

'Ah, Jensen,' Augusta calls, 'Miss Isolde and her friend will be staying with us a few nights. Can you please make sure the rooms are made ready?'

'Yes, ma'am,' he replies.

Izzy had thought she would have to beg her aunt to be allowed to stay, but her shock over how quickly things have moved in her absence has done the job for her.

'Perhaps you both need some time to rest before dinner is served. It must have been a tiring trip down here,' her aunt is saying, and Izzy nods in agreement, happy to go with the flow.

'I am sure we would both like to freshen up a bit and, um… compose ourselves,' Basia says nervously.

Izzy knows it is she who's supposed to be taking care of Basia, who is out of her depth in this timeline. But it's the other girl who helps her upstairs and into the hallway outside her old bedroom.

'Your room is here, Miss Trelawney,' Jensen says as he indicates the door opposite Izzy's room. 'The gong to

56

dress for dinner will sound in an hour,' he adds before departing, leaving them alone in the hallway.

Basia wants to ask about dressing for dinner but instead leads Izzy into her room. 'Are you all right?'

'Yes, sorry. It's just....'

Basia pats her hand. 'You've had a shock. Perhaps we both need a bit of a rest and time to regroup before dinner.' She takes a tentative step backwards. 'I'll give you some time alone, but I'm here if you need me.'

Izzy doesn't move. She's aware of Basia hovering, and part of her hears Basia gasp, 'A four-poster bed, how gorgeous.'

Finally, she shakes herself out of her stupor. 'I'll be fine,' she tells Basia as she bundles the girl out of her room and shuts the door.

Izzy studies her bedroom. It's exactly the same as she left it. She sinks down onto the bed, then lies back, her legs dangling over the edge. She had almost asked Basia to swap rooms with her because this one holds perhaps the worst memory of her life.

It was here that she last spoke to Josephine. Here that she made one last-ditch effort not to have her life torn apart. She closes her eyes and tortures herself by replaying the scene in her head.

She pulled Jo into her bedroom and closed the door before clasping Jo's hands in hers and announcing triumphantly,

'I have told Father I will never marry Lionel, that I intend to remain unmarried until I find someone I love.'

Instead of appearing relieved, tears welled in Josephine's eyes. 'No, Isolde—tell me you did not turn down Lionel's offer.'

'It was not a real offer but one he was forced to make by his father,' Izzy insisted. Josephine's face remained stricken, so she continued, 'I cannot marry him when you hold my heart. I mean, I do love Lionel like a brother, and he would not be a bad husband. It is.... Well, I promised my mother never to be forced into marriage unless I love the person. I love you, and I cannot marry you—ergo, I will never get married.'

'Isolde, do not be so dramatic. The love you have for Lionel would be enough,' Jo admonished her. 'And, unlike some, he would allow you the freedom to live your life as you want.'

'True, I would be financially independent, and he would never stop me from doing anything, but society would treat me as his wife, not as Isolde. If that were not bad enough, I would have to give up my dream of becoming a journalist because no newspaper would employ a married woman.'

Josephine squeezed her hands, forcing Isolde to look at her. 'Would it really be so bad, though? You would live in London, and Lionel has such influential friends, you would be right in the intellectual thick of things. There would be plenty for you to write about—if you could not work for a newspaper, you could write pamphlets.'

Izzy shook her head, not believing the words coming from Jo's mouth. 'Do you want me to go away, to leave you alone here?'

'I will not be alone.' Jo's voice was barely above a whisper.

'What?' Izzy asked, then paused. 'Oh, Jo, what have you done?'

Josephine withdrew her hands. She tilted her chin, and when she spoke, her tone was defensive.

'Izzy, I am not like you. I cannot disappoint my father, and I do not want to be ostracised from my family and friends. I am going to marry Stanley and return to the family estate in Dorset.'

Izzy's chest tightened, and her head felt light, as if her heart had stopped beating. 'Jo, you cannot do this. You do not love him, and he does not love you—he is only interested in your money. If he were going to inherit the family estate instead of his brother, he would not look twice at you.'

Josephine shrugged. 'I dare say that is true. In spite of that, though, we like each other, and we both know what we are getting into. Besides, Isolde, people like us cannot expect to marry for love, so I am at least lucky I like my future husband.'

Izzy paced the room in agitation. 'But why—*why* must we settle for less? You love me, I know you do—remember that first kiss under the apple tree and that day we spent by the river? Can you give that up so easily?'

Josephine grabbed hold of Isolde's arm as she passed and swung her so the two were face to face. 'If you marry Lionel, you can settle on your father's estate, and Lionel can move his valet in. We can be "friends forever." Nothing need change. It might even be better.'

'It will be different. I cannot write the types of articles

I want to write in the country. Also, they are far more conservative down there, so we would be even more constrained by our husbands' wishes.'

'Oh, Izzy, that is simply nonsense,' Jo snapped impatiently. 'Both Lionel and Stanley are modern sorts of men. They would allow us to live our own lives—you know they would.'

Izzy smiled slyly. 'Would Stanley be happy with our arrangement? He is already talking about visiting your father's property in Australia. He wants a great adventure. If you go with him, nothing will be the same.'

Jo faltered. 'We would only be away for a few years—'

'Or forever.... Once we set our feet on different paths, we will have different things influencing our actions, and we will be pulled apart,' Izzy said, pleading her case, all the while knowing she was losing this battle.

Jo confirmed this when she straightened her shoulders and schooled her face into an iciness Izzy had never seen before. 'I have made up my mind.'

Izzy's stomach lurched, and she feared she may be sick. Ignoring the pain, she clenched her fists and defiantly said, 'Then so have I. I am going to London.'

'Izzy, you cannot. How will you survive?'

'I have been offered some work with the NUWSS, and I have the allowance my mother left me. I am sure I can get by.'

'Izzy, why go like that when you can go with Lionel as your husband and live in your father's house?'

Part of Izzy wanted to find a way through this. In her heart she knew Josephine would never defy convention, and yet Izzy would never break the promise she'd made to her mother to only every marry for love. So she said, 'I want to make a stand. I want to show that women do not need husbands to have a good life. I want to do this so that in the future, women like us do not have to settle for less.'

Izzy opens her eyes and stares at the rosette on the ceiling. *Was that truly only a couple of months ago in this timeline? I've seen so much since then, and it's been exciting and exhilarating, but also so very lonely. That loneliness smudges what once seemed black-and-white into grey.*

'I thought I could make things better, but I haven't changed anything, and it certainly hasn't been better for me,' she says, and her voice echoes in the heavy silence of the room. *What about Josephine? Is she happy? Will she be pleased to see me, or will I still be a problem for her to solve so she can have her cake and eat it too?*

The bell to dress for dinner sounds, and Izzy lets out a deep sigh before hauling herself off the bed. These questions certainly won't be answered tonight, and she owes it to Basia to introduce her properly to Winchester society.

Heading to the closet, she leafs through her clothes and extracts two evening gowns. She places them on the bed before taking a moment to push aside the memories she longs to forget. Tonight she must think of Basia first. She'll be excited about dressing for dinner and about living in one of her historical novels.

During the short walk to Basia's door, she plasters a smile on her face and calls brightly, 'Want to come into my room and dress for dinner?'

Basia flings open the door, her face an image of barely contained excitement. 'I thought you would never ask.'

Dinner turned out to be a rather stilted affair, with conversation limited to "please pass the salt". It seems Izzy and Augusta had said everything of importance at teatime. Fortunately Basia is happy enough to amuse herself with the novelty of being waited on for the first couple of courses. She even pinches herself to make sure she isn't dreaming when the maid in a black dress and white apron appears to remove her plate.

The novelty soon wears off, and she finds herself unable to stand the tense silence any longer. Making conversation, she asks Augusta, 'Have you had a lot to do with the suffragist movement?'

Augusta smiles and turns to her. 'I have been campaigning for women's rights for as long as I can remember and have assisted with gathering signatures for many a petition to Parliament to extend the vote to women.'

'Have you met with members of Parliament yourself?' Basia is excited to be talking with another person who has a history in fighting for women's right.

'A few, yes, at political salons. Of course, I used to spend time with the Kensington ladies when I was younger,

and I joined the National Society for Women's Suffrage in Manchester when I married.'

'Yes, Aunt Augusta is acquainted with all the great and the good in the suffragist movement,' Izzy says, her tone a little bitter.

As August's face hardens, Basia's hands clench in frustration. Izzy's comment is certain to return the tension to the room.

'And I know the suffragettes as well, young lady. Just because I do not agree with their violent tactics does not mean I have not worked with them in the past. After all, they also sponsor peaceful activities aimed at extending the vote to women.'

Izzy's cutlery clatters to the table. 'You sneer at their tactics, but what did your petitions and all those signatures achieve?'

'More than your friends and their throwing stones through windows and chaining themselves to railings ever have,' Augusta retorts. 'At least we won some important parliamentarians over to our side.'

Izzy's jaw juts defiantly. 'At least the suffragettes have everyone talking about votes for women.'

'And forced the undecided to become our opponents,' Augusta comments sourly.

Sensing a fight brewing, Basia knows she must tread carefully, for although the women seem to agree that females should have the vote, they clearly disagree on how to achieve that goal. Trying for a mutually safe topic, she asks, 'What do you think of the Women's Pilgrimage?'

If she expected an easing of tensions, she is disappointed. Augusta turns in her seat, deliberately blocking Izzy out,

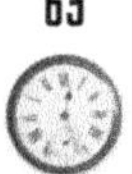

and says, 'I think it is a grand initiative. With public opinion turning against votes for women, I wholly support the idea of marching through the country, showing everyone that most of the women who want to vote are peace-loving citizens like they are.'

'But what will it achieve in the long run?' Basia asks the question before Izzy can, and with way less animosity.

'Perhaps not much,' Augusta concedes, 'but it is also a great opportunity for women to talk directly with people without the filter of the press. At least they will be able to set the record straight.'

Basia smiles, pleased she finally managed to change the tone of the conversation. 'Will you be marching at all?'

'Oh, my dear, I am far too old for that. Though I will be taking the train to London to join the rally in Hyde Park on the twenty-sixth of the month.'

Izzy's laugh sounds harsh in the quiet dining room. 'And you think the police will allow such a large group of suffragists to walk through the streets of London? There will likely be a riot. Already reports of locals attacking groups on the march are starting to filter through.'

Basia catches a brief look of pity on Augusta's face before she rearranges it into a haughty mask. 'Isolde, I know you think very little of us, believing we have accepted the slow pace of change. Even so, you should at least trust us enough to believe we will run an orderly march and that we have spoken with the correct authorities.'

'I do respect you and your ladies, Aunt, but you cannot deny many of those opposed to women's suffrage will stop at nothing to throw our cause into disrepute or to ensure we do not succeed.'

'On *that* we do agree,' Augusta say. 'Now, shall we take tea in the drawing room?'

Great, another torturous hour of this. Basia is exhausted from tiptoeing through the minefield of this family relationship, and it's taking the shine off her first experience of a life she's read so much about.

'If you will excuse me, I am tired and not the best of company.' Izzy stands, offering her aunt a tight smile. 'Good night to you both.'

It's all Basia can do not to heave a sigh of relief.

After Izzy's departure, Basia follows Augusta into the drawing room, smiling to herself at the delicious sound her sea-green silk skirts make as she walks.

For the next hour, the two women sit by the fire playing the exciting new game of gin rummy. When Basia wins the fifth hand in a row, Augusta exclaims, 'You have luck on your side tonight, Miss Trelawney.'

'Please, call me Barbara, and I do seem to be lucky at cards tonight,' Basia demurs, unable to tell her hostess that she's been playing the game for years with her family when it's only recently arrived in England.

'Another hand?'

Basia stifles a yawn and responds, 'My apologies, I am a little tired after the travel today.'

'Of course, my dear. Do you know the way to your room, or should I call a maid?'

'I shall be fine, thank you,' Basia says as she rises to her feet and heads for the door. As she reaches for the handle she turns. 'And thank you for a lovely evening.'

'Oh pish,' Augusta says, but the smile tugging at her lips shows she's pleased with the compliment.

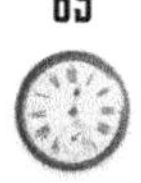

CHAPTER THREE
FACING OLD HURTS

Everyone is turning, distracted by some guy waving a gun around and yelling about the fall of civilisation. He is clearly a maniac. Her attention is still on Allan. His wound isn't healed, so she's come along to support him. Sweat beads on his forehead, and she's worried he has taken on too much. She's still watching when his eyes widen in surprise as a sharp crack fills the air followed by a red bloom spreading on his shirt. He sways and collapses as she reaches out to support him, but he drops to the ground in spite of her efforts.

'No.'

'No.' Basia sits bolt upright, the bedsheet clasped in her hands. It takes her a moment to realise she's in the guest room of Aunt Augusta's house in Winchester in 1913 and not watching Allan die yet again years in the future.

Finally, her breathing slows and the shaking stops. Her grief at the loss of Allan churns her insides. It's all that's left of him.

She lies back on the pillows. 'I should not have promised I would carry on your fight to bring the people of our world together.'

Although there's no one in the room to answer her, saying the words out loud is soothing, and the well of grief weighing her down doesn't seem so heavy. Trying to lighten it even more, she continues voicing all her fears.

'Perhaps we would have been better off allowing time to end, because it will take strong, committed leaders to mend the rift between the people left above ground and those who escaped below.'

A tear slides down her cheek. 'I'm not strong enough to lead them, and I don't have the commitment and passion you did.'

Of course, no one answers and tells her it's all right to be scared. Still, there is something cathartic about speaking aloud the words she's held inside for so long, even if she's left feeling hollow and alone.

A soft knock at the door has her closing her eyes, hoping whoever it is will go away. No such luck. The door opens quietly. Whoever enters must be tiptoeing, as the next thing Basia hears is the click as it closes.

She opens an eye and finds a discreet maid has left a bowl of warm water and a fluffy white towel on the dresser. Sighing, she forces herself out of bed, reluctant to start the day. After the strained atmosphere at dinner last night, she's in no rush to make her way down to breakfast.

No doubt Izzy and her aunt will maintain a stoic silence interspersed with short, sharp exchanges, as they had last night. This morning, Basia will not make the same mistake of trying to thaw the chill.

Now dressed appropriately, she hopes, in a shirt and blouse, her hair in a plait, Basia pulls back the heavy curtains to find out what the day is like.

The street below bustles with people, carriages, horses and carts, and the odd motorcar. Watching them go about their lives is like seeing a scene in one of her books come to life, and she has to stop herself from clapping her hands like a small child. She can't wait to get out and about and immerse herself in the story.

She swiftly crosses the hall and knocks on Izzy's door. She opens it when she hears a faint 'Come in.'

She's happy to find her travelling companion dressed in a similar outfit to her own, but Basia bites back her exclamation of relief when she sees how pale her friend is and how listless and dark-rimmed her eyes are. Izzy looks like she hasn't slept a wink.

'Are you all right?' Basia asks.

Izzy attempts a smile. 'It's nothing a cup of coffee won't fix. Hopefully my aunt or one of her staff has remembered I prefer it in the mornings to tea.'

Feeling guilty about her earlier reluctance, she hooks her arm through Izzy's. 'Let's go and see, shall we?'

Downstairs, the breakfast room is blessedly empty. Izzy literally sighs with pleasure when she sees the coffeepot on the sideboard. She bypasses the breakfast trays and pours herself a cup of the black liquid before taking a seat at the table and enjoying a long sip.

SUFFRAGETTE

Lifting the lids of the hot dishes, Basia is faced with a difficult choice. Along with bacon, eggs, and sausages, one dish contains some odd fish and another something made with rice that smells faintly spiced.

'The fish are kippers, and the rice is kedgeree,' Izzy says, standing and making her way towards the food. Picking up a plate, she serves herself a little of everything before returning to her chair.

Basia is more circumspect, taking some sausages and egg and adding a little of the kedgeree to try. As she is about to sit, Augusta sweeps into the room with a bundle of black-and-white fur tucked into the crook of her arm.

'Good morning, my lovelies. And what a grand day it is too. I want you to meet Cuddles, my new companion. He arrived today.'

Izzy chokes on her food as she snorts a laugh. Augusta's frown forces her to pull herself together. 'You called your dog Cuddles?'

Ignoring the disdain in Izzy's voice, Augusta says, 'Yes, and a most apt name it is too. He only arrived this morning, and all he has done is cuddle with me.'

Izzy stops eating. 'He came today?'

Augusta continues to serve herself breakfast one-handed, then takes a seat with the dog settled in her lap before answering. 'Yes, the man who delivers our meat has been promising me a pup from one of his litters for some time.' She feeds the dog a morsel of sausage before starting in on her breakfast.

Izzy sends Basia a meaningful look. Basia shakes her head, not having the least idea of what Izzy is trying to tell her.

Izzy's voice sounds inside her head. *Sigma, is that you?*

'What are you doing?' she leans in and whispers close to Izzy's ear.

Izzy nods meaningfully at Augusta before answering in mindspeak. *Sigma said he might try to meet us here, and I'm pretty sure that's him.*

Basia stares at the dog sitting placidly in Augusta's lap. Sigma, the Time Guardian who helped save the world, could not get any further from his last animal disguise if he truly has taken the form of Cuddles. She had met him when he was Bruno—a German shepherd working as a tracker for the military.

She shakes her head as she takes in the now snoozing dog. 'I do not think that is him. Or maybe the Time Fixers stripped you of your powers when they sent you back.'

'You could hear me talking, could you not?'

Basia nods.

'Then I can still mindspeak.' *Sigma? Cuddles?* Izzy sends again. 'Maybe he does not want to upset Aunt Augusta by talking with us,' Izzy says when there's no response.

'What are you girls whispering about?' Augusta interrupts them, her tone terse. 'Isolde, you look dreadful. There are crow's feet forming around your eyes—it must be that London air.'

Or the fact that I'm five years older than I was when I left.

Basia wonders if Izzy knows she mindspoke what was likely meant to be internal dialogue.

'Isolde, perhaps you could do something with your day. Like taking Barbara for a stroll in the park.'

Basia almost leaps from her seat at the suggestion,

70

but Izzy is slower to move.

'Come on,' Basia says. 'The fresh air will do us both some good.'

Izzy rises listlessly and makes eye contact with the dog in Augusta's lap. Cuddles raises his head expectantly, but Basia can't sense any mind contact.

Twenty minutes later the two girls arrive in the hallway, coats on, hatted and gloved. Jensen opens the door for them, his face impassive. Yesterday's animosity seemed to have disappeared when Augusta invited the girls to stay.

As Basia rushes down the stairs to the street, excited to get going, Izzy falls behind. She turns to find her friend in conversation with the butler. When Izzy rejoins her, she asks, 'What was that about?'

Slipping her arm through Basia's, Izzy says, 'Nothing important. Jensen was admonishing me not to hurt my aunt again or he wouldn't admit me back into the house—ever.'

'Wow, he's really protective of your aunt, isn't he?'

Izzy chuckles, and colour appears in her cheeks for the first time that day. 'You know, I always thought Jensen was sweet on Augusta, and he just confirmed it.'

Basia's free hand covers her mouth. 'You don't think they're....'

Another laugh escapes her companion. 'I wouldn't put it past Augusta. She's always been more egalitarian than most. However, I think that may be a step too far even for her.'

'Shame,' Basia says. 'Wouldn't it be nice if she were spending her time with someone she's close to when you're not here?'

71

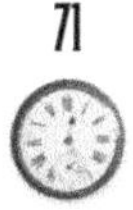

Izzy wrinkles her nose. 'Jensen? No, I don't want to think about it.'

'He's not that bad,' Basia laughs.

'Come on, enough with the romance. Let me show you the famous Winchester Cathedral, followed by a visit to the most excellent teahouse in town.'

Winchester High Street is a bustle of well-dressed people window shopping, walking, or stopping to talk with friends and acquaintances. Basia's head swings left and right until she becomes dizzy trying to take everything in.

It's not only the sheer number of people and the sense of having fallen into one of her favourite novels—it's also the experience of walking through a town that hasn't been devastated by nuclear bombs and seeing buildings left to rot because no one lives in them.

To say she's overwhelmed would be an understatement. That sensation only increases when Izzy leads her round the corner into the Cathedral Precinct. Winchester Cathedral itself is a stunning vision in creme stone outlined by a cloudless blue sky. It is beautiful and amazing and awe-inspiring. Basia gasps, but Izzy continues walking, unmoved, as if this is a building like any other.

Catching Izzy up, she asks, 'Can we go inside?' She's aware that she sounds like a small child asking for a treat, but she's so excited, she doesn't care.

Izzy doesn't alter her course, circumnavigating the

park in front of the building, deftly avoiding the headstones dotted around. 'Maybe another time. I am a little tired for it today.'

Turning to her friend to object, she finds Izzy's pallor has returned, and she's looking more washed-out than ever. Making an effort to quell her disappointment, she takes pity on her friend and says, 'I know what will pick you up—a nice cup of tea.'

The smile Izzy forces at the mention of tea doesn't reach her eyes, and Basia begins to worry her friend is falling sick. No, her eyes are clear, and she isn't exhibiting any signs of a fever. Perhaps this is more a sickness of the heart than the body.

Izzy picks up the pace as they return to the high street, slowing down only to enter the teahouse. When Basia sees the cakes in the window, her eyes almost pop out of her head. The teahouse in London had been utilitarian compared to the confectionary delights on display here.

The shop is well lit but still dull against the bright sunshine outside. Basia grins when their waitress appears. She's dressed in a black ankle-length dress with a white apron over top, just like the maid last night. This will never get old. As the woman leads them through the room, Basia comments on how few people are sat at the tables.

'It is a little early for morning tea, miss. Are you sure you want to sit back here in the dark? A table is free by the window. Most people find it enjoyable to watch passers-by as they take their tea.'

'This will do fine, thank you,' Izzy says as she takes a seat. When the waitress tuts disapprovingly, she adds, 'I have a touch of a headache and prefer the dark.'

Basia runs her hand over the white lace tablecloth. It's been starched within an inch of its life and is so pristine, she hopes she won't embarrass herself by soiling it.

The waitress takes their order for English breakfast tea and two slices of their speciality—a spiced marble cake.

After the waitress departs, Basia angles her chair to get a better view of the shop. Izzy glares and shifts so her face is obscured from the rest of the patrons.

'What's the matter?' Basia asks. 'You snapped at the waitress, which is not like you at all.'

'Nothing is the matter. I am fine,' Izzy insists. 'Look, here are our drinks.'

They have their morning tea in an awkward silence. The cake is as special as Basia expected—the mixture of spices creates a taste explosion in her mouth. Having heard her mother talk of the spices they used in food before World War Three, it's a real treat to finally experience it.

She wonders how she will ever be able to go back to eating bland food when she returns home and opens her mouth to say so to Izzy. Then she promptly shuts it again when she sees the closed expression on her companion's face. It's not the time for idle chitchat.

Izzy pours them a second cup of tea, and Basia takes the opportunity to study the rest of the customers. The shop has become much busier since their arrival, with most of the tables occupied by women dressed in an array of colourful outfits, and the occasional man dotted here and there. Basia drinks in the sight, committing everything to memory.

'Would you like another pot?' Izzy asks when they've finished their drinks.

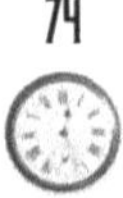

In spite of Izzy's reluctance to leave, Basia is itching to get back out into the world. 'No, I'm good. I wouldn't mind a walk around the shops if you're feeling up to it.'

'That should be fine,' Izzy responds without much enthusiasm.

Izzy calls for the bill, and when the formalities are done, Basia leads them back through the shop, only to have a gentleman step into their path when they're almost at the door.

Glancing up, Basia starts. 'Lionel?'

The man grins, and his green eyes sparkle with good humour. 'Not quite, but we do look rather alike. I am Stanley, Lionel's better-looking cousin. Pleased to make your acquaintance....'

Stanley has such a way about him, and he looks so much like Lee that Basia immediately feels like she's in the presence of an old friend, so she offers up the name Izzy chose for her without a second thought. 'I am Barbara, and my friend is—'

'Isolde and I have known each other since we were children. Nice to see you back in Winchester,' he says, looking over Basia's shoulder at Izzy.

Basia half turns in the small space between the diners to find her friend whiter than a ghost and frozen still, staring fixedly at the girl still seated at the table beside them. Recognition hits Basia like a lightning bolt—she needs no introductions.

She's Johan.

As the thought enters Basia's head, the girl's eyes flick up, slide over her, and lock with Stanley's. Something unspoken passes between them, and Stanley nods. He takes Basia's hand, tucking it in the crook of his elbow.

'Since we are clearly to be good friends, I wonder if you would do me the honour of taking a turn round the cathedral gardens with me?' He winks conspiratorially. 'I think these two have a lot to talk about, and we will just be in the way.'

'Um... Isolde?' She turns to seek her approval, but from the look on her friend's face, she's forgotten Basia is even here.

As Stanley leads her to the door, Josephine says, 'Take a seat, Isolde. I will order us a fresh pot of tea.'

Basia pauses in the doorway, waiting for some sign that Izzy is all right.

'Come, I promise you will be safe with me,' Stanley tells her, and she reluctantly lets him lead her away, sensing Izzy needs this time alone with her Jo.

From the recesses of her mind, Izzy watches Stanley leading Basia away, and that part of her acknowledges that this is not right. Not just because she's responsible for Basia, but because Stanley has the knack of getting people talking, and she's worried Basia might let something slip. As they head down the street, she can already see they are deep in conversation.

I should follow them, make sure Basia is all right. A great idea, but she can no more move and leave the teashop than she can stop herself from breathing. She takes a seat opposite Jo, her eyes still firmly stuck on Basia's retreating back.

Finally, she allows herself to look at Josephine, and a tumult of feelings rushes through her: love, regret, hurt, and then finally, she settles on anger. With shaking hands, she pushes her chair back, intending to follow Basia, but Jo reaches for her.

'No, please do not run away again,' Jo entreats her, and the hurt in her voice freezes Izzy in place.

Uncertain of her next move, Izzy whispers, 'I am not sure we have anything to say to each other anymore.'

A waitress arrives with tea, and Jo busies herself pouring while Izzy resists the urge to drink in the sight of her. She loses the battle. Jo has attempted to tame her thick chestnut hair into a bun, but already bits are escaping and forming curls around her face in the humid air. Her dark brows draw into a frown as she concentrates on the task at hand.

Most people would find her face unremarkable—that is, until she turns her chocolate-brown eyes their way. When she looks up at Izzy, she's lost for a moment in those eyes, and all her fears melt away.

'I am sorry.' The words tumble from her lips before she realises she's saying them.

Jo pauses, the teapot hovering over the table. 'Sorry for what?' Her voice is strained, but she holds Izzy's gaze.

'I am sorry for running away. Sorry for not taking you with me. Sorry for.... Oh, I do not know... everything.'

Jo puts the pot down, then reaches across the table and clasps Izzy's hand. The touch is brief, the merest brushing of skin against skin, but Izzy shivers in response.

Soon that hand is raising a cup to Jo's lips, and Izzy takes a sip of her own brew, desperate for Jo to respond.

'Where did you go?' Jo finally asks. 'Was it London?'

Izzy nods. 'Yes, I took up the position writing pamphlets for the NUWSS. I have travelled a bit too.' *You have no idea how I have travelled.* She wants to tell Jo everything. They had shared all their deepest secrets ever since they met when Jo's father purchased a manor in the same county.

Izzy's father, a member of the aristocracy, was at first disdainful of the new money from the North moving in. However, the two men soon found they had much in common and met frequently, allowing Jo and Izzy to get to know each other. Of course, it helped that Jo's mother had come from 'good stock'—as her father put it.

'Have you been up to Manchester? I hear their branch has been quite active lately.' Jo's voice is maddeningly polite, giving none of her feelings away.

Izzy nods. 'Just the once.'

'Funny, we may even have been there at the same time, as Father took me up last visit. He decided I should start learning the business since I am to take over the reins.'

Izzy's eyes widen. 'I thought he would be training up Stanley.'

Jo's nose wrinkles. 'I am not sure Stanley sees himself managing a fabric and clothing factory. He is far more interested in the sheep producing the wool than how we turn it into cloth and then into clothing.'

'So you still intend to take over the factories and start improving conditions for the women and children who work for you?' Izzy tries to keep the surprise from her voice, but she can tell from the frown on Jo's face that she hasn't succeeded.

'Of course. Why would that change?' Jo's tone is guarded.

Because you're marrying Stanley. The unspoken words settle between them, and they fall silent, not quite able to find the old rhythm of their relationship.

They finish up their tea, and then they both rise as Jo places a few coins on the table before joining Izzy. In a last-ditch attempt to resurrect their friendship, Izzy threads her arm through Jo's as they leave the teashop.

Jo stiffens a little at her touch but doesn't remove her arm. 'Come, let us catch the others up,' she says.

With Jo close by her side, Izzy finally plucks up the courage to raise the subject that has haunted her since last night. 'Aunt Augusta said you are to be married in two weeks.'

Jo moves away a little, placing some distance between them. 'No point in waiting. Is that why you are back—to try and stop me?'

The question throws Izzy off balance, and she slides a look at Jo, trying to gauge how she should respond. 'No.... Yes.... Look, I do not know why I am back. I just know that I missed you. I—'

'Isolde, please. I am at peace with my decision. If you have come back to cause trouble, then we had best part ways here and now, and you can return to London.'

Izzy's stomach clenches, and she feels sick at the thought of being parted from Jo so soon after she's found her again. They walk along in silence for a bit, and Izzy considers whether the price of being friends with Jo might be too high for her to bear after all.

Being her friend and nothing more. Always seeing her

with Stanley. Is it enough? She had thought she wanted to come back to this, but perhaps distance made things look rosier—or perhaps she remembers Jo's feelings as having been stronger.

Taking a deep breath, she makes a decision—for today, a little bit of Jo is better than none. She can worry about the future later.

'What are your plans for after the wedding?'

Jo's step falters, and she glances sidelong at Izzy, as if trying to get a sense of her motivation. 'We will go down to Dorset for a while. I will open the house, and Stanley will see to the farm. Then, after a time, he will go to Australia and sort out some problems we are having with the sheep station. It has been left to a caretaker manager for too long.'

Izzy's world tilts on its axis. She doesn't want to ask the next question, but she also needs to know. 'And... will you go with him?' She dare not breathe while she waits for Jo's answer.

'I do not know.... There is so much to think about—the farm, the factory, our holdings in Australia—but I am considering it.'

But you don't mention what Stanley wants. Is this a marriage or a business arrangement? Izzy is wise enough not to voice her opinion.

'Ah, look—there is Stanley with your friend,' Jo says, changing the subject.

Izzy allows herself to be dragged along the path towards Stanley and Basia. All the while she wonders how it's come to be that she can no longer share her innermost thoughts with the person she was once closest to in all the world.

SUFFRAGETTE

Stanley chats away, pointing out the sights of Winchester and telling Basia about some of the more colourful residents as he threads their way back towards the cathedral grounds. She finds him pleasant and diverting, and he's obviously well liked, going by the number of people who smile and say good morning to him.

'It was such good luck that we ran into you and Isolde at the teahouse this morning,' he says as they take a turn round the Cathedral Precinct. 'Josephine has sorely missed her friend since she went away.'

Basia isn't quite sure what to say. It isn't only that she's nervous about talking to anyone in this time, but also because, although she knows how Izzy feels about this man's fiancée, she's unsure if Stanley is fully aware of their relationship. She decides to change the subject with a simple sentence even she couldn't get wrong. 'So, you and Josephine are getting married soon?'

'Yes, in two weeks' time, I shall be a married man.' Stanley sounds neither excited nor upset by the prospect. In fact, he could be talking about a business transaction for all the interest he shows.

Basia isn't quick enough to mask her confusion at his answer.

Stanley stops and takes her hand in his. 'Perhaps you think I am a cad because I do not love Josephine, or at least pretend to love her. Maybe you think I am only in this for her money. Or maybe you think she and Isolde are more suited?' His eyes twinkle with mischief.

'Um....' Basia chews on her bottom lip, unsure of how to answer such a direct question from a virtual stranger. She needs to be careful with her words and remember that he isn't a friend—no matter how familiar he feels to her.

Stanley isn't going to let her off the hook that easily, though. 'Maybe you wonder how I can bear to be around such an abomination... a woman who loves another woman? Or is it you cannot understand how I can marry a woman whom I know loves another?'

Stanley studies her, head cocked to the side, waiting for an answer.

'Well, more the second, I guess,' she finally replies.

Stanley smiles. 'It is true that many people will find the idea strange, which is why we only talk about such things with close friends. I am sure we can trust in your discretion.' An eyebrow rises in question, and Basia nods.

'Yes, you can trust me. I am great at keeping secrets.'

'Good.' He pats her hand, and they carry on wandering. 'You see, I have no interest in, um... that side of things— physical things between people.'

He pauses, perhaps waiting for a reaction from her, or maybe because that's all he's going to say. Basia opens her mouth to speak, but Stanley continues before she can utter a word.

'You appear to be good friends with Isolde, and I am sure you will hear the whole story sooner or later.'

Or perhaps not at all, Basia thinks, not sure where this conversation is going, or if she even wants it to continue.

Stanley appears unaware of her discomfort as he continues talking. 'And at least you will hear it from me. I have read about it in books, of course, and some of the chaps have talked about different things, but it is all alien to me. I do not know whether it is because I am yet to find the right person, or perhaps I am not built that way… the way you need to be to feel physically attracted to someone.'

Basia isn't sure where to look.

Stanley finally seems to remember she's there. 'Ah dear, I did not mean to tell you all of that…. It is perhaps because you are one of those rare women who listens more than they speak.'

He stares at her as if expecting a response. There's so much going round in her head, she's unable to form a single coherent thought. Although she had come across studies on asexual humans while learning medicine from her mother, she's never had such a frank conversation with anyone about their sexuality. She understands the theory that some people are asexual from birth, but her sampling of humanity has been so small, she hasn't come across anyone quite like Stanley before.

'Oh dear, have I horrified you?' Stanley's face is a study of concern, and she almost falls over her own words in her effort to reassure him he hasn't.

'No, no! Of course not.' She pats his arm. 'It's just, I've never had someone speak so openly about their sexuality before. But I'm okay with it… with you, I mean.'

As the words leave her mouth, she realises her mistake—she's answered as Basia, not Barbara. Her eyes widen with dismay as Stanley's brows draw into a frown.

Closing her eyes, she sighs inwardly, wishing Izzy were here to help. She isn't, though, and Basia is going to have to use her own wits to get out of this. Opening her eyes, she lowers her gaze to show her dismay.

Offering an apology to the real Barbara Trelawney, Basia invents an excuse straight out of one of her many books.

'Oh, Stanley, please do not say anything. I am from the wrong side of the Trelawney family, and we are not quite proper. Although I was at school with Isolde, it was only because my uncle paid the fees. Sometimes I forget where I am and drop back into my regular speech. I have to be careful because we are staying with Isolde's aunt, and she would not have me in the house if she knew where I really came from.'

Stanley studies her, as if trying to assess the truth of her words.

Please be the true gentleman I believe you are, Basia prays.

He nods once, as if her words have convinced him.

'It seems you and I are both to hold each other's secrets. We really are best of friends now.'

He places her hand back into the crook of his arm, and they continue walking. Then he carries on talking as if her slip had never happened.

'Of course, once Josephine and I are married, I will do the right thing and father an heir. It is my duty and all that, what with Josephine being an only child. All part of the deal, really. After that, I suspect we will both fill our lives in other ways. Society will be appeased and will let us get on with our lives in peace, and we will both find some measure of happiness in this arrangement.'

SUFFRAGETTE

While Stanley continues talking about his plans, Basia grows quiet and more than a little sad. Like Stanley, she had grown up in an age where same-sex relationships, nonbinary, and asexual people were frowned upon. At some point in history, the world had begun to accept people's differences, only to have that tolerance disappear when faced with the prospect of human extinction.

Procreation is at the heart of societal norms in both times. Here they protect bloodlines and inheritances, while in the future, they ensure there are enough people for humanity to survive.

Suddenly they stop walking again, and Stanley appears to be waiting for her to speak.

Unsure of what he'd asked, she fumbles for something appropriate to say. 'It is nice you have found a solution that works for you and Josephine.'

'But not for Isolde.' Stanley shakes his head slowly. 'She wants to take on the entire world and change it. I am afraid it is all or nothing for her, and that is what saddens Josephine the most.'

'And you would be happy to have Isolde in your lives?' Basia asks, not really believing someone would be all right with sharing their partner.

'If it makes Josephine happy…,' Stanley chuckles. 'Even if it did not make Josephine happy, I enjoy Isolde's company. I am not sure she likes mine so much, though.' He appears genuinely saddened by that thought.

Part of Basia wants to agree with Stanley, that leading a good and peaceful life is something to aspire to. Then she remembers how stifled she'd felt before Allan arrived and opened her eyes to the possibility of change. 'But surely Isolde is right to challenge things. How else will anything ever get better?'

'Challenging is all right, but expecting radical change?' Stanley shrugs. 'People's minds and their beliefs are not that easily altered, especially those who have a death grip on power. Besides, society has to have rules, you know, or we would descend into chaos.'

Basia stares at Stanley, unable to believe he's prepared to accept that he must hide his real self. 'But do you not long to be who you are, for people to accept you?'

Such a look of sadness crosses Stanley's face that Basia immediately regrets speaking so forcefully. Then he nods towards a couple across the park. The thin, darkhaired young man is arguing earnestly with the dainty blonde woman.

'There are worse things than marrying for friendship and position. Take my friend Nathanial over there. He is head over heels in love with Hannah, and they have been betrothed for more than a year. Every time he even suggests getting married, she comes up with another reason they should wait a little longer.'

Intrigued, Basia watches the couple as their fight becomes more animated. They both have a look of hopelessness about them, and it pulls at Basia's heart.

'Why does he not simply give her an ultimatum? "Marry me or I will find someone who will"?' Basia asks.

Stanley sighs. 'Because he loves her, and he cannot imagine himself happy without her in his life.'

A single tear escapes Basia's eye as sadness presses down on her—she empathises with Nathanial. She had met her soulmate in Allan, and then he'd died so soon after. The world is not as rich a place without him.

'Oh dear, I did not mean to sadden you. I mean, really, it is not as bad as all that. Come, I will introduce you,' Stanley blusters as he steers her towards the couple. 'I will prove to you I was exaggerating to make a point.'

His panic over her lone tear is sweet, as is his wanting to make everything right. Basia wipes the tear away, her mood a little lighter now.

As they approach, Basia can't help but overhear the conversation between Stanley's friends.

'Is a month too long to plan for? And we can still meet our commitments while planning a wedding. It does not have to be anything too spectacular. In fact, from my perspective, the quieter the better,' Nathanial is saying, almost begging.

Hannah places her hands on her hips. 'Are you suggesting we put ourselves before our duties? As educated people, we have a responsibility to help those less fortunate.'

'So, what, we put our own lives on hold indefinitely—oh, hello, Stanley.' Nathanial turns to them, his face red, but Basia can't tell whether it's from his anger or embarrassment at someone overhearing their private conversation.

'I am so sorry, old chap, I did not mean to interrupt,' Stanley apologises, although from his tone, Basia thinks he intended to do just that.

'No, no problem, simply a bit of a misunderstanding,' Nathanial says, trying not to look at his fiancée.

Hannah plucks at something on her floral-patterned skirt, studiously not meeting anyone's gaze.

'Nathanial, Hannah, I would like to introduce you to a friend of mine, Barbara. She is newly arrived in Winchester

and is staying with Isolde Fielding.' In contrast to the tension surrounding the group, Stanley's voice is friendly, as though he thinks he can single-handedly clear the air.

'Does Josephine not mind you walking around with lovely young women?' Nathanial asks as he shakes Basia's outstretched hand.

Stanley runs a finger nervously around his collar. Basia wonders how many of these everyday comments he must endure and if it ever annoys him, living up to society's conventions.

'Um, well, Isolde's close friend Barbara and I are out for a friendly stroll in public, so there is nothing for her to worry about. Besides, she knows she can trust me.'

Hannah's skirt suddenly seems to be fixed, and she raises her eyes. 'Of course she does. Nathanial, leave him alone. He clearly only has eyes for Josephine. I mean, have you ever seen him spend more than a moment with another woman in the whole time we have been in Winchester?'

Basia flushes with embarrassment on Stanley's behalf as an awkward silence falls over the group. It's broken by Hannah before it's allowed to become too uncomfortable.

'We must make our apologies, Stanley, Barbara. We are expected for lunch with my parents. We should have dinner soon, Stanley, before the wedding.'

'Yes, we must. I will mention it to Josephine,' Stanley agrees as Hannah slips her hand into Nathanial's and virtually drags him away.

When they are well out of earshot, Stanley says, 'See? He is madly in love with her, and she leads him round like a child.'

Basia's lips curl into a smile. Stanley's defence of his

friend is heart-warming. 'He seemed to be holding his own when we arrived,' she says, because she feels someone should be standing up for Nathanial. Though, in truth, she agrees with Stanley.

'He would jump into the jaws of hell for her, and she would let him. I much prefer the arrangement I have with Josephine. It is an honest bargain, and I still get to be my own man.'

As she watches the couple cross the common, she wonders if she had felt empathy for Nathanial because she's so like him—following the one she loved even if it wasn't in her best interests. When she was with Allan, she had lost sight of her own goals.

Of course, she truly believes uniting the disparate groups in future Hampshire is the best way to prevent another war. What she worries about is whether or not she's the best person to lead people towards that goal, in spite of her deathbed promise to Allan.

'Barbara? Are you all right? You have come over all pale. Have we overdone it? Shall I find us a place to sit?'

Basia pulls herself back to the present to find a concerned Stanley clasping her hand. Unable to explain her scattered thoughts, she's relieved to see Izzy and Josephine approaching.

'I am fine, Stanley, and here is your fiancée and Isolde.'

With the others joining them, Stanley is so distracted, she doesn't have to explain her sudden sadness. As they return to Aunt Augusta's, she happily follows the others. Her excitement at being in the world where some of her favourite authors penned their stories has been washed away by the intrusion of her real-world problems.

CHAPTER FOUR
SIGN OF THE TIMES

Walking arm in arm with Josephine, Izzy begins to relax. They may not be talking, but their silence is at least companionable. Izzy catches sight of Basia and Stanley across the park.

'They are over there.' She points, but Jo is distracted by the couple who rudely brushes past them, heading for the high street.

'They do not look very happy. I wonder what is wrong now?' Jo comments.

Izzy squints, trying to get a better look at the pair, but can't place them. 'Do we know them?' she finally asks.

Jo's laugh tinkles. 'Goodness no, they are friends of Stanley's. Hannah's family have taken a house down here for the rest of the year while her father does something with the local regiment.'

'Oh.'

'We had them over to tea last week, and they did nothing but bicker,' Josephine says. 'Stanley wants me to invite them for dinner, but I am not sure... though I guess I should for his sake.'

Izzy raises an eyebrow. 'Perhaps you should invite them to the theatre with you. They cannot argue while a show is on.'

Josephine chuckles. 'Isolde, you are naughty. Still....'

'Hello, you two,' Stanley says before Jo can finish her thought.

'Did you invite Nathanial and Hannah to dinner with us?' Jo asks as she releases Izzy and links her arm through Stanley's.

Stanley's face flushes. Not a good look for someone with pale skin and fair hair. 'No, I did not think.... Besides, they had to rush off for lunch.'

'Good,' Josephine says, 'because Isolde has given me a much better idea. Speaking of lunch, though, we should head back.'

A cheeky grin crosses Stanley's face as he catches Izzy's eye. 'I rather thought we would invite ourselves to lunch with Augusta. She always enjoys our company, and I am sure you and Isolde still have a lot to talk about.'

Jo sends him a thunderous look, but Izzy can't help but grin back at Stanley. In all her angst over losing the love of her life to him, she'd forgotten what fun he could be. It's difficult to stay mad at him for long.

'I warn you, she was not in the best of moods this morning. Then again, you always could charm her, Stanley.'

Jo glances from her friend to her fiancé and sighs.

She knows when she's beaten. Basia, on the other hand, looks like she would rather be any place but here.

'Are you all right?' Izzy asks Basia as they follow Stanley and Jo.

'Mmm.'

Izzy places a hand on her arm. 'Basia,' she whispers, 'is something wrong?'

Basia shakes her head slowly, almost as if she isn't quite with them. Izzy's worry eases a little when her friend says, 'It's just…. Let's just say my conversation with Stanley was a little unsettling. He raised some ghosts I'm not yet ready to face.'

Izzy slides her arm around Basia's waist and gives her a swift hug. 'We travelled such a long way in time that it is easy to forget you only lost Allan a few days ago. You need time to mourn and to find a new path for yourself. Don't force it.'

Basia closes her eyes for a moment, then whispers, 'I feel like a fraud, missing him so much.' She wipes a tear from her eye. 'We were only together for such a short time. I don't feel I have the right to be this sad.'

Giving Basia another hug, Izzy leans her head on her shoulder. 'Love and loss have no time limit. If you are sad, go ahead and be sad. There is no right or wrong way to mourn a death.'

Basia leans into her for a moment, as if drawing some extra strength, before pulling away and giving her a tear-laden smile. 'How did it go with Jo?'

'Ah, changing the subject, I see,' she chuckles. 'I have the opposite problem to you. I've had time to consider what I want from Jo, but it's only been a few weeks for her, and she's still angry with me.'

'But you two seemed okay when you joined us, and she *is* coming to lunch.'

'If Stanley hadn't suggested it, she would have been more than happy to leave us.' Izzy can't keep the pain from her voice. It hurts her that Jo is coming to please Stanley and not her.

As they turn the corner into Augusta's street, Basia chuckles out of nowhere. 'Um, I guess I should warn you, Stanley thinks I'm not as well-bred as I ought to be.'

Izzy's eyes widen in shock. 'What did you do?' she asks as a dour Jensen opens the door.

Basia is saved from answering as he ushers the group inside, saying in his tartest voice, 'You are late. Madame is already in the dining room.'

They remove their outdoor wear and hand it to a maid under Jensen's watchful eye.

'Can you please set two more places, Jensen? Stanley and Josephine are staying for luncheon,' Izzy says.

A flicker of annoyance crosses Jensen's face, but he is too well schooled to speak out. 'As you wish, miss.' His words are more clipped than usual.

Normally she wouldn't have been so high-handed with the butler. Although her aunt won't mind her asking Jo and Stanley to lunch, in the past, Izzy would have waited for her to issue the order for more settings herself.

It seems she can't strike the right note with anyone. Five years with the Time Fixers have changed her enough that she can't slot back into being Isolde.

When Jensen opens the dining room door, she almost bolts. With the tension between her and Jo and Basia still making slip-ups, she's uncomfortable enough as it is. She doesn't think she can sit through a meal with guests.

'Isolde, do not hover in the doorway,' Augusta orders, and Izzy obeys, letting the others pass by her into the room.

'Oh, Stanley, such a pleasure. Are you joining us? And you, too, Josephine. The more the merrier,' Augusta carries on, not noticing Izzy's reticence.

Before Izzy can make her excuses and leave, Augusta says, 'For goodness' sake, Isolde, come in and take a seat.'

Augusta sits at the head of the table with a thin birdlike woman of around her own age on her left. Izzy has met Mrs Trimms a number of times, as have the others. Stanley takes a seat beside the older woman and immediately begins charming her.

On Augusta's left is a familiar face, but it takes her moment to recognise Maisie Ottaway from the train. Basia is quicker off the mark and takes the seat beside their travelling companion.

Josephine and Izzy wait for Jensen to lay the additional places before sitting opposite each other. She and Jo have spent many hours at this table with Augusta, discussing politics and imagining a different future. Sitting across from Josephine now, all of that old camaraderie has gone.

As if sensing her discomfort, Augusta's new companion pokes his head out from under the table. His fluffy body brushes against her leg as if to give her comfort. Leaning down, she picks Cuddles up and places him in her lap, absent-mindedly stroking him while the first course is served.

Sigma, is that you? I hope it is. I need your help. I've

no idea why I came back. Nothing here has changed, but I have. I missed Jo so much, and I had hoped she missed me, too, but she's moved on with her life. If you were here, you would tell me to take my time and get to know everyone again. Why won't you talk to me and tell me yourself?

'Isolde, what are you doing? You are almost choking poor Cuddles. Here, bring him to me.'

The room slowly comes back into focus, and Izzy realises everyone is looking at her. She glances down at the dog, and he stares back at her with loving but vacant eyes. Slowly she rises to her feet and hands the dog to her aunt.

'What is wrong with you?' Augusta hisses.

'Nothing,' Izzy mumbles before returning to her seat. Perhaps Cuddles is not her friend Sigma in animal form after all. The very thought that he isn't here leaves her even more alone.

After the second course is served, Izzy tries to pay more attention. Mrs Trimms brings up the Pilgrimage, and it sets off a lively conversation.

'In our day it was all petitions to Parliament, Augusta, but this march through England is such an inspired idea.'

'Do you really think people will change their minds about women getting the vote by listening to speeches?' Stanley asks, and Izzy silently applauds him.

Mrs Trimms's eyes narrow. 'Are you against women having the vote, young man?'

'Me? Goodness no,' Stanley laughs. 'I think we would all be better off with women running the show. Well, they could not make a worse job than we men have been doing.'

Again Stanley has smoothed over a wrinkle, and Izzy

wishes she didn't like the man so much. In truth, the only thing she has against him is that he's going to marry Jo.

Basia moves into the seat next to her. 'Isolde, do you think we could join the march? It goes through Portsmouth. Or perhaps we could meet it at Petersfield or Haslemere? Maisie says Miss Fielden is to deliver her speech at Haslemere.'

'I see no reason why we should not go and hear Miss Fielden speak,' Izzy says and is instantly rewarded with a beaming smile from Basia.

Reminded that she's actually here in Winchester to do a job, Izzy leans around to catch Maisie's eye. 'Do you think Miss Fielden would speak with me if we went to the rally in Haslemere?'

Maisie winces. 'I am not sure. She does not like to speak to the press because they often twist her words. If I tell her how kind you have all been to me, perhaps it might convince her to talk to you.'

'Thank you, Maisie,' Izzy says. 'When do you go and join her?'

'I shall be staying with Mrs Trimms for two more days yet. I received a telegram today that Miss Fielden has some additions to her speech. They should arrive by post tomorrow. Once I have the notes, I must write a clean copy of the new version and have it ready for her when she arrives in Haslemere.'

'She is lucky to have such a diligent secretary,' Augusta says, patting Maisie's hand. 'Now, shall we have tea in the drawing room?'

Stanley's expression is rueful as he says, 'I am sorry, but we must refuse. Josephine and I have an appointment at the solicitors that we simply cannot be late for—another time, perhaps.'

Izzy hopes her relief isn't too obvious as she watches Josephine and Stanley take their leave.

'You two are family and are always welcome,' Augusta says as she bids the two farewell.

'I am afraid I must be excused as well,' Izzy says once Stanley and Jo have left the room. 'Lionel will be here tomorrow, and I have very little to give him on the march that he would not be able to find himself from the newspapers.'

'If I may suggest,' Mrs Trimms said, 'you might start by talking to some of the shop assistants on the high street. They have been quite active in our local suffragist group.'

Izzy already knew this information, but Mrs Trimms was only trying to be helpful.

'Thank you, Mrs Trimms. I will take your advice. Barbara, would you like to join me?'

Basia glances up from her conversation with Maisie. 'If it is all right with you, I would prefer to stay here for a while. I find myself a little tired.'

Izzy shrugs. Catching Augusta's frown, she interprets it as 'Girls of breeding do not make such common gestures.'

Are you all right? she sends.

Basia gives her a slight nod. *I'm still feeling a little sad after this morning. Besides, I would just be hanging around while you ask questions. At least here I'll be able to talk to Maisie.*

'Of course, Basia. Coming with me would be boring for you, and you must be tired after this morning's activities.' She turns to her aunt, and in an attempt to

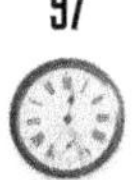

make amends for her unladylike behaviour, she says, 'I will be back in time for tea, Aunt Augusta.'

Basia settles onto the sofa and accepts a cup of tea from Izzy's aunt. While the others chat away, she stares into the crackling fire, surprised at how weary she is after the emotional turmoil of the morning. She'd done very little compared to a normal day on the family farm, but she's finding it difficult to concentrate on what the other women are saying.

Sipping her tea, she marvels at the smoky taste. It's unlike anything she's drunk before. When there's a pause in the conversation, she asks, 'What type of tea is this?'

'Why, just common old Darjeeling,' Augusta tells her. 'Although I have to say, my supplier does have the best quality tea in all of England. Do you not have it at home?'

'I don't th… I do not believe so. It is delicious,' Basia stutters, holding her breath and hoping Augusta didn't notice.

Fortunately Izzy's aunt simply flushes with pleasure. 'Before you go, I will give you my supplier's details so you can pass them on to your mother.'

'Thank you' is all Basia says because she can't say, 'Tea and spices are severely limited in the future, where I come from.'

Taking another sip of tea, Basia decides she's going to stop wallowing and make the most of everything before

she has to return to her time—even if it means she won't be able to fit into her clothes when she gets back. With a renewed sense of purpose, she focuses on what Augusta and Mrs Trimms are talking about.

'My dear Augusta, because you run your poor dead Harold's business affairs, you are treated differently to us mere wives and mothers. Men respect your opinion, whereas it never occurs to them that I would have one at all,' Mrs Trimms is saying.

'And as I have said more times than I can count, if you do not stand up for yourself and make yourself heard, how will men ever consider that you want to have a say in politics, let alone a vote?'

Mrs Trimms's eyes narrow, and Basia senses she's ready for a fight.

Before she can speak, Maisie sits forward in her chair and says, 'We do have to be careful, though. Those Pankhurst women and their followers have gotten men so scared of a violent overthrow, any time a woman stands up for herself, she is tarred with the same brush.'

Augusta snorts. 'We must not let those women speak for all of us, yet we must not be cowed into the shadows either.'

'What do you propose we do, then?' Basia asks, genuinely interested.

Augusta's head tilts slightly as she considers her answer. 'We simply must not stop pushing for the vote, but perhaps for a time, we must not push quite so hard. The Pilgrimage is an inspired idea. We must find more ideas like this.'

'And you do not believe the more radical women are

helping by keeping the issue forefront in everyone's mind?' Basia presses.

'An interesting question,' Augusta says, sending Basia an approving smile. 'Although I cannot condone civil disobedience and lawbreaking, I can understand why they choose to take direct action. And, if I am honest, they have gotten people talking.'

Maisie sits forward, her eyes blazing. 'There is no excuse for their behaviour.'

'Ah, the convictions of youth. My dear, I have been a part of this movement for a long time, and I know change has come slowly—too slowly for many. And it is that snail's pace that has driven women to violent acts.' Augusta looks into the fire. 'Many of my old friends have not been well treated by the authorities. I shudder to think how demeaning being force-fed must be.'

Maisie's lips form a line, and she clearly wants to say something. Eventually she can hold it in no longer. 'If they did not break the law, those women would not be in prison. If they were not in prison, they would not need to go on hunger strikes to make a point.'

'And then they would not need to be force-fed. I understand your argument. However, many of them have been sentenced under the flimsiest of pretences. I think perhaps their biggest mistake is not the violence or the unruly protests but more that they have not recognised that their actions are creating a reaction of fear which affects us all.'

'And that fear is causing men to hold on to what they have with an iron fist,' Mrs Trimms says. 'Which slows the pace of change even more. Ah, it is a vicious circle.'

The room falls silent as the four women follow their

own thoughts. Basia can't guess what the other women are thinking, but she's pretty confident their paths are miles from hers.

From her study of history, she knows it will take a world war before a small number of women get the vote in England and another war before women are allowed into many professions—although they will soon be pushed out of those jobs once the men return home. It has her wondering if it will take another war for people to work together in her time.

No, she can't let that happen. The population is barely holding on as it is. They can't afford to lose good people to senseless fighting. There has to be another way.

'Well, this has been an interesting end to a lovely lunch,' Mrs Trimms says as she stands to leave.

'Perhaps a reflection of the times we live in,' Augusta replies as she pulls the bell.

As they wait for Jensen to come and show the guests out, Maisie says, 'Barbara, I would love to meet with you and Isolde tomorrow if you have time. I am sure Miss Fielden would be interested in what she has found out from the local women.'

'I will see what we can arrange,' Basia prevaricates. She would enjoy seeing Maisie again, but Izzy had been in such a strange mood over lunch that Basia can't predict what her response to the invitation will be.

In fact, Basia would bet her life that Izzy's need to go out is less about writing her story for Lionel and more about dealing with her feelings after spending time with Josephine.

Placing her pen on the bureau, Izzy stares at the words on the page. They had flowed from her hand as if someone else were directing her. Having heard the lofty ideals of the leaders of the Women's Pilgrimage, she's been brought back to earth by the words of the local working women.

Like everyone else involved with the march, they hope to sway enough hearts and minds to support another 'votes for women' petition to Parliament.

However, they're more pragmatic than the movement's leaders and believe there will need to be many more such marches before public opinion swings their way and politicians are forced to vote for change.

They're also questioning the timing of the Pilgrimage while so many are angry at the actions of the suffragettes. Already, accounts of women being attacked on the march have been coming through, and they report being afraid for their welfare when attending local meetings.

At first they had been reluctant to talk about it. Winchester is a small community, after all. However, with a little prompting, and promises of anonymity, they admitted that a group of men had started lying in wait for them to leave the meeting hall.

Some were bold enough to follow them home, taking note of where they lived. They threatened women and their families with violence if they continued with their wicked ways, and the threat has been escalating in both intensity and frequency.

'I tell you, our meetings are only half the size they once were since they started hanging around,' one shopgirl had told Izzy. 'Some of us have young children, and others have not told their husbands what they are doing, and so it is easier not to come.'

The girl sounded apologetic, almost guilty, that some of her friends had put family over the cause. Izzy won't stand in judgement of them, though. She knows all too well that there will be more violence and more fear before women get the vote.

'Everyone must do what is right for them,' she had agreed. 'Those who are unable to openly support the cause can assist in other ways, I am sure.'

Izzy knows the fight for equality will only ever move forward in small, hard-won steps. Once women have the vote, there is still the fight for other forms of equality, like equal pay for equal work. History shows that they don't meet this goal before the world falls into its last and final war. It all seems so futile.

Flopping down on her bed in a way that would give her aunt conniptions, Izzy stares at the ceiling. Writing an article in support of the march is advocating for social change, but she's become used to taking more direct action.

She can't remember when she had last gone more than a couple of days without being thrown into a difficult situation while trying to set the world on a better course of action—one that would see all people treated with respect and would not end in the horrific holocaust of World War Three.

Now that she's back home, she's frustrated both at the lack of direct action and at the hope many hold about future change. Has she always been this pessimistic, or is this the result of five years more experience and a knowledge of the future?

A tap on the door sees her shoot upright. Straightening her clothes, she attempts to hide her surprise as Jo slips into her room.

'Jo, what are you doing here?'

'I have not got long. Stanley is waiting for me downstairs,' Jo starts but is unable to continue.

Izzy holds herself still, not wanting to frighten Jo away, but she's unsure of how to help her.

Jo takes a deep breath, and the words rush out. 'Why did you come back, Izzy? If it was not for my wedding and to wish me well, and it was not to ask me to give Stanley up, then why?'

'Because—'

'Because I was starting to get over you. Now... now I am confused.' Jo's hands are tying themselves in knots, and she fixes her gaze on the carpet as if waiting for a blow to descend.

Izzy sighs. There are so many things she could say. She should tell Jo something that will cut their ties and allow her to move on, but she hasn't come back to live a lie. Perhaps this last time, she'll tell Jo how she feels.

'I missed you. The world is not so bright without you in it.'

Jo doesn't move. 'Is that it?'

All or nothing, Izzy thinks. 'And, if I am honest, I hoped you missed me.'

'And?'

Does Jo truly want me to say the last words out loud?

The room remains silent. Izzy guesses she must. 'And that because you missed me, you had changed your mind about Stanley.'

Jo raises her head. Tears glisten in her eyes. 'Isolde—'

'I am aware it is selfish and self-serving, but you asked for the truth.'

'Isolde, I told you about our arrangement, and you still rail against it.' She takes a step towards Izzy but stops herself.

'I know, I know.' Izzy tries to keep the impatience out of her voice but fails. 'Marry, produce an heir, go your own ways.'

'I owe my father that, Izzy. He deserves an heir to pass his business on to. Unlike you, I have no brother to take up that burden, and I do not have the luxury of holding out for a love match as you insist you must.' Her eyes silently beg Izzy to understand.

Izzy starts to reach for Jo, but then her hand drops to her side. 'I understand your reasons, but I cannot bear the thought of Stanley.... I just can't—'

'We all have responsibilities, and my love for you does not wipe those away.' Jo takes another step, and Izzy thinks her heart might burst from her chest.

The two women stand an arm's-length apart now. Izzy wants nothing more than to cross that void and take Jo into her arms, but so many things hold her back.

In all the years she's been a Time Fixer, she never found out what happened to Josephine and Stanley. Did they survive the war? Did they have a child? Was there actually a way for her to fit into this world if she stayed? Or would she simply be ruining Jo's life?

'Jo, I want so much for the two of us to be together. You believe you have space for both of us in your life, and I do not see anywhere for me to fit. I miss you so when I am not here—' Her voice catches, and she swallows down the lump in her throat. 'Perhaps I should not have come back.'

As the words spill from her, Izzy's chest tightens, making it hard to breathe. *Is this it? Is it truly the end?*

Jo closes the gap between them, taking hold of both of Izzy's hands. 'There is a way forward for us, a way that should be acceptable to everyone if you can only move past that one little hitch.' Jo leans forward, her lips grazing Izzy's cheek. 'Can you think about it... for me?'

Their eyes meet briefly, but before Izzy can answer, Jo dashes from the room as the tea gong sounds.

Taking a deep breath, Izzy tries to centre herself before appearing downstairs, but she can't shake the feeling that she doesn't belong here anymore. She quickly checks herself in the mirror and is not surprised that she looks every one of her twenty-four years. A part of her knows she should use some concealer to hide the fact that she isn't the nineteen-year-old who left home, but she's too shattered to care.

Of course Augusta has to notice she isn't herself when Izzy joins her and Basia in the drawing room.

'Isolde, you look positively ancient today. You have certainly lost the bloom of youth while living in London. I will ask Jenkins to pour you a tonic before dinner.'

'Thank you, Aunt,' she mumbles, wishing she had taken the extra time to get ready before coming down.

Basia shoots her a sympathetic glance, and her mood

lightens a little.

Izzy has no idea how she manages to make it through afternoon tea, let alone dinner that night. Basia's presence certainly helps. She manages to keep up a conversation with Augusta and then to include Izzy in the teatime conversation when she asks how her research had gone that afternoon.

For the first time since arriving home, Augusta's attitude towards her thaws a little, and she even asks to read what Izzy has written so far. Izzy takes her notes down at dinnertime, and much to her surprise, her aunt even comes up with some ideas on how to improve the content.

Still, it's like someone else is going through the motions while she watches from within. Finally, dinner concludes, and she's free to retreat to her room without seeming rude, using the excuse that she wants to update her work before Lionel arrives tomorrow.

She's almost finished her amendments when someone knocks tentatively on the door.

'Izzy, it's only me.' Basia opens the door a crack and pops her head in. 'Are you okay? You seemed a little… off today.' Basia hovers in the doorway, her face pinched with worry.

'I'm getting there.' That's all she intends to say, but the sadness in Basia's eyes is her undoing, and the words come of their own accord. 'I still have some things to work through, but at least now I'm almost sure I don't belong here anymore. My mind's telling me this. I just need to get my heart on board.'

'Oh, Izzy. I'm so sorry.'

She takes a deep, calming breath and offers her friend

a small smile. 'It's okay, Basia. Time will mend my heart.' It's as if saying everything out loud has freed her, and suddenly, as if she's laid down a heavy load, she is lighter. However, she's said enough, and it's time to stop being so self-absorbed.

'What about you? How was your day?'

Basia's smile is tremulous. 'I'm loving this world. The sights, the sounds, the tastes…. It's like a fantasy come to life, but, like you, I don't fit in here. I can't show how I'm really feeling, and it's exhausting being someone else all the time.'

'Yes, isn't it?' Izzy agrees.

'I believed it would be worth it, though. I mean, Sigma was so sure I would find the answers I need here. I thought so too. Now I'm not so sure.'

Izzy chuckles. 'Mmm, he was sure, wasn't he? And he hasn't even had the good grace to turn up and help us, or at least let us tell him how wrong he was.'

A look of understanding passes over Basia's face. 'That's what you were doing with the dog at lunch, wasn't it? You were convinced Cuddles was Sigma, and you were trying to get him to speak with you.'

Izzy nods sheepishly, and the two girls burst into laughter. When they finally settle down, Izzy says, 'Sigma may not have turned up in person to help, but that laugh at his expense did the trick.'

'For me too,' Basia agrees, a genuine smile on her face. The weight on Izzy's shoulders lightens even more. 'Sleep well,' Basia says, closing the door behind her.

CHAPTER FIVE
GOING BACKWARDS TO GO FORWARD

A loud snick tells Basia the maid has left the room. She rolls onto her back and stretches her body, resisting the urge to curl up and go back to sleep. Through a gap in the curtains, she can just make out the crimson sky. It's almost dawn, too early to get up yet.

At home she would be up and inside the barn, milking the cow by now. Mum would be in the kitchen, making porridge for breakfast, and her father and Johan would be preparing for the day's work—either getting ready for a hunt or hauling out farm implements. She doesn't miss the early wake up or the work, but boy, does she miss her family.

Glancing over at the steaming bowl of water, she sighs. Here she might have the luxury of a maid bringing her water to wash in the morning and food she's never eaten before, but nothing is familiar, and she can't be herself. Hell, she can't even speak normally. It's time she returned, but to what?

Not to the role Allan wanted her to take up, and also not to her home in the country where she would be expected to find someone to spend the rest of her life with.

It's a big decision giving up her promise to Allan—to be a leader in the movement uniting their people. She mentally shakes her head. No, she isn't giving it up—she'll merely approach it from a different angle. If there's one thing she's learned from Maisie, Augusta, and Mrs Trimms, it's that not all change is brought about by confrontation or by great leaders. Societal change can also be effected by small acts by a number of individuals.

Word will spread in the underground town, Portsdown, of the changes in the world above. Many will want to leave, and she'll work with her local communities to ensure they have somewhere to go.

She won't be at the centre of it all, and it won't be as exciting as running away from home with a boy hunted by soldiers from Portsdown. What she will have, though, is a real purpose in her life, and she'll still be close to her family, who she's sure will support her.

Suddenly full of energy, Basia is keen to embrace the day. She throws back the covers, and the cool morning air hitting her skin wakes her more fully. She quickly washes and dresses—well, as quickly as she can in Edwardian clothing. Now that she's made up her mind, she's impatient for Izzy to take her home.

Unfortunately her momentum is stalled when she

enters the breakfast room to find herself alone. Heaping her plate with food from the heated silver salvers, she takes a seat at the table and picks at her breakfast.

Where is Izzy? Should I go and wake her? She's convinced herself to do just that when the door opens and Izzy herself appears. Although she's impatient to get going, she waits until Izzy is sitting with a cup of coffee and some toast before she broaches the subject.

'I am ready to go home,' she states.

Izzy raises dull, lifeless eyes to her and nods. 'I am meeting with Lionel to give him the story at two. We can leave after that.'

Basia wants to ask why they can't leave now. Surely Jensen can arrange for Lionel to get the piece for the newspaper. Then she takes a closer look at Izzy.

Last night Basia had sensed her return home had not been all she wanted it to be. Now it seems the experience has taken a bigger toll on the woman than she first thought. The strong, confident woman she first met has turned into a lost little girl.

'Izzy, are you okay? Do you want to talk about it?'

From across the table, Izzy's eyes stare blankly at her. Slowly they focus, and Izzy smiles wanly. 'No, I am not okay, and I do not think I have been for some time.'

She takes a sip of coffee, and Basia wonders if she'll say more.

Izzy puts her cup back down and continues, 'I have been running away from something painful, and yesterday I finally faced up to it. So, while I am not all right, I believe now I have a chance to be.' Her hands tremble as she picks up her coffee again.

III

'Are you coming back here once you take me home?' Basia asks.

Izzy shrugs. 'No, probably not. I do not think I belong here anymore. Maybe I will go back to the Time Fixers. Perhaps Cynthia and Beta will find a place for me in their new—'

The door bangs against the wall as Augusta flies into the room, Cuddles tucked under one arm and a sobbing Mrs Trimms hooked through the other. 'You sit down, and I will fix you a nice cup of tea, Minnie.'

Augusta leads her friend to the seat beside Izzy and plonks Cuddles on her lap. Mrs Trimms absently strokes Cuddles, and the dog curls into her as if sensing her distress. Over the clatter of cups, Izzy asks the distraught woman what's wrong.

'Mai… Maisie went to a… suffragist meeting last night…. She thought she could encour… encourage some of the girls to join the march.' Mrs Trimms sniffs, fiddles round in her pocket for a handkerchief, and then dabs at her eyes before continuing. 'When I awoke this morning, I was informed she did not return last night.'

Mrs Trimms dabs at her eyes again, then in a woeful tone adds, 'And I cannot find the copy of the speech she wrote for Miss Fielden. I know it was on her writing desk yesterday….'

Izzy and Basia lock eyes. *This isn't good,* Izzy sends.

Augusta places a cup of tea in front of the crying woman and takes a seat on the other side of her. 'All will be well, Minnie—'

'But it will not, Augusta. Some of the girls have been followed home and subjected to abuse after the meetings….'

'Now, now, please do not upset yourself.' Augusta pats her friend's hand. 'It is likely she got talking, realised how late it was and that your house would be locked up, and elected to stay with one of the girls.'

Basia catches Izzy's eye. Izzy had spoken with some of the local suffragists yesterday, and Basia now wants to judge her friend's reaction. Izzy is white as a sheet, and when her eyes meet Basia's, it's clear she thinks something bad has happened to Maisie.

'Perhaps we should check the hos—'

A glare from Augusta stops Izzy midsentence.

'Just in case something is not quite as it seems, I have had Jensen call for the police. I am sure they will be able to track her down if she has not yet returned to your home, Minnie.'

Before anyone can say anything more, the door opens, and Jensen enters. The four women turn expectantly, but Maisie isn't with him.

'Miss Josephine and her young man have arrived. Shall I tell them the timing is not convenient, ma'am?'

'They are family, Jensen. Please show them in,' Augusta says.

Izzy's knuckles turn white as she grips her cup more tightly, and Basia guesses her friend would rather not have Jo and Stanley around this morning. After a sleepless night and with her decision to leave just made, Basia is sure Izzy doesn't want her goodbyes to be said like this.

'No, wait,' Augusta says, and Izzy relaxes a little. 'Show them to the morning room. We will join them in a moment— and please arrange fresh tea and coffee.'

'As you wish, ma'am.'

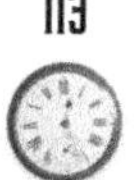

The door closes behind the butler, and Augusta's eyes sweep the table. 'I am sure no one feels like finishing their meal,' she says.

Basia looks down at the bacon and eggs that had earlier seemed so appetising, but now her stomach is churning so much, she couldn't eat another mouthful.

'I think I am done,' she confirms.

When they join the others in the morning room, a chintz-inspired affair with a large mahogany desk directly opposite the drawing room, they find Stanley has disappeared. Josephine is sitting by the empty fireplace, a cup of tea in hand.

As they arrange themselves, Stanley returns, followed by Nathanial and Hannah. The latter's pursed lips tell Basia she is none too happy to be here.

'Look who I saw wandering by,' Stanley says and is surprised by the cold response from most of the room.

'Stanley, now is not the time for visitors,' Augusta says tartly. 'Not when Mrs Trimms's house guest has gone missing.

'What?' Stanley splutters at the same time Nathanial gasps, 'Pardon?' and the room erupts into a cacophony of questions and explanations.

More tea and coffee are brought in, and amongst all the chaos, Izzy leans in to Basia and whispers, 'I have decided to leave my article with Jensen. I am ready to go when you are.'

Basia almost drops her teacup. 'We cannot go yet. Why are you all right to save complete strangers in my world yet leave Maisie, whom you have met, to her fate in yours?'

Izzy's mouth forms a hard line. 'You and I cannot interfere anyway because we might be changing history. I mean, we are not even sure Maisie is not meant to disappear. Besides, she must be returned safe and sound because I am pretty sure Miss Fielden gives her speech.'

Basia's jaw drops. 'What is wrong with you?' she hisses. 'You know Maisie. How can you just abandon her? The Izzy I followed here was prepared to do anything it took to do the right thing—no matter what.'

Izzy stares into the fire and says, 'I thought you wanted to go home.'

'I do, but I cannot abandon a friend, even if you can.' Izzy picks up her tea and takes a sip. *Ah, I might have a way to convince Izzy to stay.* 'What if our being here changed the timeline somehow, and that meant Maisie was taken or hurt in some way she would not have been if we had not come?'

Beside her, Izzy's blank look is now replaced with a flicker of interest. 'That is a possibility, but unlikely. If this is an abduction or a murder, it would require direct intervention, which is not allowed. And I do not believe either the Time Fixers or the Time Guardians would send operatives out while I am here—especially as our presence would already have caused small ripples.'

Basia stares at the dog sitting in Augusta's lap. *If only you were Sigma, you would know how to jolt Izzy from her apathy.* The dog returns her gaze with liquid brown eyes, and in that moment, Basia makes up her mind. Izzy can do what she wants, but she isn't the type of person to walk away from a friend when they're in trouble.

She stands and joins Stanley by the window in time

to see a man walking up the steps. Her stomach drops and her head swims. He looks so much like Allan, it's painful.

'Barbara, are you all right? You have come over quite pale.' Stanley cups her elbow and leads her to a chair.

She wraps her arms around herself and resists the urge to rock. Perhaps staying isn't such a great idea after all.

Izzy sits wrapped in a cocoon of her own misery. Having made her decision to leave last night, she thought the actual departure would be easy. This time she even planned to say her farewells before leaving. Then she saw Jo again, and her resolve crumbled.

All the hours of loneliness and of missing her soulmate crashed down on her, and she wasn't sure she could go back to her solitary existence. In typical Izzy fashion, though, instead of revisiting her decision, she decided to double down and leave earlier than planned.

When Basia had questioned her about ripples in history, Izzy had been pretty sure Maisie would have spent the night out in the original timeline... or had she? When an operative returns to their time, there's bound to be some small changes. Because of this, permission to return is only granted on rare occasions. Perhaps it *is* their fault that Maisie didn't go home after the meeting last night?

Stirring from her self-imposed exile, Izzy considers her options. If she and Basia caused this, then it' up to

them to fix it. If they didn't cause it, then they will leave as planned.

Before she can act on her decision, the door opens, and Jensen slips in.

'Ma'am, a Detective Barker is here.'

'Well, show him in,' Augusta snaps, and the room falls silent, waiting for the detective.

Jensen holds the door for the policeman to enter. Izzy's first thought is that he is younger than she expected. Everything else about him screams early twentieth-century detective, though—from his well-made but inexpensive woollen suit, to his immaculately shined shoes, and to the trilby that sits on the top of his head.

As Jensen takes his hat and coat, she does a double take. He pushes his jet-black hair out of green eyes, and her mouth falls open. It's Allan.

Izzy's eyes slide past him to Basia, and the shock drawn on her pale face tells Izzy she's already noticed the resemblance.

Izzy's concern for her friend is temporarily put on hold as the significance of who is present in the room becomes clear to her. She taps her index finger against her lips. All four of Sigma's team are here—Jo, Stanley, Basia, and now Allan. Time would not have brought their reincarnations to this place unless it was important. Is there something more going on here than a girl staying out for the night?

She turns to study her aunt's dog. *If you're not Sigma, then where is he? Or am I reading something into this situation that isn't there?*

As Izzy's attention returns to the room, the detective is taking a seat beside Mrs Trimms.

'Now, tell me in your own words what happened,' he says in a deep, soothing voice.

At the sound of the detective's voice, Basia releases a small whimper but quickly hides it with a cough. Izzy wants to go and comfort her, but she also doesn't want to draw attention to the woman's distress.

Mrs Trimms appears a little calmer now, but her voice is barely more than a whisper as she repeats her story.

'With the unrest caused by the Women's Pilgrimage to London, I am a little surprised you let a young lady go out unaccompanied,' the detective says after Mrs Trimms has finished speaking.

This apparent criticism affects Mrs Trimms more than everyone's concern had. She straightens her back and says, 'Young man, Miss Ottaway is from London and travels by herself around the country all the time. She is no wilting flower needing to be chaperoned everywhere.'

'Still…,' the policeman muses.

Every woman in the place leans forward, seemingly about to give the detective a piece of their minds, but it's Augusta who gets the first word out.

'Perhaps you should consider not blaming the potential victim,' she snaps, her face screwed into a scowl. 'If a lone woman is attacked by a male, it is not her fault for being alone but the man's fault for attacking her.'

The young detective shifts uncomfortably in his seat as Augusta continues. 'And are you sure you are old enough to be a detective? You hardly look to have left school.'

Red starts to creep up from under the man's starched collar. 'I must confess, I am newly appointed to my position, but the captain is not going to send a seasoned man out to check on a woman who did not come home last night.'

Augusta nods her approval, and Izzy smiles. Testing new people's mettle is one of her aunt's favourite pastimes. Augusta can't bear to be around people who won't stand up for themselves.

Having taken back control, Detective Barker says, 'Now, it is likely Miss Ottaway stayed with a friend last night because it was too late to walk home, is it not? I mean, you said she is a sensible girl.'

Mrs Trimms nods, but Izzy's unease has been growing as time has been marching on. It's almost morning teatime, and no one from Mrs Trimms's household has arrived to say Maisie has returned.

'That was our original thought,' Izzy says, 'but the suffragists Maisie met with were mostly shopgirls or in service of some kind. They would have left for work early this morning, and it is unlikely Maisie would not have reached home by now.'

The detective's cool green eyes bore into Izzy as he considers her words. Nodding once, he reaches into his pocket and takes out a notebook, writes for a moment, then asks Mrs Trimms, 'Have you spoken to your neighbours? Asked if anyone has seen her?'

Izzy cringes with embarrassment. If she hadn't been so wrapped up in her own misery, she would have thought of this already, and they would be well on their way to finding Maisie.

'No,' Mrs Trimms says. 'I was all in a fluster, and I came straight here because I knew Augusta would know exactly what to do.'

'Where do you live, Mrs Trimms?'

'On Clifton Road, looking over the park. It is close, not five minutes' walk away.'

'All right. You and I shall return to your home and start by questioning the neighbours.'

He stands to leave, and Augusta rises to her feet. 'I will come with you, Minnie. You should not be alone.'

'Wait,' Stanley says. 'We cannot just stay here and do nothing.'

Detective Barker takes the group in and dismisses them. 'These things are best left to the professionals, sir.' He turns to help Mrs Trimms from her chair.

Izzy is not to be put off. 'I spoke with some of the suffragists yesterday. Basia and I are going to go talk with them to see what we can dig up. Jo and Stanley, how about you go and see if you can find out anything from the morning cathedral walkers.'

'What about us?' the girl Stanley introduced as Hannah asks.

Izzy had forgotten about them, or perhaps had disregarded them, as they aren't part of Sigma's team. Still, many hands make light work.

'Perhaps you and Nathanial could talk to people on the high street and see if that turns up anything.'

'Hold on now,' Detective Barker says. 'This is a police matter. I cannot agree to your all becoming involved.'

Izzy is now sparked up, and she isn't going to let anyone tell her what she can or can't do. 'Little more than a minute ago, you were prepared to write this off as a woman staying with friends. Now you want the police to handle it?'

Detective Barker blinks a couple of times, as if he can't believe Izzy is speaking to him like this. Before he forbids them to become involved, she adds, 'What is more, we can cover far more ground if we all pitch in. After all, I believe the first few hours after someone has been abducted are critical, are they not?'

Detective Barker holds her gaze, and she gets the sense that he's still going to refuse their help.

'You are not trained to ask questions. How will you know whether you have something useful or not?'

Izzy's eyebrows rise. Allan's reincarnation has always been the brains of the group. 'You cannot be serious. We are generally intelligent people. We can ask questions without causing a catastrophe and are more than capable of sifting the wheat from the chaff.'

'This is all getting out of hand,' the detective says, running a hand through his hair.

Jo steps forward. 'How about we gather what information we can and then meet back here in... say two hours to share everything with the detective.' She pauses, waiting for the others to agree. 'Then you can decide how best to proceed, Detective.'

Izzy mouths a thank you to Jo, who smiles back.

Detective Barker studies the two of them, a thoughtful expression on his face. 'That plan is acceptable. But be careful. And please, if you find something, do not act alone.'

With that admonishment, he leads the ladies from the room, followed closely by the other teams. Izzy is left alone with Basia, who appears to have been frozen in her seat since the detective entered.

'Basia, are you good to do this?' Izzy asks.

Basia turns to her. 'It's Allan,' she says, amazement colouring her voice.

'Yes it is. But not your Allan,' Izzy tells her gently, then regrets her words when a tear slips from Basia's eye.

'I know,' she says, 'but it's difficult because he is so like him.'

Izzy wraps her arms around Basia and gives her friend a hug, wishing she could take away the pain of her loss.

After a few minutes, Basia pulls away and wipes the tears from her eyes. 'Come, let's go find Maisie.'

As they retrieve their outdoor clothes, Izzy sends a thought to Sigma. *Where are you? I could really use your help with whatever the hell is happening here.*

As Beta scrolls through the report on the tablet, a frown forms between his brows. He takes a seat on the orange leather sofa and again marvels at how Cynthia has furnished her place in 1960s retro. Only it probably isn't retro to her, as she was recruited from the '60s.

He waves the tablet in the air, thinking of how it isn't nearly as satisfying as waving a paper report. 'And they're sure of this?' he asks Cynthia.

Today she's dressed in capri pants, a white button-down shirt, and ballet flats. With her hair teased into a beehive, she so completely fits into the room he can't help but smile.

Her lips purse, as if he's criticising her rather than

trying to clarify the situation. He's still an outsider in Time Fixer headquarters, so he needs to choose his words more carefully until he gets the lie of the land.

'As sure as they can be without having someone on the ground,' she tells him.

'The report says there are usually some minor changes when agents go back to their original timelines. Are we able to confirm we don't have an incident on our hands without sending someone in?'

Shaking her head, Cynthia says, 'I don't believe so. What do your guys say?'

'They, too, are reporting minor anomalies that are not part of the historic timeline. So far they haven't affected any major events, and they're taking a wait-and-see approach.'

Beta reaches forward and places the tablet on the coffee table. Leaning back in his chair, he closes his eyes to better process what he's read. Opening them again, he studies Cynthia's face. She's projecting a calm demeanour, but there's a tightness around her lips that suggests she isn't comfortable with something and, knowing her, he'll have to prise it out of her.

'What are you not telling me?'

Her smile is distracted. 'Nothing for you to worry about.'

'Now I'm even more concerned. If you don't let me in, I can't help.'

'The Council was discussing whether to bring Izzy back or not?'

Ah, now they've reached the crux of the matter. When Izzy returned home from her last mission, she had requested a visit to her own timeline.

Unlike the Time Guardians, who train their operatives during many lifetimes and ask them to join at the end of their life cycle, Time Fixers recruit their agents from any time or at any age. They also allow occasional returns to their lives to keep in contact with family and friends, giving agents a chance to reaffirm their commitment or return to their lives.

Although this process is controlled, it does cause some disruption. Agents are monitored to ensure they don't make too many waves and are immediately pulled out if they might cause too big a disruption.

'What did they decide?' he asks.

'To monitor and meet again tomorrow and decide whether or not to intervene,' Cynthia replies.

He studies her again, this time noticing her posture has still not relaxed. He reaches out and takes her hand. 'What is it?'

'Something doesn't feel right about this. The potential Time Guardians you've had working with Sigma are all there. That has me anxious.' Her fingers squeeze his. 'I don't want Izzy pulled out, but....'

'But you think the situation will turn bad?'

She nods.

He considers their options. With Sigma on a well-earned sabbatical, the only Time Guardian he would trust to treat this with the delicacy it requires is Theta.

Although his new position allows him to contact other Time Guardian councillors' agents without going through them, Theta is close to Alpha and would likely report her assignment to him. Then it would be goodbye to the gentle touch.

A sigh escapes his lips. 'You knew when you brought me that report that the only option was to ask Sigma to come back to work early, didn't you?'

'Harold, he is the only one I would trust in this situation and the only one Izzy would too,' she confirms. 'Besides, his team is assembled and waiting for him.'

Cynthia speaking his real name throws him off balance for a moment, and he wonders if she had meant to do just that. Or has he become too cynical from working with the Time Guardians for so many years?

'Well, it seems neither of our people are going to get the time they need to recharge. I hope this disruption doesn't turn them off coming back to us after their respective breaks.'

When Cynthia doesn't respond, he says, 'All right, leave it with me.'

CHAPTER SIX
YOU CAN'T ESCAPE TROUBLE

With only a couple of days left until the Women's Pilgrimage passes through Portsmouth and Haslemere, the streets of Winchester are bustling. Supporters from outlying areas are gathering in the city to take advantage of the buses the local WSPU organised.

In general the atmosphere is festive, at least among the women and their male supporters, but Basia notices a few disgruntled faces as she and Izzy walk to the high street. A couple of men are outright hostile, jostling women and calling them names even Basia has never heard in mixed company. The anger and aggression send a shiver of unease down her spine, and she stays close to Izzy.

In spite of keeping a low profile, one of the hooligans jostles Izzy and snarls, 'Think yer better than us, do yer?'

Izzy's fists clench, but before she can take action, a constable moves between them and the man. 'Move along, you, and leave the ladies be.'

The man thrusts his chest forward, and for a moment, Basia thinks he's going to refuse, but the constable bustles him away. Before they can voice their thanks, he goes to help another policeman break up a scuffle across the street.

'With all this activity, I am surprised the police were able to send anyone to investigate Maisie's disappearance,' she says to Izzy as they duck into the doorway of a clothing store.

'He said he is only newly appointed, so perhaps they did not mind sending him,' Izzy replies as she opens the door, sounding a lot calmer about the situation than Basia.

A bell tinkles, calling a figure from the back of the store. When she sees who's entered, a look of alarm crosses her face before she schools it into the mask of a professional saleswoman. 'Good morning, ladies. What can I assist you with today?' she asks, her voice bright and chirpy.

Izzy frowns. 'I was in here yesterday—'

'Ah, yes, I remember. You were looking for a new blouse.' The young woman moves to a rail by the door. 'It was this one that took your fancy, was it not?' She takes an apparently random piece of clothing from the rail and walks towards them.

When she's close by, she whispers, 'The owner is in today. You will lose me my job if I am caught chatting with you on her time.'

Izzy nods her understanding and plays along. 'Yes, it

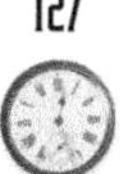

was. I brought my friend along for a second opinion.'

'I think it would look lovely on you, but a friend's opinion is always best. What do you think, miss?'

Basia reaches for the blouse, feels the fabric, then holds it up to get a better look. The simple white shirt doesn't require a second opinion, but she pretends anyway so Izzy can talk with the shop assistant.

'It is a little plain for your tastes, Isolde. Let me see if I can find something a little more suited to you.'

She slips past Izzy and the assistant and moves to the rack of blouses. Placing herself between the back room and the two girls, she begins flicking through the clothing, all the while keeping up a constant inane prattle to cover their voices.

'No, this is too big, and this one is too fussy. This one, the cotton is too… stiff. Ah, I like this one. It is much nicer than the other one.' She holds up a blouse with a Chinese collar and pin tucks down the front. 'What do you think, Isolde? Do you not think it will go nicely with your blue serge jacket?' she asks just as the gap in the curtains widens and a thin, stern-looking woman with a pair of pince-nez perched on the end of her nose joins them.

'That is one of our most popular styles,' she says in a dry voice and with little enthusiasm.

Izzy peers around the shop assistant and says, 'I knew I was right to bring you with me today, Barbara. I will take it. Could you please wrap it and send it round to Mrs Augusta Hartfield? I believe she has an account here. The address is—'

'I know the address, thank you,' the woman interrupts, peering down her nose at them. 'She is one of our most valued customers. I believe I have seen you with her before, although not for a while. You are her....'

'Niece,' Izzy provides. 'Yes, I have been in London for a bit, but I am back now.'

'Ah. Daisy, do not stand about gawping like a fishwife. Get that package wrapped and sent around to Mrs Hartfield's.'

'Yes, Mrs Mirth. Right away.'

Daisy's heels click on the wooden floor as she takes the blouse, and Basia bites back a laugh. Mrs Mirth! That woman was anything but mirthful.

'Thank you, Daisy. You have been most helpful,' Izzy says, looping her arm through Basia's and leading her out of the store while saying, 'Come, Barbara, there is the most adorable hat in a shop just up the road, and we still have time to buy it before we are expected for luncheon.'

Still chuckling to herself, Basia follows Izzy as she threads their way through the crowd. They stop for a minute in the entrance of a side street to regroup.

'What a dreadful woman,' Basia says. 'Did you manage to learn anything useful from Daisy?'

'Yes. She said Maisie left the meeting with a girl named Alice. She works in a hat shop at the other end of the high street,' Izzy says.

'Let us hope we do not have to buy anything there to get information, or else Aunt Augusta might not be too happy.'

Izzy grins. 'Do not worry, Augusta will charge my father for everything I buy. And, so long as they are items to make me pretty and more marketable as a bride, my father will pay up without a murmur.' She winks, then laughs. 'So it is a good thing none of my contacts work in bookshops, or I would be out of pocket.'

Izzy's laughter sounds hollow, and Basia squeezes her arm in sympathy. At least her own parents have always been happy for her to be who she wants to be—the people in their community, not so much. They want her to fit into the mould of wife and mother, whether she wants to or not.

'Come on, we need to move. By the time we work our way through the crowd, we will not have much time to talk with Alice before we have to head back.' Izzy takes hold of Basia's hand, pulling her through the ever-growing throng of people.

They enter the small millinery shop ten minutes later to find a tiny black-clad woman run off her feet. Pinning some stray stands of grey hair back in place, she can't keep the exasperation off her face when Izzy asks to speak with Alice.

'I am sorry, Alice is not in today.'

She moves to serve someone else, but Izzy places a hand on her arm. 'Is she ill?'

'Are you a friend of hers? I have not seen you in here before.' The woman eyes them suspiciously.

'I am a member of her women's group, and some of us were worried. Another member has gone missing.'

'Dear me,' the woman gasps, a hand flying to her mouth. 'It is all so dreadful. Her younger brother popped in to say she had been attacked walking home from her meeting last night. I told her no good would come of joining those—'

Basia grips Izzy's arm, but her friend maintains a professional demeanour as she interrupts the shop owner. 'Do you know where she was attacked?'

'Yes, I believe it was near Clifton Terrace, by the park there—the one with the historic whatnot in the middle.'

'Oram's Arbour,' Izzy offers, turning white.

Basia's stomach churns, and what little breakfast she'd eaten threatens to come up. While she tries to keep everything down, Izzy asks, 'Do you have Alice's address?'

'Oh, I am sorry dear, I am unable to give out that sort of information, not to a complete stranger. I am going round to her place as soon as my sister arrives to take over here, so I can pass on your good wishes if you would like.'

Basia expects Izzy to take offence, or at least argue vigorously. Instead, she says, 'Thank you. Tell her Isolde Fielding asked after her, and if she needs anything to send a message care of Mrs Augusta Hartfield.'

'I will, dear. Now, if you are finished, I must attend to my customers.'

Izzy leaves the shop at speed, and it takes Basia a while to catch her up. When she does, she says, 'I thought you would put up more of a fight. I mean, do you not want to talk with Alice?'

Izzy stops and turns to Basia, her face showing a determination previously missing. 'We know Maisie and Alice left the meeting together and that Alice was attacked near Mrs Trimms's place. Something bad has happened to Maisie.'

'Yes, I get that. But we need to talk to Alice so we can find out exactly what happened during the attack,' Basia presses, unsure why Izzy doesn't feel the same sense of urgency.

'I agree we need more details, but I think our detective friend might be able to find them more easily than we can. I mean, he has to be good for something. Come on, we should go back to Augusta's and set him off in the right direction.'

Half an hour later, after Jensen lets them in and then guides them to the morning room, Basia becomes less certain about coming face to face with the detective again. Fortunately, they're the first back, much to Basia's relief. Jensen leaves them alone after advising coffee and tea would be arriving soon.

Basia takes a seat by the window so she can watch for the others' arrival, but Izzy can't settle. She paces the room and only sits down when the maid brings in the tea tray.

Stanley and Josephine are the next to return, followed minutes later by Nathanial and Hannah. Both groups have nothing to report other than tensions seem strained in Winchester with the influx of suffragists.

When Basia begins to tell them what they found, Izzy shoots her a warning look. 'We should wait until Detective Barker comes back before we share. After all, we only want to tell it once,' she whispers as she hands Basia some tea.

Izzy then returns to the table to get herself some coffee, and Nathanial joins her in the window seat. Basia places her teacup on the table to hide her surprise. The two times she had met the couple, Nathanial had been glued to Hannah's side, almost as if he thought that if he left her alone, she would disappear.

'I thought I might help you keep watch for everyone,' he says, a shy smile forming on his lips. 'I have a feeling that when they arrive back, things will really take off.'

Basia searches his face. He looks like Nathanial and sounds like Nathanial, but something is definitely off about him. She wonders if he and Hannah had another fight, and this time one of them had said something that had altered their relationship forever.

Through her lashes, she glances over at Hannah, studying the girl as she talks with Stanley and Jo. She appears engrossed in the conversation, but every now and then, she sends questioning glances Nathanial's way. He continues to sit with his back to her, completely oblivious.

Interesting, Basia thinks, but she's distracted by the appearance of Augusta swooping down the street with Detective Barker striding in her wake.

'Apologies to you all for being tardy, but we stumbled on some interesting information as we were on our way back,' Augusta blusters as she blows into the morning room.

'Where is Mrs Trimms?' Jo asks before Izzy can get a word in.

'My dear, she is so dreadfully upset, I left her at home. She has taken a tonic, and her housekeeper is sitting with her while she rests. Oh, is this tea still hot? I am parched.'

Izzy tries to hide her impatience as Augusta pours herself a cup of hot tea, then sits beside Jo on the settee.

Before her aunt has a chance to settle in, she starts, 'Basia and I found out—'

'Isolde, manners, please. I was in the middle of explaining why we were delayed.' Turning to the room, Augusta carries on speaking. 'On our way back here, we ran into Mrs Joyce, who owns the millinery shop just off the high street.' She turns to Izzy. 'I bought you that dear little hat from there before you left for London.'

Izzy nods, willing her aunt to move on so she can tell everyone what she and Basia had learned.

'Well, she was all in a fluster. She was on her way to visit one of her girls. Someone attacked her last night as she walked home from a meeting. Well, that set off Mrs Trimms, who almost fainted, so we had to take her home and make sure she was all right before we came back here.'

Augusta pauses to take a sip of tea, and Izzy uses the break to jump in with her news.

'We spoke to Mrs Joyce, too, in her shop, and to Daisy, another friend of Alice's. Basia and I found out that Maisie left the meeting last night with Alice, the girl who was attacked, and we believe it might all be linked.'

She spoke so fast, it takes a moment for her words to sink in with the others. She watches as their faces change from mildly interested, to concerned, to genuinely worried.

'You are right. It is linked.'

Izzy turns to see Detective Barker standing in the doorway, a manila folder in his hand. 'I sent a runner to the station to get the police report of the incident and bring it here. According to this, Miss Ottaway and Alice were walking together when they were attacked by two men. Alice was knocked unconscious, but she was pretty sure she saw Maisie being dragged away before she completely passed out.'

'So your people are already following up?' Izzy asks.

The detective shakes his head. 'With so many constables assigned to keep the peace in and around town, we have not had the resources to do anything other than search the park to make sure Miss Ottaway has not been left lying injured somewhere.'

In her head, Izzy is putting all the pieces together, but they aren't adding up. Her mind is sluggish from a restless night, and she can't make out what's missing until Basia says, 'Why was Alice attacked and Maisie taken away? It does not make sense.'

'A good question,' Detective Barker says, beaming at Basia as though she's a star pupil.

Although Basia is finding it difficult to look the policeman in the eye, his praise brings a small smile to her lips. *Interesting,* Izzy thinks as she turns to hide her own smile.

As the detective leafs through the report again to see if there's something he missed, Basia joins him, reading over his shoulder. He moves so she can get a better look, and Izzy half turns to hide her smirk. There's obviously a budding attraction between the two of them, and they look so right together.

Basia reaches over and points at something, and Detective Barker asks, 'You think that may be important?'

'Everyone has been talking about it, so maybe,' Basia answers.

The detective shuts the file. 'According to Alice, as they were walking, Miss Ottaway was complaining to her about the number of versions she had written of the speech her employer, Miss Fielden, is to give in Haslemere.'

'That seems an odd thing for the two women to be talking about,' Nathanial says.

'Not so odd given she had taken a draft speech for the women to read. Some of them wanted to add comments, and Miss Ottaway was worried she would now have to give two versions to Miss Fielden so she could choose which one to use,' the detective informs them.

'And you think she was taken because she had the speech with her?' Jo asks. 'That is a little far-fetched. I mean, surely they would just take the speech.'

'She had obviously copied it many times. Maybe they need Maisie to locate all of them,' Hannah says.

Basia frowns. 'Perhaps, but Mrs Trimms said she had seen the speech in Maisie's room earlier in the day, but it is not there now—which is odd.'

The cogs in Izzy's mind have finally warmed up. 'Maybe it is not only about the speech. Although there might be many copies of it floating around, only Maisie knows where and when she is to meet up with Miss Fielden to hand it over. Delay her long enough, and Miss Fielden will have nothing to deliver to the crowds in Haslemere.'

'One speech in a small country town cannot be that important,' Stanley laughs.

It is, Izzy thinks. In the future, Miss Fielden's words and how they inspired onlookers is one of the few things reported from that day. Perhaps her speech motivated people to support the march or changed their minds about giving women the vote.

Only she can't say any of these things because she would have to explain too much. Would they even believe her if she told them she had travelled to the future and seen how altering one little thing like this could change the course of history? It's more likely they'd think she's going crazy.

She rises to her feet and paces around the room. *Why was Maisie taken? There must be a reason.* If the group here couldn't understand how a minor change could affect the future, nor could Maisie's kidnappers. So why would they have abducted her rather than beat her like they did Alice?

Could the Time Fixers be involved here? It can't be the Time Guardians—they're sticklers for protocol and would never do anything to alter history.

Basia joins her on her circuit of the room. 'What is it?' she asks, keeping her voice low so the others won't hear.

'I am not sure,' Izzy whispers. 'Miss Fielden's speech is spoken of well into the future, which raises the possibility that her inability to give it may have a very real impact on women getting the vote in England.'

Basia's brow furrows. 'Okay, I see it is important to find Maisie and make sure she delivers the speech to her employer, but how does that help us find her? I mean, her abductors are not able to see into the future.'

'No, they cannot, but there must be a reason they chose her. Maybe they are trying to sow the seeds of fear by abducting one of the people from out of town who have arrived here to support the Pilgrimage. Or they may even know about her connections.'

Izzy and Basia both start at the voice. Neither of them had realised they'd drifted towards the window until Nathanial joined their conversation. Izzy looks to Basia, whose wide-eyed surprise tells her she's worried too—how much had he overheard?

'Of course, that is the most likely explanation,' Basia says, perhaps louder than necessary, as if trying to cover their earlier conversation. 'They probably overheard her London accent and decided they would cause more mischief and fear by taking her rather than Alice.'

'A sound analysis,' Detective Barker says as he approaches them.

Basia's cheeks pink at his words, and Izzy fears a full-on blush will soon appear.

Leaving her friend to the detective, she turns back to Nathanial. If he had indeed heard their entire conversation, he seems completely unaffected by them discussing the future impact of Miss Fielden's speech.

Nathanial meets her gaze and raises an eyebrow, and the corners of his mouth twitch as if about to form a smile—or a smirk.

'Shall we join the others, Izzy, and see if we can find our Miss Ottaway?'

Before she can react to the use of her nickname, Nathanial has joined the others. He waits patiently for a break in the conversation and asks, 'Detective Barker, Alan, how many men can the police assign to the search for Miss Ottaway?'

'Nathanial, what are you doing?' Hannah asks, her tone conveying surprise.

She isn't the only one startled by Nathanial's actions. He had called her Izzy, and he called the detective Alan, even though the man hasn't told anyone that's his name.

Oh Lord, he has the same name as Basia's Allan. She searches for her friend, who's listening intently to the conversation. The only sign she gives that the detective reminds her of her dead lover is the way her fingers are wrapped so tightly together, her knuckles are white. Basia smiles wanly, acknowledging Izzy's glance of support.

'I am looking out for someone who needs our help, just like you have always wanted me to,' Nathanial responds to Hannah's question as Izzy's focus returns to the group.

He turns back to the policeman, missing the shock on his fiancée's face, but Izzy doesn't miss it.

What's happening here? Who is Nathanial, and why did he call me Izzy?

The door swings open, and two maids enter carrying trays with more tea and coffee, Cuddles close at their heels. Izzy follows the dog as he pads around everyone, sniffing them and cataloguing their scent.

If only you were Sigma. We could do with some Time Guardian help about now.

You thought I was the dog? That dog? How long have you been trying to talk to him—I mean me?

Izzy's eyes fly upwards to meet Nathanial's amused smile.

You? You're Sigma? You're taking human form now? Wait. Where's the real Nathanial?

Nathanial simply stares at her and waits for the penny to drop. Izzy fights the urge to palm her forehead.

You were Nathanial? Then Hannah is... will become

Theta. Oh…. Still, that doesn't explain what happened to Nathanial.

Nathanial shrugs. *I'm not quite certain. I seem to have… integrated with him, or maybe I've boxed him away somewhere. I can't really tell. Beta sent me here on short notice, and my best option to place myself in the middle of things was to come as me. Beta assures me Nathanial will be fine when I leave.*

Izzy glances at Cuddles, then back at Nathanial.

If Cuddles was here, why not come as him? It would be less messy.

It would be too weird being here and interacting with myself. Besides, Cavaliers are home dogs, and I need to be out and about if I'm to be of any use.

Hannah steps between them, momentarily obscuring Izzy's view of Nathanial.

'Nathanial, we have lunch with my parents, and there are enough people here that they no longer need us.' Hannah's voice holds an undertone of command.

'I cannot leave now, Hannah. Things are only just starting to get exciting,' Nathanial tells her. 'You go ahead, though, and please give my apologies to your parents.'

Hannah's head swivels, and she glares at Izzy, instantly making her the cause of Nathanial's defiance. 'No, I will stay too. We will ask Jensen to send a message to my parents.' She links her arm through Nathanial's, and he follows her out to search for the butler.

Izzy moves to the table to pour herself some coffee. She's sipping it thoughtfully when a maid enters and hands Detective Barker a note. He reads it, nods once, then calls them all to order.

SUFFRAGETTE

Taking the seat closest to Detective Barker, Basia sends a questioning glance to Izzy as her friend takes the seat opposite. Something has been going on between her and Nathanial. Hannah may think they're flirting, but Basia knows it must be something else. "Later," Izzy mouths, and Basia nods.

'So, my captain informs me he cannot spare anyone else to look into Miss Ottaway's disappearance—I am instructed to investigate on my own.'

'But that is outrageous.' Stanley stands. 'I shall go and have a word with him.'

Josephine smiles indulgently and reaches out an arm, pulling Stanley back down beside her. 'Let the detective finish before you go charging off,' she tells him.

Detective Barker smiles at Jo, and Basia's heart literally flutters. What's going on here? Her head knows this man isn't her Allan, but her heart is taking time to catch up, and her physical reactions—well, that's a whole other level.

Perhaps it's that her loss of Allan is so recent. She would give anything to look into his green eyes one last time, to hold his hand and tell him how much she misses him. This must be a stage of grief—yes, that must be it.

Detective Barker starts, 'Since—'

The door opens, and Nathanial and Hannah return. Nathanial is actually smirking, but by the set of Hannah's lips and the storm brewing in her eyes, she is furious.

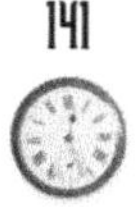

Izzy catches Nathanial's searching gaze and drops her head to hide her chuckle.

Putting on her best schoolmarm face, Basia glares at Izzy. "Stop it," she mouths, and Izzy attempts to look chastened. Basia glances from Izzy to Nathanial and wonders what the two of them are up to. She doesn't have time to work it out, though, as the detective has started talking again.

'Since you were all so helpful this morning, I am hoping you will agree to assist me in the next step of the investigation,' he continues.

They all murmur their assent except for Augusta. 'I am afraid I must return to ensure Mrs Trimms is all right. Besides, I am told I can be a little... off-putting. I would not like to hinder your efforts.'

Basia's lips curl into a fond smile at Augusta's words. The woman is certainly a force to be reckoned with, and Basia can see how people might be a little intimidated by her presence.

'What would you like us to do, Detective?' Jo asks.

Just like her Johan, Jo is the one keeping them to task—the glue holding them together.

'Pretty much what you have been doing already— asking people if they saw anything unusual last night. This time, however, we will be a little more targeted because we are pretty certain Miss Ottaway was taken from the park. We will be questioning people who live around the streets near Clifton Avenue, and those who are walking in the park itself.'

'That sounds pretty straightforward,' Jo says. 'Will we be in the same pairings as before, Detective?'

'Probably—'

'Before you go, Jensen has set up a light lunch in the dining room. You will need sustenance before you tackle this new round of investigation,' Augusta adds.

And a toilet break, Basia thinks, unable to remember when she's had so many cups of tea in such a short time.

Arriving in the dining room after the others, she loads her plate with dainty sandwiches and pastries before finding there are only two empty places at the table.

One is beside Hannah, who seems to be haranguing Nathanial between mouthfuls of food. Basia seats herself beside Detective Barker and begins to eat self-consciously, all the while hyperaware of how close the detective is to her.

'Miss... um—'

'Oh, please call me Barbara.'

He smiles. 'And I am Alan.'

Of course you are, Basia thinks.

'So, Barbara, how is it you are staying with Mrs Hartfield and her niece?'

An odd question. Then again, perhaps being a detective, he likes to know how everyone fits in.

'I have a little time before I start my nursing studies in London, and when Isolde decided to come to Winchester, she asked if I would like to accompany her,' Basia tells him, outlining the cover story Izzy had created for her.

'Fascinating. So you want to be a nurse? And are your parents supportive of your choice?'

Is this what it's like to be interrogated? Should I tell him they would rather I became a doctor, but that road is as difficult in my time as it would be now? How would he react?

Suddenly she doesn't want to know. If he is one of those men who wants a woman at home rather than working, her attitude towards him would change. It's selfish, but she's enjoying how his presence soothes her battered soul too much to want this budding friendship to end. *Still, this attraction isn't real. It's simply a spillover from losing Allan so recently,* she reminds herself.

'They are happy for me to find my own way in the world,' she said. 'How about you? How did your parents react when you told them you wanted to become a policeman?'

He chuckles. 'Surprisingly well. I am a younger son, and I always knew the money my grandfather left me would never be enough to live on. My father would have preferred I took a commission in the military, but I have always been intrigued by solving mysteries.'

Basia could easily imagine the serious man as a child curled up with Sir Arthur Conan Doyle's latest offering, imagining himself as Sherlock Holmes.

'When I announced my intention to join the police, my uncle introduced me to the captain here in Winchester, and he took me on to repay an old favour, I believe.' Alan's eyes drop to his food, and Basia wonders if he's finished speaking. 'I aim to make sure he has no cause to regret that decision.'

Alan says these last words with such intensity, Basia is a bit taken aback. She decides to lighten the tone. 'So are you enjoying being Sherlock Holmes?'

Alan smiles wryly. 'I am afraid I am more of a Dr Watson. I still have much to learn before I make Sherlock status.'

Basia nods and fiddles with her sandwich as she considers how useful this newly minted detective will be in the search for Maisie.

Alan chuckles. 'Ah, I see you are now wondering how much help I will be in finding your friend. Or perhaps you are thinking the captain sent me here today so I would keep out of the way of the main action.'

'No....' She turns towards him, eyes wide, worried she'd offended him.

'And that is fine. I believe it is probably true. I only joined the force last week, so my police training is rather limited. I suspect the captain sent me here to appease a lady whose name carries a lot of weight in this town.'

'But—' His words don't inspire confidence.

'Oh, do not fear. I aim to show the captain that assigning me this case was the right thing to do by finding your Miss Ottaway. Sometimes a man who has something to prove can be more effective than one who does not.'

Basia sends him a shy smile. 'Then I hope we can help you achieve your goal.'

A slight frown furrows his brow as he answers, 'For some reason I am even more sure of succeeding with all of you helping.'

Of course you are. With you here Sigma's team is all assembled. If only the Time Guardian were—

It hits Basia like a punch. She raises her head to find Nathanial staring straight at her, a cheeky grin on his face.

'Why is it you have smiles for everyone else but me today?' Hannah complains, her tone more angry than hurt, and Nathanial is pulled back into whatever battle the two are having.

Before the argument becomes too heated, Alan rises to his feet and addresses the group. 'If you are all finished, perhaps we can get started.'

CHAPTER SEVEN
THE GANG IS HERE

Basia tries not to let her disappointment show. Before they left Augusta's, Detective Barker split them into two groups to cover more ground and also so they would remain safe.

It wasn't being split up that disappointed her, but more the fact that he sent her off with Josephine, Stanley, and Hannah. They're to proceed up Clifton Hill and follow the line of houses round until they meet up with the others on Clifton Road.

It was obvious the detective separated Nathanial and Hannah so their constant arguing wouldn't interfere with the afternoon's work. Nathanial had readily agreed— perhaps too readily. Hannah hadn't said a word, but the sour expression on her face spoke louder than anything she might have said.

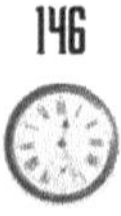

Meanwhile, Basia is brooding. Why had the detective not wanted her with him? Not that she's too bothered either way, but it would be nice to know.

Stanley drops back and falls into step with her. 'I think our young detective is quite sweet on you,' he teases.

Heat rises from Basia's collar. 'What makes you think that?'

A smirk pulls at his mouth. 'Perhaps the way his eyes always seek you out first when he walks into the room and how he always manages to be close to you.' He nudges her gently with his elbow as Jo half turns to join the conversation.

'I think what clinched it, though, was his sending you along with us instead of Isolde,' she adds.

Basia doesn't want to rise to the bait, but she can't help herself. 'How does that show he likes me?'

'Why, because if you are with us, he can concentrate on doing his job,' Stanley says, a twinkle in his eye and a chuckle in his voice.

'I am sure I have no idea what you mean,' Basia responds a little too tartly, causing Jo to smile knowingly and sending Stanley off on another bout of laughter.

'Of course you don't.' He winks conspiratorially.

It's hard to stay annoyed with Stanley—he's just so likeable. Besides, it's such a beautiful day, and the world is a happy place now that she no longer feels the sting of rejection.

If only Stanley could work some of his magic on Hannah. Basia turns to the girl following them silently, dragging her feet, and clearly not engaged. When they questioned passers-by, she had stood to the side, her eyes wandering, saying nothing.

Basia racks her brain for something that might lift Hannah's spirits, but she doesn't know her well enough, and Hannah has been rebuffing her efforts at conversation with terse, dismissive replies.

After an hour of disappointment and no new clues, they finally meet up with the others in the centre of the park. When she finds they have nothing unusual to report either, dread seeps its way into Basia's bones.

Although she has always felt that there's something untoward going on, she's now beginning to fear something more sinister happened to Maisie. Coming to a stop by Hannah, Basia listens to the intense conversation as the others argue over what to do next.

'That nurse has been pushing her pram around for a while,' Hannah comments.

Basia follows her gaze. 'The poor woman looks half-asleep,' she sympathises.

'Yes.' Hannah taps her chin thoughtfully. 'Almost like she has been walking that child around for hours.'

Without saying another word, Hannah strides off purposefully towards the nurse. Basia drifts along in her wake, interested to find out where this is going.

'...notice anything unusual today?' Hannah is saying as she catches her up.

The nurse scrubs a hand over her tired face and studies Hannah wearily.

'A friend of ours has gone missing, and we are searching for her,' Basia says. 'You look like you might have been around the park for a while. Perhaps it is something you do quite often? Maybe if you noticed something, even if it is just little, you might be able to help us find her.'

A wail comes from inside the pram, and Basia leans over to find a newborn baby screwing its face up, readying itself for a good scream.

Standing up, Basia says, 'Come, let us help you. We can walk a while and let the baby settle while you think.'

Basia places her hands on the handle of the pram, guiding it onto the path. The nurse drops her arms with a sigh of relief, and Hannah, to Basia's surprise, slips the woman's hand over her arm.

As soon as they're on the move, the baby's eyes begin to flutter and are soon closed.

'Is the baby always this unsettled?' Basia asks conversationally.

'Always, and it's worse after she's been fed. She screams and is forever sicking up. She's such a fussy one. I hardly sleep at all, and I'm out walking her all hours of the day and night. If I'd known she was going to be this difficult, I would never have taken the job.'

'I have seen many babies with similar problems. They have what is called reflux. Maybe this little one is one of those,' Basia says.

'Naming it don't help much,' the nurse grumbles.

Basia smiles at her grumpy reply. 'No, it will not, but there are some simple things you can do to help. Here, I will show you.' Basia reaches out and adjusts the mattress in the pram until the baby is a little propped up. 'If you keep the baby gently raised up, she will be a little more comfortable. Also, stirring a teaspoon of ground wheat into her milk to thicken it should help a little.'

As Basia adjusts the baby, her face relaxes, and in a

couple of minutes, she's already looking more contented. Basia stands to find the nurse and Hannah staring at her in amazement.

'I help my mother out, caring for newborn babies. This is more common than you would expect.'

'Still, I'm grateful,' the nurse says as the three of them start walking again, this time in silence.

Perhaps it's the mention of her mother, or perhaps it's the peace and quiet of the common, but Basia's thoughts are pulled home, and a wave of longing sweeps over her. She had been on her way back when all this started, and now she's stuck here until they find Maisie. In this moment, trying to prevent the end of the world in her time is not as daunting as trying to find the missing suffragist here.

'You know,' the nurse says, interrupting her thoughts, 'I do recall something odd from this morning. When the policeman asked me earlier nothing came to mind, but now that the baby has settled, and I can take a moment to think....'

'Do tell. It may not appear important to you, but it might help us,' Hannah encourages.

'Well, grumpy Mr Parsons down the road is forever yelling at me when I'm out early. He says the baby crying wakes him up. So rude, he is. Lulu was especially noisy this morning, and I didn't hear a peep from him.'

'That is interesting,' Basia says, not sure how this is relevant but pleased to have something from their efforts this afternoon.

Hannah, however, has a glint in her eyes. 'And you are sure that it was not because he has gone to visit

relatives or is too poorly to leave his bed?' she asks.

The nurse shakes her head. 'He has a nephew who comes and visits, but only at Christmas. My mistress says it's only because he hopes the old man will leave him something in his will. And he's too curmudgeonly to get sick. Besides, I'm sure he's home, because I saw two men go inside just before midday, and he opened the door for them.'

For the first time that day, Hannah's mood brightens. 'Where does Mr Parsons live?'

The nurse points across the park. 'Over there, at number 54. The big, creepy house with the overgrown garden.'

'Thank you so much. I am sure this will help.' Hannah smiles. 'Come, Barbara, let us rejoin the others.'

'There is nothing more we can do at the moment,' Alan says for the umpteenth time. 'Not until we have some new leads.'

'There must be something. We cannot just leave her to fend for herself.' Izzy doesn't try to hide her frustration, which is being fed by the growing fear that something is very wrong here.

She catches Nathanial's eye, and he shakes his head. *Does he also think this is a wasted effort, or does he want to lose the detective and strike out on our own? No, he can't want that because Alan is a part of that team.*

Izzy tries again. 'Perhaps we could—'

'Leave everything up to the police. We are the right and proper people to investigate this,' Alan tells her before she can outline her plan.

'Yes, Isolde, we should leave it up to the police,' Stanley says.

Clenching her fists, Izzy stares at each of them in disbelief. She had at least thought Nathanial would support her efforts to continue the search.

'Let us go back to Augusta's and have some tea,' Josephine suggests. 'A bit of distance might give us a new perspective.'

Under the weight of their objections, all the fight goes from Izzy. 'I guess that is almost a plan.'

'Wait,' Hannah's voice rings out. 'Hold up.'

The group turns as one towards the sound to find Hannah practically running towards them with Basia close behind.

'We have a lead,' Hannah says to Alan. 'Tell me, did your group question the owner of number 54?'

Alan takes his notebook from his pocket and flicks through the pages. 'Um, yes, let me see. A Mr Parsons, who reported nothing unusual in the street.'

'Of course he would say that.' Hannah turns to Basia, who nods approvingly. 'It appears our Mr Parsons has been hiding something.'

'According to a local, he has some guests staying, which is very unusual, and he has not been out bothering the neighbours as he normally would,' Basia chimes in.

'How does that help us?' Stanley asks. 'So he has guests, and he is not harassing the locals. They should

be grateful.'

Hannah's eyes capture Nathanial's, and Izzy senses she's looking for some softening there, perhaps even his support as she argues her case.

'It seems he is not the type to have visitors. And he usually complains about any noise in the street, but he was strangely quiet this morning,' Hannah explains, relaying what the nurse had told them.

There is a heavy silence once she finishes, and Izzy fears she hasn't convinced anyone this is indeed a lead. She's about to voice her support and suggest this warrants a follow-up when Nathanial slowly nods his head. 'If it is strange behaviour for him, then perhaps we should look into it.'

Stanley sighs. 'If we must, let us go over now and ask him what is going on. The sooner we clear this up, the sooner we can have some tea.'

'Whoa, wait a moment there.' Josephine places a hand on his arm. 'We cannot just go barging in, asking questions. If he does have Maisie, then he has already lied to the police, and he is not likely to tell us anything.'

Stanley puffs out his chest. 'Then Nathanial, the detective, and I will force our way in and demand to look around.'

'We will do no such thing,' Alan tells him. 'We do this by the book or not at all.'

'If we do it your way, then we might not get anywhere,' Izzy says, unable to keep the frustration from her voice.

Nathanial holds up his hands in a placating gesture. 'Surely we can find a middle road.'

Even though Alan might be the authority figure here,

the Time Guardian is still the one galvanising them as a team and leading the way.

'And that would be?' Alan asks.

'We need to watch the house for a bit to see if we can find if anything unusual is going on there,' Nathanial outlines.

'What, all of us?' Stanley asks. 'It will be a little obvious, do you not think?'

Izzy bites back a sigh. Stanley is a lovely guy, but he really wasn't blessed with great intelligence. 'If we take it in turns, it will not look suspicious. This is a popular place for walking and picnicking, so I suggest we pair off and plan some surveillance.'

'I am not sure this is a good idea, all of you getting involved like this,' Alan worries.

Basia moves close to him and asks, 'Do you not need to go back to the station to update the captain?'

The detective holds her gaze for a moment, and his whole body seems to soften as he contemplates her words, or perhaps Basia herself. In response, Basia leans towards him and adds, 'A walk together would be pleasant. And, if you are not here, you can turn a blind eye to what the others are doing.'

'And we will not do anything stupid, like storm the house, until we have spoken with you,' Josephine assures the detective.

'But—'

'Stanley, I want your word,' Josephine says, confronting her fiancé. 'No heroics.'

'I suppose,' Stanley mumbles, sounding so much like a thwarted child that Izzy chuckles under her breath.

SUFFRAGETTE

Now that Stanley has been tamed, all eyes turn to Alan, who's staring at the ground as if it might provide him with a solution. 'But if something happens to you… to any of you….'

'Nothing is going to happen to us. Best case, a crazy old man has some unexpected guests and there is nothing going on. Worst case, Maisie is being held in that house, we confirm it, and meet back this evening at Augusta's to formulate our next steps.' Izzy's gaze rakes over the others, begging them to agree with her.

'We promise not to do anything without talking with you first,' Stanley says.

The others nod their agreement.

'I suppose when I leave, you are just going to do what you want to anyway,' Alan says, almost defeated.

They all have the sense not to answer.

'I guess what I do not know….'

Basia places her hand on the detective's arm and says, 'Come, you can walk me to Aunt Augusta's on the way back to the station.' Basia quickly smiles over her shoulder at Izzy as she steers Alan away.

Izzy admires how deftly Basia dealt with the detective, leaving the rest of them to plan how best to observe Parsons's house without anyone noticing—not that it was any hardship for her if that glint in her eye was anything to go by.

'Nathanial and I will take the first turn,' Hannah says before anyone else can offer.

Given the tension between the two of them this morning, Izzy expects Nathanial to object. Instead he says, 'I think that is a perfect idea. Shall we stroll?'

He holds out his arm, and Hannah takes it, leaving Izzy with Josephine and Stanley.

'Well, Stanley, I think you and I should have a picnic tea in the park later this afternoon,' Josephine says.

Stanley smiles. 'Always happy to oblige when food is involved.'

'Aunt Augusta's cook can sort something for you, I am sure,' Izzy tells them.

'Will you join us?' Stanley asks.

Izzy shakes her head, and Stanley's face droops in disappointment. 'You are not still holding a grudge against me, are you?'

To Izzy's surprise, she finds she isn't. 'No, Stanley. It is just, if I picnic with you, who will accompany Basia when it is her turn to take watch?'

'Perhaps we will already know what is going on by then,' Stanley says before his eyes twinkle at another thought. 'Or perhaps the charming policeman will accompany her.'

'Come, you two, we do not need to decide now. Let us return to Augusta's and plan in comfort.' Josephine links arms with both Stanley and Izzy and leads them back through the park.

In spite of the gravity of the situation and her worry for Maisie, for the first time since she returned home, Izzy feels like she belongs.

It's a beautiful day for a walk, and Nathanial would be enjoying being back in his normal time, enjoying the scenery, if only the years between didn't weigh so heavily on his shoulders. Then again, it's hard to relax when Hannah's nervous energy is radiating off her in waves with such intensity that Nathanial imagines he can actually touch them.

He wants to reach out to his fiancée and reassure her that he's just excited about the adventure they're on and that everything will return to normal once Maisie is found. The problem is, there's a gulf between them, only Hannah is blind to it.

This Hannah has no idea that in a few months, they'll meet the Time Guardians Alpha and Beta. Or that in a little over a year she'll decide to become a Time Guardian herself, ready to abandon him if he doesn't join her.

He sends a sidelong glance her way. Even with her lips pursed, she is beautiful, and his heart skips a little.

As if sensing his attention, she turns and catches him watching her.

'What?' she snaps.

'Nothing. Well, I know you are upset with me. Why not tell me what I have done wrong, and I will apologise and try to fix it.'

He sighs inwardly. Falling back into old patterns is so easy. She's always taken the lead in their relationship— why change things now? He steels himself, waiting for her to outline his latest list of transgressions.

'Oh, Nathanial, and here I was, thinking you had grown a backbone today,' Hannah whispers almost as if to herself.

What? His toe hits a protruding tree root. He stumbles, rights himself, then catches Hannah up. They carry on walking as if nothing happened.

Had he heard her correctly? He can't have. She's mad at him for making decisions without consulting her, and for talking to other women, and for perhaps a hundred other little things he doesn't know about.

Is she actually implying she approves of his behaviour? He chews his bottom lip thoughtfully. Had he gotten it wrong all those years ago? In trying to be exactly who Hannah wanted him to be, had he pushed her away?

They complete a circuit of the park, and Nathanial's mind is still in turmoil, questioning the actions of his younger self. He'd fallen hard for Hannah when they first met—no doubt about it. It took time for him to convince her to actually consider him as a serious suitor, and even more time for her to accept his marriage proposal.

He'd tried to change himself into the man she wanted, but it never seemed enough. Had he altered himself so much that he pushed her away? If he'd been true to himself, would things have turned out differently?

Hannah's hand on his arm interrupts his thoughts. 'Nathanial, did you see that?'

'Sorry, no, I was… elsewhere.'

A frown creases her brow. 'If you are not going to take this—'

'Hannah, I lost focus for a moment.' He knows his tone is terse, but this isn't the right time for one of her lectures. 'Why not just tell me what I should be looking at.'

She turns to face him, taking his hands in hers as if they're having an intimate moment, and looks into his

eyes. 'There are two men walking towards us, heading across the common in the direction of Parsons's house. Something about them is not right—I am pretty sure they do not belong here.'

Nathanial raises her gloved hands to his lips as if to kiss them while at the same time turning his head slightly to get a better look. As he does, his breath catches in his throat.

Straight away he sees what had alerted Hannah. One of the two men has a military-style haircut but is dressed as a day labourer. The other has the look of a thug—perhaps he's hired muscle. At a quick glance, they appear to be labourers, perhaps employed in one of the houses around the green.

It isn't just the unusual haircut of the military-looking one that makes him question what he sees. It's more the fact that they're walking through the park in the middle of the day, one of them carrying what looks to be a bag of groceries, when any real labourer would be working.

The pair draw closer, and it's only Nathanial's training that prevents him from dropping his fiancée's hand, stomping over to the man with the military haircut, and punching him in the face. Anger bubbles inside him. How could he be here after everything he's done?

As they walk by, Nathanial forces his gaze back to Hannah. 'My love, I know you want to carry on walking, but I think we should return home, else your parents might believe I have kidnapped you.'

Hannah's mouth opens as if to snap a snarky retort, but she bites it back as he turns to follow the men's retreating backs. Not taking his eyes off them, he releases one of her hands as he slips the other into the crook of his elbow. Arm in arm, they follow the strange men.

'But, Nathanial,' Hannah simpers, and the oddity of that tone coming from her lips almost has him stumbling again. 'I am so enjoying our stroll. Maybe we might stay a little longer?'

He realises she's playing along with the ruse and says, 'I would love to, my sweet, but I have some business I must attend to this afternoon. Besides, we will be together again at dinner tonight.'

'Of course you must visit with your lawyer, but I shall miss you so.' Hannah pouts prettily, and it's all Nathanial can do not to snicker. This performance is so the opposite of his independent, confident fiancée.

For a brief moment, he wonders if things would have worked out between them if she were more like she's pretending to be now. No, the thing he admires most about her is her drive and her independent nature. He wouldn't put up with someone who bent their will to his.

Then it hits him like a sock to the jaw. He'd be frustrated by a woman who puts his needs first all the time... yet that's exactly what he's done with Hannah. Is that why she's grown increasingly terse and distant with him?

He shakes his head. This is not the time for deep soul-searching. He needs to keep his mind on the job.

They've only walked a couple of paces when the larger of the two men swings round and stalks back, stopping only when he's standing toe-to-toe with Nathanial. His eyes are ice cold, and menace wafts off him. Hannah gasps but stands her ground.

'You follow'n us, pretty boy?' His voice is rough and

raw, and Nathanial has to force himself to swallow the lump in his throat before answering.

'I have no idea what you are talking about. My fiancée and I are simply returning home after our walk.'

The man turns his head to look at Hannah. With her face obscured by the hat she wears, he contents himself with raking his eyes up and down her body, leering lasciviously, before focusing back on Nathanial.

'Well, y' keep yer distance if you want to keep that pretty face for your luscious lady.'

Hannah's grip tightens on his arm. The thug still holds Nathanial's gaze even after speaking, his looming presence causing Nathanial's heart to pound. Still, the man keeps his attention on him rather than on Hannah.

'Come on, Barry, leave the locals alone. We have business to attend to.'

The voice carries the tone of command, and its familiar sound sets Nathanial's teeth on edge. In spite of the physical threat from the man in front of him, it's the owner of that voice who scares him more.

'Huh. Can't a man 'ave a bit of fun?'

The thug lifts his arm and pokes Nathanial in the shoulder. 'I'm a-watching you,' he almost purrs before turning on his heel and catching up with his mate, who's almost at the edge of the common.

As the men walk away, Nathanial calms his racing heart, squares his shoulders, and pulls Hannah a little closer. 'Shall we continue?' he asks.

'But...,' Hannah starts, and he senses her gaze on his face. Perhaps it's the determination she sees there that stops her from finishing what she started. 'Of course.'

As they reach the end of the common, they're in time to catch the men entering Parsons's place as expected. Rather than going round the rear to the servant's entrance, they boldly walk up the steps and open the front door.

If their threatening manner hadn't confirmed that these men are not part of the normal social scene of Winchester, their entering the front door of the house does.

'Come on, we must report back to the others,' he says to Hannah, leading her away from the house and towards the centre of town.

When he glances down at her, surprised by her acquiescence, a small smile plays across her lips. Is she actually enjoying his taking charge? Or is this reaction because he hadn't backed down when threatened? His heart is racing again, and this time it's from joy rather than nerves.

Before the house is completely out of view, he chances a quick glance back and starts in surprise as a face appears at one of the upper windows. He stops and half turns to get a better look. A woman seems to be trying to pull the window open, but it's well and truly stuck. Her face twists in fear, and she backs away as the thug fills the space, pushing her back into the room. Moments later he's replaced by a familiar face, who reaches out and pulls the curtains shut.

Nathanial quickens his pace. This is not good, not good at all. He must contact Beta and find out what the hell is going on, and then Izzy and Basia need to be warned.

CHAPTER EIGHT
LOOK WHO'S BACK

Beta dumps the papers he's been reading onto the table and reaches his arms above his head, stretching out his spine. There are certainly some advantages to being back in a body, but the aches and pains he could do without.

Standing, he stretches again, then paces the room. He isn't just trying to loosen his muscles but is also trying to force his jumbled thoughts into some semblance of order.

The reports he spent the morning reading were proposals for the second joint Time Guardians and Time Fixers mission—their second attempt to nudge humanity away from a future war that would set it on course for extinction.

It's against his training and beliefs to interfere in history, but their recent success in stopping a major war had highlighted the potential benefits of limited intervention.

As Cynthia had pointed out on more than one occasion, history would not let them change anything too drastically without removing them from the timeline and using someone else to redress the balance.

Still, choosing where to make changes is fraught with pitfalls he hadn't had when planning his missions for the Time Guardians. Trying to keep history on track is black-and-white, whereas amending it is too many shades of grey for his liking.

Sighing, he has to admit he needs Cynthia. Not only is she more experienced with planning these types of missions, but she would also see problems he couldn't even imagine.

Beta?

He stops pacing. He only put Sigma in place this morning. Surely he wouldn't have anything to report yet.

Sigma, what is it?

You should have told me Jason was at the heart of this mess before you sent me in.

Jason? Jason is in Winchester with the others?

Are you sure?

Of course I am. I've seen him with my own eyes.

Sigma sounds angry. Surely he doesn't believe they sent him to Winchester knowing full well Jason is around?

Is Jason meant to be here? I mean, is he from this time?

What? No! Jason is from twentieth-century London.

Okaaay.

There's silence as the two Time Guardians reflect on the situation. Sigma breaks the silence first.

Beta, before we proceed, I need to know if I'm working for the Time Guardians, limiting a Time Fixers mess, or

am I working for this new combined agency, and I'm somehow supposed to be helping him?

Beta's head spins. As far as he knows, Jason had been placed under house arrest until he decided whether to retrain or leave the Time Fixers. He isn't supposed to be anywhere near 1913 and definitely not on an assignment.

Umm... I can assure you that Cynthia and I have not chosen our next mission. I'm not sure—

So Jason is working for the Time Fixers. I thought all but essential missions had ceased until you and Cynthia finalised the new agency set-up. And Izzy is here. Don't they have some rule about that?

Beta stares out the window, his head pounding as he tries to make sense of Sigma's report.

Beta?

I'm here. Just give me a moment.

Beta, you sound a bit... if you don't mind me saying... uncharacteristically woolly brained.

Sorry, Sigma, but this information is as much a shock to me as it is to you.

How do you want me to proceed?

For the first time in his afterlife, Beta not only has no idea how to advise his agent, but he also doesn't know where to start to find the answers. Nothing makes him angrier than having someone on the ground he's unable to support.

Beta, are you still there?

Ah, yes. Let me think. You need to brief Izzy, of course, and try to hold off from taking any further action until I can clarify the situation. And under no circumstances are you to confront Jason.

Beta, he's the one holding the young woman captive. What happens if we believe her life to be in danger? I mean, Jason is hardly the most stable of characters.

Obviously, if you fear for her life, you must intervene immediately, but please try and hold off doing anything, and I'll try to get answers as quickly as I can.

Please do. I would like to wrap this up as soon as possible. Not only for Maisie's sake but also because people have started to notice I'm not quite myself. I'm not comfortable with this whole "being me" situation.

Beta chuckles, enjoying Sigma's discomfort. This is his first mission in a human body, and time constraints had forced him to take over his own. It must be quite the distraction for him.

Yes, of course. I'll do the best I can, but I must proceed with some delicacy, as our agency isn't exactly meant to be running missions yet.

The connection winks out, and Beta strides to the door to his apartment, trying to remember where Cynthia said she would be this morning. As he marches through the corridors to her office, his anger grows. *What in god's name do the Time Fixers think they're doing, running a mission in the same timeline Izzy has returned to?*

Flinging open the door, he launches himself towards Cynthia's desk. 'Why on earth did you guys send Jason to 1913 with the others? I mean, *Jason*? And a mission in the same time period as a returning agent?'

As he says the words, he realises how ridiculous he sounds, and Cynthia's stunned expression tells him she thinks he's lost the plot too.

'What nonsense are you accusing us of now?'

Her voice chills him to the core, and his heart sinks as he realises he may have damaged their relationship with his accusations. He needs to remember that Cynthia is not his Time Guardian nemesis, Alpha, and that not everything with her has to be a battle.

Taking a deep breath to calm himself, he also takes a seat. Leaning forward, he rests his arms on his knees and starts again. 'I'm sorry, Cynthia. I just had some disturbing news, and my imagination ran off on me.' He gives a self-deprecating laugh. 'I guess this trust thing between us will take some getting used to.'

Cynthia's stony face doesn't soften as he had hoped it would, but her voice when she answers him is a few degrees less chilly. 'Your apology is accepted. Now, please explain what's going on.'

'Sigma—Nathanial—just informed me that Jason is the one who kidnapped the suffragist. It's him causing the timeline variations.'

Cynthia blanches and clasps her hands in front of her, and he senses it takes quite a bit for his partner to control her reaction to that piece of news. She rises slowly to her feet and, in clipped tones, says, 'If you will excuse me, I have to go make some heads roll.'

The murmurings of the others intrude on Basia's calm as she stares out the window, not exactly waiting for Alan to return but hoping he'll arrive soon. Life is so much brighter with him in the room. *Goodness, Basia, you're acting like a lovesick girl from a romance novel. Get a hold of yourself. Alan is not your Allan, and it's unfair to him for you to treat him as though he is.*

She forces herself to turn around and sit on the window seat. Jo and Izzy are talking animatedly, and Stanley lounges in his chair, watching them, a self-satisfied smile on his face.

What's he up to? Basia rises and wanders to the tea trolley to refill her cup and to eavesdrop.

'What is the point of getting the vote if all we are able to do is vote for men? Why must men always represent us?' Josephine's voice is tight with frustration.

'Because society does not change with great leaps forward. It takes small, incremental steps,' Izzy argues.

Josephine's face breaks into a triumphant smile. 'Yet you would have them leap to accepting same-sex relationships when they cannot even countenance women governing.'

Izzy is wide-eyed and stunned into silence as she realises Jo has trapped her. The atmosphere is heavy. Almost as if the entire room is holding its breath, waiting for her response.

'Well, you walked right into that, Isolde,' Basia says.

Izzy turns to her, then laughs. 'I guess I did. Well played, Josephine.'

Stanley regards his two companions fondly, and in that moment, Basia is able to imagine the three of them building some sort of life together.

She hopes for Izzy's sake that she'll come to see it, too, because she's a better person when she's around Jo

168

and Stanley. Besides, it seems to Basia that there's as much, if not more, for Izzy to focus on changing here in her own timeline as there would be traipsing back and forth at the beck and call of the Time Fixers.

If only her own dilemma were as easily resolved. Walking back to Augusta's with Alan had been enjoyable. It's clear he admires her, is perhaps even attracted to her. She also has to admit that, in spite of the recent death of her Allan, the attraction is reciprocated.

This disturbs her, not least because she can't work out whether she's falling for Alan himself or if it's because he's so like her Allan, it's uncanny. Then again, one of them is a reincarnation of the other, so does it matter?

Either way, she needs to take a step back because she isn't staying around. Or… is it possible she can stay here a little while longer and see where this is heading? No, that wouldn't be good. One or both of them would inevitably get hurt because she can't stay here forever.

Not only does she have a life to get back to, but there would always be the risk that she might overstep and inadvertently change something, and then history would dump her back home, not caring how or where, and that might cause her and Izzy problems explaining things.

Also, at some stage, she and the person she's the reincarnation of might end up in the same area. From what Izzy had said, that might change history as time worked to keep them apart.

History? Oh no. A hand flies to her mouth as her brain catches up with her ramblings, and she turns away so the others can't see her face. Next year, these young people will be embroiled in a war themselves, and not all of them will survive—perhaps not even her detective.

'Barbara, are you all right? You have gone quite pale,' Stanley says from her side. When had he moved?

'Yes, I am. I just thought of....' She doesn't know what to tell him, but fortunately she's rescued from having to say anything at all as she glimpses two figures rushing down the street.

'Nathanial and Hannah have returned early, and they do not look very happy,' she says, drawing Stanley's attention to the approaching couple.

'I hope they have not had another fight,' Josephine says as she joins them.

As one, the four people head out into the hallway to meet the Nathanial and Hannah, arriving just as a maid is closing the door behind them.

'Whatever is the matter?' Izzy demands before they have a chance to even catch their breaths.

Nathanial glances around, taking in the maid as well as the butler emerging from the morning room. 'Perhaps we should find somewhere a little more private to talk.'

Izzy turns to Jensen. 'We shall be in the library. Please show Detective Barker up when he arrives.'

'As you wish, miss. The fire has been lit. Would you like any tea or refreshments?'

Izzy takes in how distressed Nathanial is and says, 'Thank you, Jensen. If you could bring up some tea and perhaps a decanter of claret. It looks like we might need some fortification.'

'Very good, miss.'

Izzy leads the party up the stairs to the first floor. As she opens the door to the library, she asks, 'What was

wrong with the morning room?'

No one answers until everyone is inside and the door is firmly closed.

'Nathanial is being a bit overdramatic,' Hannah says. 'I believe this is his attempt at complete privacy. Although why we need it is beyond me. All we have to report is that we saw some suspicious men, followed them, and, as we suspected, they were headed for Parsons's home. As we were turning to leave, a distressed woman appeared at the window—we believe it may be your Maisie Ottaway.'

A stunned silence follows Hannah's words, and then everyone talks at once. Nathanial holds up his hand for silence. When he has it, he says, 'There is more to the story. Hannah, I did not tell you that when I was in London last week to see my lawyer, I believe I was in the same teahouse as Isolde and Barbara.'

Hannah eyes him suspiciously, but he explains, 'I did not recognise them at first, and when I tell you the whole story, you will understand why.'

'All right, go ahead,' Hannah tells him, arms firmly crossed in a defensive position over her chest.

Butterflies erupt in Basia's stomach, and she leans forward, eager to hear what Nathanial has to say. *Because I'm pretty sure I wasn't in London last week. I was hundreds of years in the future, attending a peace conference, so this should be good.*

'I had tea in a shop on Fleet Street and was paying the bill when a ruckus started up outside. A man was yelling and shouting and waving a gun, threatening to kill another man. The gun went off, and the victim fell to the ground. I was quite disturbed by the whole thing, and I decided there and then not to share the incident with you.'

'And seeing Barbara and Isolde?' Hannah pressed.

'Well, it was only when I saw that man again today that it must have jolted my memory. I believe the two women sitting at the table by the window last week were Isolde and Barbara,' Nathanial explains.

Basia stares blankly at the Time Guardian. What is he talking about?

Nathanial returns her gaze, and his eyes widen, as if he's willing her to do something—but what? A man with a gun? Last week? Then it dawns on her—last week, one of the Time Fixers shot her Allan. Was he saying that that man was here—in this timeline? She looks from Nathanial to Izzy and back again.

'Yes, I believe we were there,' Izzy confirms, sending a look to Basia that says, 'Please back us up.'

'We were,' Basia says somewhat hesitantly.

Nathanial nods and continues. 'Well, you would have seen the wild cast of his eyes and heard the nonsense he was spouting. He was unhinged and very dangerous.'

'But… but the authorities got him,' Izzy says. 'Surely he is not here. He cannot be.'

'Perhaps he escaped.' Basia's voice is barely above a whisper. 'I mean, it's… it is the only explanation.

'I hope that is what happened,' Izzy says, her voice crisp. 'One cannot be too sure about where the authorities sit on this.'

'Isolde, of course the authorities will be on the right side of the law,' Stanley almost bellows. 'How can you think otherwise?'

SUFFRAGETTE

Josephine places a hand on Stanley's arm. 'You have such a good heart, Stanley, but even you must see how the police have been manhandling and arresting suffragettes—even those who have not broken any laws.'

'But... but...,' Stanley splutters, unable to conceive that those who keep law and order might not be perfect.

He's still coming up with a response when Alan enters the library.

'I see I have arrived in good time to hear you denigrating my fellow officers.' Although his tone is stern, it's softened somewhat by his good humour as his eyes rake over the room, falling finally on Basia. He sends her a warm smile before turning to the others. 'Am I guessing correctly that you at least have something to report?' he asks.

The gong to change for dinner sounds as Nathanial quickly fills the detective in, including their suspicions that one of the men might be a wanted criminal.

'I must say, Nathanial, I have not read any reports of escaped prisoners, or indeed of anyone apprehended for a shooting in London,' Alan protests. 'Are you all quite sure the man from London is in fact the man you saw today?'

'I am completely sure,' Nathanial says.

Heat rises to Basia's face, and she's sure she must appear guilty of something as she struggles to come up with a way to support Nathanial's story.

Izzy, however, is quite at ease with lying—a skill she's no doubt honed on her many Time Fixer missions.

'Of course, I cannot say anything about the man Nathanial and Hannah met today. What I can tell you is last week, I watched one man shoot another man. He was yelling and raving, and the crowd in the street went wild. Because of the ensuing chaos, I cannot swear that he hit his victim, but I can assure you, everyone in the teashop had a good view of the gun wielder's face. We also saw the policemen who led him away. If Nathanial says it is the same man, then I believe him.'

It would be difficult for anyone to question Izzy's firm assertions, but Alan is not so easily mollified.

'Well, I can assure you, no one has escaped custody. We would have had a report and been directed to be on the lookout for him. So it cannot be your man.'

Before anyone can further argue the point, Nathanial steps in. 'Does it matter whether he is the man from London or not? We have discovered where Miss Ottaway is being held. It is likely that, whoever her captors are, they are armed and dangerous, and we should take that into account when we go rescue her.'

'Well said, Nathanial.' Stanley raises a glass of wine to his friend.

Alan is not so supportive. He takes the glass of claret Izzy hands him and has a small sip before saying, 'Identifying the location of the missing girl has been most helpful of you, but now it really is time to let the professionals take over, gentlemen. Not only do we have the experience, but we also have the numbers.'

'The six of us here stand ready to help you. Do you really believe the police force will release enough officers today, given everything going on in Winchester?' Izzy asks, and Alan's eyes widen in what Basia thinks can only be shock.

'But... but you cannot possibly mean to.... I mean, you women cannot be involved in any rescue.'

174

'Piffle,' Josephine snorts. 'I am a better shot than Stanley. No one can punch harder than Isolde. And I warrant you, Barbara and Hannah have some hidden talents as well. Detective, write us off as feeble women at your peril.' The look on Josephine's face challenges Alan to deny their usefulness.

Alan opens his mouth as if to respond, then closes it, almost as though he knows this is not an argument he can win. When he does speak, it's to reiterate that they should leave this to the police now.

'When do you think you can get someone organised to retrieve Miss Ottaway?' Stanley asks.

Alan frowns again, and he appears reluctant to answer. 'Well, um, rather a large number of people have been misplaced in Winchester today, so the captain doubled patrols this afternoon in light of Miss Ottaway's disappearance.'

'So more women have been abducted,' Josephine gasps.

'I am sorry, I should have chosen my words better under the circumstances. With the number of visitors in the city, people have lost members of their groups. We have more constables out and about to provide directions and try to reunite stragglers with their friends.'

'Oh, thank goodness. I thought things might have escalated beyond our ability to help.' Josephine breathes a sigh of relief. 'So, when will the constables be freed up to rescue Miss Ottaway?'

'Perhaps later this evening, but more likely tonight,' Alan answered.

Nathanial, who was shaking his head before the detective had even finished speaking, says, 'Not only is that too long to wait, but if their captors are smart, they will be expecting a night-time rescue by the police.'

Izzy nods. 'Yes, and if we go in now, perhaps with a frontal approach to throw them off-guard, we might succeed. Josephine and Hannah will be the best to send in as decoys. No one will expect two women looking for their friend to be part of a rescue attempt.'

'Good thinking,' Basia says. 'And the chap from London will not have seen them before and so will not be suspicious—'

'Except when I was in the park this morning, they walked right past me,' Hannah butts in. 'But if I change my dress and hat, I will seem like someone completely different to all but the most observant of people.'

'Yes, you could borrow something of mine,' Izzy agrees. 'We are much the same size.'

'So, while Josephine and Hannah are at the front door, causing a scene over—' Stanley starts, and the entire group except for the detective forms a circle, bandying around ideas. Alan turns from one to the other as they speak, a look of bemusement on his face.

'Asking about the disappearance of one of our suffragist sisters, of course,' Josephine interrupts. 'That should get them aggravated enough to drop their guard.'

Alan places his wine on the table, clearly not comfortable with the runaway plan but seemingly not sure how to stop it. Basia wishes she could say something to include him, but Maisie must be rescued as soon as possible, and this plan is coming together nicely.

'But, my dear, what if they try to abduct you too?' Stanley's face creases with concern.

'Then you will be inside, having come through the back

door, ready to help,' Hannah says, a smile on her lips.

As Hannah speaks, Nathanial rises to his feet and excuses himself from the table. 'Please carry on. My stomach is just a little upset,' he says as he rushes from the room.

What is it, Beta? Nathanial asks as soon as the door closes behind him.

You still sound angry, Sigma.

Sorry, I had to make an excuse to leave the room. I'm with people who have no idea Time Guardians exist, let alone ones who can mindspeak.

So you couldn't have just gazed out a window?

Hannah already thinks I'm acting strangely enough, and I don't want to give her any more reason to think I'm not her Nathanial.

Nathanial is annoyed, and though he's pretty certain the interruption isn't the cause, he is not quite certain what has gotten him so het up.

Of course, it could be because he was taken from this first ever holiday during which he'd been trying to get some perspective on life so he could make some serious death decisions. Or maybe because he's been dropped into a situation that appears to be going from bad to worse. Or it could be because he doesn't like cleaning up someone else's mess—and that someone else should definitely have cleaned Jason away some time ago.

If he was being honest, though, what's gotten under his skin is the fact that Hannah appears to like this new version of Nathanial far more than the old one. It has him questioning his whole past life, and one does not need a life crisis in the middle of a mission.

How he wishes he were back in the holiday simulation, lazing on a beach, reading books, and drinking ice-cold beer.

Well, it's never easy going back into your own timeline, Beta says, and his holiday vision recedes.

A little less of the pop psychiatry, if you please.

All right, I have an update for you.

Beta is being his usual chatty self and taking time Nathanial does not have. *I thought as much, but please make it quick. I've excused myself to use the facilities, so I can't be away for long.*

All right. Cynthia's investigations found Jason has escaped from house arrest and is hellbent on ruining Izzy.

Izzy? Why not all of us? Nathanial asks.

The enquiry into his actions last week caused some doubt over his past performance. They reopened the investigation into the mission he went on with Izzy, and some judges are thinking perhaps her version of events may be closer to the truth. So now Jason blames her for everything that's happened to him.

That is nonsense. Izzy wasn't even involved in his decision to interrupt the peace talks.

Beta's sigh is clearly audible. *You can't argue with crazy, and this guy has definitely lost the plot. Unfortunately for us, there are enough supporters of his family who are prepared to listen to his nonsense, including his parents themselves.*

You mean there are Time Fixers helping him? Nathanial asks, sure his shock has transmitted through to Beta.

He was under house arrest, which means he had a bracelet preventing him from portalling anywhere. Someone must have removed it or opened a portal for him if he's in Winchester.

Unbelievable.

And that's not all. He's spun some yarn about needing to go and clean up Izzy's mess because she's been taking action contrary to Time Fixers protocols.

But that's nonsense. Izzy had barely arrived…. Ah, you mean by bringing Basia here.

Exactly.

It was my suggestion, though.

But Izzy agreed to take her.

Nathanial runs a hand through his hair. Could he have brought this mess down on everyone because he tried to help Basia?

Don't beat yourself up, Sigma. Jason would have found another excuse to attack Izzy if this one didn't exist.

He's sure Beta is right, but it doesn't stop him feeling somewhat responsible anyway.

So, what now, Beta?

We—Cynthia and I—have taken responsibility for Basia being with you. However, all this debating has created delays on our end.

Delays?

Yes. The Time Fixer Council wants to send a team to extract Jason, Basia, and Izzy before they cause any damage to the timeline. However, Jason's parents and their supporters have called for a full Council session to debate the mission and clearly define its parameters. There are some who are prepared to argue that Jason's actions will improve the timeline.

You can't be serious. How would delaying women getting the vote improve the chances of stopping the world ending? No, don't tell me. I don't have time, and it'll only make me angrier. So what now?

Cynthia is about to leave to attend the Council session, and I'm off to Time Guardian headquarters to see if they're prepared to send an extraction team for Jason. They've been strangely silent on the matter, so I'm not sure I'll gain any support.

So, what do we do in the meantime? We can't leave poor Maisie with Jason—he's clearly unhinged.

I will leave that up to you and Izzy. You need to decide what's more important—her future with the Time Fixers or saving the girl.

Not much of a choice, Nathanial says.

Whatever you decide to do, remember that Jason is no longer considered an agent of ours, as he was stood down. His actions will be considered unsanctioned until the Council votes to approve them, Cynthia's voice cuts in, her tone terse.

Has she been listening this whole time? He knows Beta trusts the Time Fixer, but Nathanial hardly knows her. He quickly reviews the conversation to work out if he had said anything he didn't want her to hear. Fortunately, he hadn't opened up too much about the awkward situation between him and Hannah. Happy he had kept things professional, he turns his mind back to Cynthia's statement.

So you're saying the sooner we get to Jason, the better for Izzy's future? he clarifies.

Exactly. Now I must be off, or I'll be late.

The silence drags out, and Nathanial wonders if Beta has gone as well until his mentor says, *I am afraid she's angry with me because I didn't trust her enough when I found out about Jason. And she's beyond angry with the Time Fixers for not telling her Jason escaped and that they were trying to find him. This new unit…. Well, it's new, and we have a few teething problems.*

I don't think anything about this situation is good for anyone, Nathanial sends. *In fact, I'm surprised that history hasn't removed Jason from the timeline for taking direct action.*

Well, we believe that's because anti-suffragette sentiment is running so high, meaning his actions are not as extreme as they first appear.

Nathanial considers this for a moment and wonders how he hadn't noticed the depth of anger towards women seeking the vote when he lived through this time before. Had he really been so wrapped up in his own life that he hadn't seen the signs that were so obvious to him now? Or was it simply because he'd been viewing the world through a male perspective? Was it any wonder Hannah had been so disparaging of him?

Sigma, if we've finished, then I must go—the Time Guardian Council awaits. Any ideas on what I should tell them?

Still caught up in his own self-reflection, it takes a moment for Nathanial to redirect his thoughts. Everyone in the room next door appears intent on taking action. The

Time Fixers are procrastinating, and the Time Guardians are unlikely to become involved.

Do you think you can persuade the Guardians not to react for a day in order to see how the timeline looks and whether history intervenes?

I can probably swing that, but what do I tell them about you and Izzy?

Do they even know you asked me to come here?

Not exactly. In my new role, I have some autonomy....

At first Nathanial doesn't know how he feels about that. It's as though he's going against the Time Guardians. Having only ever stretched the rules before, he isn't sure he's up to breaking them. Then again, not being required to follow their rules gives him a feeling of freedom.

Sigma? Whatever happens, this is on me if it goes wrong.

Nathanial's laugh is hollow. *Thanks for your support.*

No, what I mean is, I sent you to deal with the situation—you've done nothing wrong.

So why does he feel like he's about to? Putting his misgivings aside, he sends, *Right, so rescue Maisie it is!*

It's Beta's turn to laugh. *All right, my friend. In that case, I believe you have a day at the most to resolve this before one or the other of the sides chooses to intervene.*

Understood.

At the creak of a door hinge from behind him, Nathanial quickly turns and steps forward as if he's returning from the bathroom just as Hannah emerges from the library.

'Ah, there you are. I wondered if you were all right.' She smiles tentatively at him, but the question remains in her eyes, the same one that had appeared when he replaced his earlier self.

'I am fine. Just a small stomach upset.'

Her smile broadens. 'Good, because it is getting out of hand in the library, and I am sure they could use some of your newfound organisational skills.'

She takes his hand and leads him back to the fray.

CHAPTER NINE
DANCING AROUND

Hannah's description of what's going on in the library is woefully inadequate. Everyone is talking over top of everyone else. Voices are raised, hands are busy gesticulating, and no one is listening.

Nathanial watches for a moment and decides there's nothing else for it—he whistles. It's as if he's stunned the room's occupants. They stop talking and immediately turn to him.

'We are not going to get very far if we behave like a group of street thugs,' he tells them.

Big mistake, because they all start talking at him. He sighs, wondering if he is the right person to lead this group. Then again, who else is there? Izzy? She's too distracted by Josephine, and this reincarnation of Alan is too young and green, as is Hannah—although he knows she'll go on to be a formidable Time Guardian. Basia is sitting quietly by the fire and appears to have opted out of whatever is going on. So, it's up to him.

He holds up his hand for silence, and it takes a few moments, but they all eventually quieten down. When he's positive they're going to stay that way, he speaks, keeping his voice low so they will all have to concentrate or risk missing out on what he's saying.

'When I left only a few minutes ago, I thought we had agreed to rescue Miss Ottaway and were forming a rather decent plan—something about Hannah and Josephine approaching the front door as a distraction. What happened in that small amount of time to cause this chaos?'

Everyone opens their mouths, and he holds up his hand again. 'One at a time, please.' He points at the detective.

'We should not do this. We should wait for the authorities,' Alan says, predictably.

'We have gone past that point. We are going to rescue Maisie. All we need to decide is how,' Nathanial says, dismissing the detective's plea. He points at Stanley, the other person who has some misgivings about this rescue.

'I think the women should not be so directly involved. We should gather some chums and let the men take care of this,' Stanley says. 'Of course, they will need to be there to help Miss Ottaway once we have taken out her captors, but there is no sense in placing them in harm's way.'

'And I think you are being a pompous idiot,' Izzy says without waiting for Nathanial to point at her.

'Isolde, do not talk to Stanley like that.' Having admonished her friend, Josephine turns to her fiancé and says,

'And you should have more faith in us. We are perfectly capable of taking care of ourselves.'

Basia rises to her feet, frustration written on her face. 'I cannot hear this another time. We should all be thinking about what is best for Maisie, not going round in circles with this constant bickering. I shall be in my room when you are ready to plan sensibly.' With a swish of her skirts, she leaves them.

The silence following her departure is heavy. 'I am not surprised she is annoyed with you all. You do rather sound like squabbling children,' Nathanial says, smiling wryly, and the others laugh, breaking the tension.

'Look, if we want Miss Ottaway out of that house, we are going to have to work together.' He pauses for a moment, searching for agreement on the faces in front of him. They give him nothing.

Taking a deep breath, he continues regardless. 'That will mean each of us bending a little. For instance, Detective, perhaps you could send a runner and ask for a constable or two to be dispatched to help us out. You could use them to make up a team to lead a charge through the back once the ladies have distracted the men out front.'

'I guess I could do that,' Alan agrees reluctantly.

'But—'

Nathanial does not allow Stanley to complete his sentence. 'And, Stanley, maybe you could remain hidden at the front of the house to ensure help is at hand if something happens to Hannah or Josephine.'

'Well, yes, I guess that could work,' Stanley concedes.

'And if I wait with you, we four could make our way

through the front door when the others enter from the back,' Izzy adds.

Stanley grins. 'Catch them in a traditional pincer movement.'

'Exactly.' Izzy grins back.

'And that leaves Nathanial and Barbara joining the fray from the rear,' Hannah finishes.

Nathanial relaxes. 'It looks like we have the beginnings of a plan. Perhaps someone should find Bas... um... Barbara so we can finish our planning? And maybe we could have some more refreshments?'

'I will find her,' Josephine offers.

'And I shall organise more tea—that is if you do not mind, Isolde,' Hannah adds.

'That would be great, thank you. And could you please ask Jensen to hold dinner? I fear we may be a while yet,' Izzy says as the two women leave.

Everyone's playing nice again. Nathanial is pretty proud of himself until Izzy pulls him aside and says, 'You should know that while you were out, Stanley and Hannah were talking about the change that has come over you today. Perhaps you should be a little less Sigma and a little more Nathanial for a while.'

Nathanial's lips curl into a smile. 'I rather thought Hannah liked the new me.'

Izzy's eyes sparkle. 'I think you are right, but what mess are you leaving for the Nathanial who has to stay behind?' Her eyes widen. 'Or are you thinking of staying here as well?'

Seizing the opportunity to change the subject, Nathanial says, 'So have *you* decided to stay?'

'I am not letting you off the hook that easily. Answer my question—are you thinking about remaining here after this is over?'

'No, of course….' Nathanial had been about to give a vehement no, but he realises he would be lying. 'That was not my intention when I arrived, but I have to admit, I am kind of enjoying being the new me in this old time.'

Izzy's eyes narrow. 'I understand you find the rules around being a Guardian difficult, but I kind of thought you might join Beta's new team.'

'I was struggling with that decision while I was on leave—trying to decide whether to allow my soul to slip away, or wondering if I had the energy to continue and effect some real change in humanity's timeline,' he admits, running a hand over his jaw. 'But I feel alive here, for the first time in a long time—and before you say it, it is not just because I am back in a human body.'

Izzy chuckles. 'I must say, it is unusual to talk to you face to face like this, but please, do not get carried away by the excitement… or by Hannah's admiration.'

'So, it is all right for you to decide to stay but not me?' Nathanial doesn't mean to sound petulant, but he can't help it.

For the first time in a long time, he feels like he's being true to himself, and for some reason, he'd hoped Izzy would be happy for him. After all, over the past few months, he and the Time Fixer had become close, even working on missions together, and she of all people should understand the conflicts he faces in his job. Even so, why is he so bothered by her negative reaction?

'Nathanial, you are my closest friend, and—'

188

'Sorry?' he says, ready to stop her. Friends? Then he reads the concern in her eyes, and he realises she *is* his friend, or at least the closest thing he's had to a friend for some years.

'Please hear me out, Nathanial.'

He nods for her to continue, but he's only half listening, as part of him is still processing this new revelation.

'I want you to find your place in the world almost as much as I want to find my own, but your staying has such different consequences. As much as I want women to be treated the same as men, the reality is that we will not be when war comes next year. By staying here, you could be placing your life in danger.'

'War?' he reacts, suddenly paying attention. Of course, the war to end all wars is almost upon the world.

'Yes, the war in which Britain's male population is decimated. Now, it may be that Hannah will make a different decision with her new and improved Nathanial, but are you willing to take that chance only to be drawn into fighting a war that will, like as not, result in your being shot in a trench somewhere in Europe?'

It was as if she'd thrown cold water over him. 'What a grim picture you paint, Isolde.'

It had been so easy for him to be drawn into his old life, renewing his attraction to Hannah, and thinking perhaps he had found a way to make a life with her that didn't mean joining the Time Guardians. Combined with the excitement of searching for Miss Ottaway, he had totally forgotten about the war looming over the horizon.

As Great Britain spiralled towards conflict, he and Hannah had become despondent, worried about the future of mankind. They both opposed Britain going to war and worked tirelessly for peace. Hell, he'd even been leaning towards becoming a conscientious objector.

Not long after, Hannah had changed. She'd become distant and would go missing for hours on end, offering no explanation. Finally, he forced her hand, and she introduced him to Alpha, and Beta, and the Time Guardians.

She was so excited, believing she'd found a better way to stop warring factions in the world. When he questioned her some more, she asked him to come along on a mission.

He feels a hand on his arm. 'Nathanial, I am sorry. I did not mean to dredge up unhappy memories. Especially not when we should be focusing on Maisie and how to get her away from Jason. You join the others, and I will go and see what is happening with the refreshments.'

A part of him notices Izzy's departure, but he continues replaying the scene between him and Hannah after their first two missions together.

'I am going to join them, Nathanial. They say I am ready, that I have helped them in past lives, and I can now ascend.'

'And what about me? About us?' he'd asked.

'The good news is that they are happy for you to come with me. It seems it would be cleaner if we both died in an accident. Our families would find some peace, knowing we were together in death.'

The shock he felt at how she calmly planned their demise is still as raw today as it had been then.

'Beta said most guardians ascend at the end of their natural lives,' he'd countered. 'I am happy to wait until my life ends naturally.'

Her anger had surprised him. 'Of course you would be. It is not you who would be left alone for years, grieving for me.'

'What? I do not understand.'

'Alpha has explained that in the coming war, so many men die that I will likely be left a widow. So, chances are you would be given the option to ascend within the next few years. I will likely live out the rest of my life alone, without you.' Hannah's words were laced with a bitterness that cut him deeply.

He was not so ready to jump to his own death. 'If there is only a chance I might die, there is also a chance I might live, and that we will grow old together.'

The scornful look she'd turned on him cut him to the quick. 'Even your optimism cannot remain in the face of the scale of this war. I have decided. I will ascend next week. Alpha has planned the accident. I want you to join me, but if you decide not to, I hope you live a happy life.'

Turning on her heel, she'd left him standing alone in the deserted park. He reached out, trying to call her back, but he couldn't form the words. What would he say to her? What would convince her to stay with him?

Now, standing in the library in Augusta's house, his feelings of loss and betrayal return in full force. With his new knowledge, could he actually influence Hannah enough to change her mind, to have her try for the slim chance of a life together? Knowing the decision she'd been capable of making once before, does he even want to try?

As if she materialises from his thoughts, Hannah appears beside him. 'Nathanial, do you want to join us?'

The Hannah from the past wouldn't have asked. She would have assumed he would always want to be by her side.

They move to the circle gathering around the fresh pot of tea, Hannah making sure he's cut off from Izzy, and he finally sees it.

The potential future he'd seen for them was a fantasy of his own making, a vision he's holding on to, has indeed been longing for, during the years since they ascended. It's time to let it go and start making decisions for himself.

He pulls Hannah's arm through his as the other Nathanial would have done, hoping to reassure her everything is all right, but his mind has already returned to the problem of rescuing Maisie.

Basia returns to the library with Josephine after the woman promises everyone is now playing nice. As she takes a seat by the fire, she studies the group, and they do indeed appear to be getting along. She's barely had a chance to sit when Alan joins her, offering a cup of tea.

'Thank you, but no. If I have any more to drink, I think I will burst,' she tells him.

'You are quiet this evening,' he says, taking the seat opposite, the cup still in his hands.

'All this arguing and fussing is really not my style. To me, it is clear-cut. Maisie is being held by some not very nice people. The sooner we get her out of there, the better.'

Alan looks at his tea so intently, it's as if he's searching for something in the bottom of his cup.

'Extracting her will be dangerous. Surely you should leave saving her to the professionals.' The words explode from his mouth as if he's been trying to keep them in, but they have to be spoken.

Basia bites back a snort, but she can't keep the scorn from her voice. 'If it were not for us, you and your professionals would have no idea where she was being held, or by whom.'

Her companion has the good grace to colour at this. 'I have to admit, you have all turned out to be most helpful—'

'And we will also be helpful in extracting her from their clutches.'

Alan continues to study the tea, then takes a sip and places the cup back on the saucer. 'I would prefer it if we had more men. I have sent a runner to the station, but by the time they get here, it will be late, and it will be dark.'

Basia doesn't understand why he's so concerned about darkness falling when he'd been perfectly happy to wait before. 'You see that as being a problem? I thought we would be able to hide better in the dark.'

'True, we will be able to hide more easily, but if these men are professional criminals, they will know that too. If they can reasonably guess what we will do, they will be prepared—if not for our exact plan, then for something to happen.' He raises his head and looks her in the eyes, almost as though he's willing her to understand.

'That sounds logical. When would you suggest we go?'

193

Alan shrugs. 'If it were completely up to me, I would go in at first light. One of the captors will not be quite awake, and the other will be tired from guard duty.'

Basia nods, understanding his argument but not really liking it. She wants to say she can see his point, but they need to get Maisie out now. Alan is gazing so earnestly at her, she hasn't the heart.

'It sounds like early morning might be a better time. And I guess it means everyone can get into position under cover of darkness and be ready when Josephine and Hannah make their entrance at first light.'

The smile Alan gives her causes her heart to skip a beat. 'You know, if they let women on the force, you would be quite good at this.'

'Will they not be suspicious about women being out so early?'

Basia had been so focused on Alan, she hadn't heard Stanley approach.

'If we were truly worried about a friend, we would be up bright and early looking for her,' Josephine says from the other side of the room.

'I am still not completely comfortable—' Stanley starts, but he's interrupted as the door opens.

Izzy enters, followed by Jensen pushing a tea trolley loaded with cakes and sandwiches. 'Refreshments,' she announces.

'I am going to need to get a whole new wardrobe when I get home,' Basia sighs as she eyes the delicious offerings.

Izzy catches her ogling and says, 'I had forgotten how Aunt's cook likes to feed everyone.'

'I have no problem with the amount of food she sends

up,' Stanley says, placing a cake on a plate. 'She is a superb cook, and I will show my appreciation by eating whatever she serves.'

With the food having distracted Stanley, Alan presents his objections to the current plan. They take very little persuading that his option has a better chance of success with a couple of tweaks. Once they've agreed, he outlines it again to make sure everyone is on the same page.

'At around five thirty tomorrow morning, Nathanial and Isolde will take their place in the bushes in front of Parsons's house. Barbara and I, with hopefully two constables, will take up a position in the back garden with easy access to the back door. Then, as the sun rises, Josephine and Hannah, escorted by Stanley, will knock on the door and question whoever answers about their missing friend.'

'So far so good,' Stanley says, helping himself to another cake.

'When we are certain the household is distracted, those of us at the back will enter. Hopefully this will cause whoever is answering the door to return inside. After which, those at the front will be able to enter the house and head upstairs to find Miss Ottaway.'

'What then?' Basia asks. 'I mean, how will they get her out?'

Alan shrugs. 'Obviously the optimal solution would be to retreat the way we came in, but we cannot predict where people will be in the house, how many of them there are, or how they will react.'

'Should I stay at the bottom of the stairs or go up with the women?' Stanley asks.

'A good question,' Alan tells him. 'I guess that depends on how many different voices you make out downstairs when you come in. If all the action is there, you might need to stay on the ground floor with Nathanial to ensure no one goes up to disturb the getaway.'

'Understood.'

'It sounds like we have a plan,' Alan says and waits for agreement.

'I am not comfortable leaving her there for another night,' Basia says, not quite able to give up on helping the young woman escape from her prison this evening.

The faces the others turn towards her show they disapprove. Only Nathanial is nodding in agreement. 'That thug who threatened me seemed like a bit of a brute, and I certainly did not like the way he looked at Hannah. I am not sure Miss Ottaway will be safe with him in the house.'

'You do not think they would….' Hannah's voice trails off as she contemplates what might befall a young woman alone in a house full of men.

'No one is saying that.' Izzy steps forward, hands on hips.

'Perhaps when I return to the station, I will find out if one of the trainee officers can watch the house for the night,' the detective offers.

'What good would that do?' Basia asks.

'He would raise an alarm if he hears anything untoward. It is not much—'

Basia's spirits lift at Alan's gesture. 'Thank you. It may not be much, but it would make me feel better.'

Jason may be many things, but he wouldn't let anyone

defile a woman.

Basia is sure the comment was meant for Nathanial. Nonetheless, she's a little more settled knowing Izzy thinks Jason incapable of assaulting a woman—although he did appear to be okay with killing a man.

He may not be able to control his hired muscle, Nathanial sends.

I know how Jason works. If he's worried about what the man might do, he'll most likely take the night watch himself to ensure Maisie is safe.

Izzy and Nathanial lock eyes, and Basia watches them, waiting for Sigma's lead that he believes it'll be okay to leave Maisie where she is until the morning.

That's what I would do in a similar situation, so maybe it's all right to wait until tomorrow.

'Nathanial,' Hannah hisses, startling Basia. 'Stop staring at Isolde. It is beyond rude.'

Basia can't help smirking. Hannah is obviously jealous of Nathanial and Izzy. Of course, she has no idea the two are actually friends or that Izzy's romantic interest lies elsewhere.

Nathanial turns away from his fiancée and says, 'All right, the morning it is, then, unless you still have concerns, Barbara?'

Although she hates the thought of Maisie spending another night alone, she understands why a morning rescue has a better chance of success. 'I guess this is the best plan we have.'

'Good, then let us meet at the station at five o'clock. We can then proceed in small groups to our places around Parsons's house.'

It's comforting how easily Nathanial moves into his Sigma role of directing the troops. Alan and Hannah eye him uneasily. Alan probably because he believes he should be in charge, and Hannah because she isn't used to seeing Nathanial like this.

Sensing Alan's discomfort, Basia positions herself beside the detective. This plan will only succeed if the two men work together, and she has an idea on how she might achieve that. 'So, Alan, you will obviously be coordinating our entry from the back. Perhaps it might be useful to have Nathanial take the lead in the front.'

The detective looks at her, a frown drawing his brows together.

'I mean, you will be supervising the two constables and me as we capture the kidnappers. It would be difficult to also lead the rescue from the front.'

Maybe it's because he sees the sense in her plan, or maybe it's because it's her making the proposal, but whatever the reason, Alan says, 'What a good idea, Barbara.'

'Good. If we are all agreed, Nathanial and I are due to join my parents for dinner,' Hannah says, linking her arm proprietarily through Nathanial's as she glares at Isolde.

'That is, if there is nothing further to discuss,' Nathanial adds, clearly not as keen to leave as his fiancée.

'No, I think we are good,' Alan tells him, and Basia wonders if he's hoping to remove the threat to his control of the situation. Then she quickly admonishes herself for thinking badly of Alan.

Once Nathanial and Hannah have departed, Stanley decides to help himself to more tea and yet another cake.

'Stanley,' Josephine chides him, 'you will not fit into

your wedding suit if you carry on eating like that.'

Stanley turns to her, sending her his best puppy dog eyes as he holds another bite-sized sweet halfway to his mouth. 'I am unable to resist them. They are truly delightful. I have no idea how Augusta is not three times the size she is, having such an amazing cook.' Stanley returns to the vacant chair by Josephine and Izzy, cake still in hand and grinning contentedly.

The three begin talking quietly, and Basia wonders if they're doing their best to give her and Alan some privacy. As if confirming her suspicions, Alan moves in closer and takes her hand. For a moment she freezes as her mind is overwhelmed with conflicting thoughts. The touch draws her closer to Alan, and yet at the same time, it reminds her of the Allan she lost.

Completely unaware of her internal conflict, this Alan speaks. 'Um, Barbara, I was wondering if perhaps you would join me for supper, as you now have nothing on?'

Basia's first thought is to pull her hand away and respond with an adamant no. It's too close to Allan's death, and although this Alan is so like her love, he isn't him. Besides, she isn't sure she wants to spend an intimate evening with a man calling her Barbara—it's difficult enough to remember to respond under normal circumstances.

Still, her hand tingles from his touch, and a warmth spreads across her cheeks. Maybe she could let herself enjoy an evening with the detective. He's so handsome. She likes the way his eyes twinkle, and the smile that often plays around his lips causes her heart to flutter. He'd been good company on their walk back to Augusta's earlier, talking on a wide range of topics: his family, the current political situation, and his role as a policeman.

Yes, she would enjoy an evening getting to know him. Perhaps it might even end with a kiss.

She shakes her head. Tempting though the thought is, she shouldn't toy with Alan's affections like that. In a few days, she'll return to her own time, and she doesn't wish to do so knowing she left behind a broken heart or perhaps taking one with her.

'I am sorry, Alan, but with such an early start tomorrow, it would not be such a good idea.' She allows her all-too-real disappointment at turning him down to ring through her words, hoping to soften the blow.

'Ah, I see. Yes, that is certainly sensible. Maybe after this is over?'

'Maybe,' Basia agrees, feeling guilty that she doesn't have it in her to be strong and completely reject his attentions.

'It is a shame, though, because I had hoped to spend the evening convincing you to stay at home tomorrow morning. Now that I have changed the time, I am sure I can find another officer to replace you.'

Basia's sympathy for the detective disappears at these words. Withdrawing her hand, she says rather primly, 'If you thought that, then you have completely the wrong impression of me.'

A familiar smile plays around his lips. 'No, Barbara, I think I am beginning to know you quite well. I said I would try. I was pretty certain I would not succeed.'

He stands and announces it's time for him to leave, as he needs to organise his men for tomorrow. Basia barely hears a word he says, as she tries to regain control

of her emotions after their teasing interplay. Dammit, she wants to ask him to stay for dinner, to spend more time with him, and perhaps have the evening end with that kiss she imagined.

Instead she rises and calmly says goodbye to him, and then Stanley and Josephine, who have also decided to have an early night. The room feels empty after their guests are gone, and Basia gravitates to the round window nestled between the bookshelves and follows Alan's retreating form until he disappears from sight.

Jensen comes to clear away the tea things and advises them that Augusta would be staying with Mrs Trimms that night.

'Would you like dinner in the dining room now?' he asks.

'What do you think, Barbara?'

'Um, pardon?' Basia pulls her gaze from the window and turns her attention to the butler. 'Ah, I think I might retire to my room, if that is all right with you, Isolde?'

Izzy's gaze holds concern for her, but she doesn't say anything. Instead she instructs Jensen that they will both take trays in their rooms.

Basia follows the butler out before heading upstairs, needing some time alone with her thoughts.

For the third time that night, Izzy crosses the corridor and stands outside Basia's door. There had been little sound from within when she checked previously. This time, though, she thinks she hears pacing.

She raises her hand to knock, then drops it back to her side. Earlier, Basia had appeared distant and… well, sad. Although she and Basia have become close over the short period of time since they met, she doesn't know her well enough to feel certain the other girl would want to confide in her—or would want her help.

'If you're going to come in, just come in,' a voice calls from inside.

Does that mean she wants me to come in, or is she just letting me know she knows I'm here?

Turning the knob, she opens the door, all signs of prevarication hidden behind the confident demeanour she normally presents to the world.

'I wasn't sure whether you were asleep or not,' she tells Basia's back. 'Since you're awake, I have something to show you.'

Basia turns from staring out the window. 'What is it?'

Her voice shows no interest at all, but Izzy ignores that. 'You have to come with me.'

She leads Basia back into her room, where she'd laid two sets of women's trousers and tailored jackets out on the bed.

'I wouldn't normally wear these in Winchester, as they attract too much attention. But I think they'll do fine for tomorrow and will give us better freedom of movement.'

Basia stares at the outfits on the bed, and Izzy wonders if she's even seeing them.

Reaching out a hand, she touches the other girl's arm. 'Basia, I think the ones on the left will be perfect for you, as they're cut to accommodate someone with more curves than I have. You'll have time to tack the trousers up a little so they fit better.'

'Yes, of course.' Basia reaches for the clothing, ignoring Izzy's hand. 'I'll get right on it.'

Turning, she carries the garments back into her room. Izzy follows. There's something wrong with her friend.

'Basia, did things go all right with Alan? You two seemed happy enough this afternoon, but... well... now you seem a little sad.'

Basia drops onto the bed, facing Izzy, the clothes resting in her lap. 'He's so charming, Izzy, and funny and serious and... and, well, he's everything my Allan was, but he's not, as well. I can't tell whether all these feelings I have are for him or if I'm simply missing my Allan.'

Izzy sits beside her friend and wraps an arm around her shoulders. 'It must be so difficult. I can't tell you how many times I've fallen for my Josephine's reincarnations— loving that person but knowing full well they aren't the one I truly want to be with. And at the same time knowing I can't fully be with the one I love more than life itself.'

Turning slightly to face her, Basia says, 'How do you cope with it, Izzy?'

'I'm not sure I ever really have,' Izzy responds, speaking from the heart. 'I mean, look at me. I came back here hoping I might salvage something with my Jo. At the moment I'm thinking it's better to be with her some of the time than with someone else all of the time.'

Izzy's eyebrows draw together. She hadn't known she was going to say that. The words just flowed from her mouth, bypassing her brain and coming straight from her heart. Now that they're out there, she recognises them for the truth they are.

'I'm pleased you've worked out what you want, but it's not so simple for me. Allan won't be there waiting for me when I return home. And you of all people know I can't stay here.' Basia sounds as though the weight of the world rests on her shoulders.

Izzy curses inside her head. Why is life so difficult for Basia and the many versions she's met of her old nemesis Barabal?

'You know, Basia, Sigma and I first met you in medieval England. You were called Barabal then.'

Basia smiles. 'I know. Sigma told me that was the only timeline he'd come across where I ended up with Allan, only he was called Alain then.'

'Sure, and they had many babies, and yet Barabal was a political force to be reckoned with in her time. I always thought it was because women were of no consequence, and she used every skill she had to make sure she mattered, and Alain respected her enough to just let her get on with it.'

Basia stood, clutching the clothes to her chest. 'I'm not sure why you're—'

'I'm telling you because not one of your incarnations I have met since then has been as confident defining their own future while still having a relationship with their Allan.'

Izzy isn't sure whether or not to go on. As Basia hasn't moved, she decides it's worth a try to get her message across.

'I next met Bebe. She was so focused on her career that when she met her Allan, she had no room for him

in her life.'

Basia sits on the bed, places her hands on top of the clothing in her lap, and stares at Izzy. 'And how would you describe me in this reincarnation loop?'

'I would like to be able to say that you're the one who found her calling... and love as well.'

'But...?'

'But at the moment, you're the one who fell in love and allowed Allan to mould your future.'

Basia's shoulders slump, and Izzy wonders if she's gone too far. In an attempt to bring Basia back, she asks, 'Who are you, Basia?'

The other girl blinks a couple of times. 'Sorry?'

'No, seriously—who *are* you, and what do you want? If Allan hadn't turned up on your doorstep, and the last two weeks had never happened, who would you be?'

Basia is motionless beside her except for the teeth gnawing at her bottom lip. Izzy allows the silence to lengthen, forcing Basia to speak next.

'I'm... I'm not sure I can answer that. I'm not the same person I was before Allan came, and I don't think I can go back to thinking like farm-girl Basia.'

Again Izzy resists the urge to fill the silence.

'What I can say for certain is, when I return home, I will no longer allow people to define my life by my ability to have children. I refuse to put off my dreams until I've contributed to repopulating the world.'

Izzy can't hide her surprise. 'You don't want to have children?'

Shrugging, Basia answers, 'I don't know. I might, one day. I've never been allowed to think of it in terms of

want. If I do, though, I'm determined that having children will be my decision, not an expectation.'

'Well, good on you,' Izzy says and mentally high-fives Basia. 'That's a step in the right direction.' But it's still not enough. She needs to ignite something in her friend, something to knock her from her dreamlike state and give her a reason to take her life into her own hands and move it forward.

Sigma had believed bringing Basia to this time would show her anyone can fight for what they believe in and that women are more than capable of leading the charge.

After a few days with Basia, Izzy now believes that in the wake of Allan's death, it's more important for Basia to find out who she is and what she wants from life.

'You were ready to go home today. Did you want to go back to your parents? Pick up from where you left off before Allan shook things up? Or did you have something else in mind?'

Basia laughs. 'Going back to the farm is not an option. I had already outgrown that girl before Allan appeared, I just hadn't admitted it to myself.' Basia's voice drifts off. She sits still for a moment, then rises to her feet, the trousers and jacket dropping to the ground.

Izzy picks up the discarded clothing from the floor as Basia paces the room.

'I thought I followed Allan to Portsdown, and I guess in some ways, I did. What I hadn't realised until now is it was my choice to go. If Allan hadn't come along, I would have found some other reason to leave.'

She paces a little more before adding, 'I think I may have been as attracted to the opportunity for adventure,

for change, as I was to him.'

'Are you saying—'

'Oh no, he was definitely my soulmate, and I wish more than anything I could spend the rest of my life with him, but—'

'He was the icing on the cake, not the cake,' Izzy finishes for her.

Basia's laugh tinkles 'What a lovely way to put it. Stanley *would* approve.'

Izzy chuckles at this and relaxes a little. Lying back on the bed, she allows the sense of crisis averted to sink in.

Basia flops down beside her. 'Now I just need to decide what it is I want to do from here.'

Izzy reaches out and curls her fingers around Basia's. 'And in the meantime, you know it's perfectly acceptable for you to have a bit of fun with a certain handsome detective.'

Basia sighs. 'After talking with you, I've gone off that idea a bit. He's not Allan....'

Izzy rolls onto her side and smiles a teasing smile. 'But he is handsome... and here.'

'So, are you actually thinking of staying?' Basia asks, changing the subject, and Izzy lets her, happy to finally tell someone about her change of heart.

'I'm still in two minds. Yesterday I thought I might return to the Fixers. Well, at least to Cynthia's new group, and I was kinda hoping Sigma would too. After today, though, I can see how a life with Stanley and Jo wouldn't be too bad. Still, what would I do with my life if I stay here? I would miss the adventure and trying to keep the world in line. And there's the problem of Josephine's attachment to Dorset. I'm certainly not going to spend the rest of my life stagnating down there.'

Basia squeezes her fingers. 'It's a good thing neither of us have to make up our minds right now, isn't it? Perhaps we should just concentrate on saving Maisie for the moment, and maybe things will fall into place for us when we're not trying so hard.'

Izzy's lips form a wry smile. 'You're such a sensible girl.'

'Not so sensible.' Basia sighs dramatically. 'I've just realised I don't have a sewing kit, so taking up those trousers could be a bit difficult.'

Laughing, Izzy forces herself off the bed. 'Come back through to my room. We can work on them together.'

CHAPTER TEN
THE GAME'S AFOOT

The morning is still shrouded in darkness when Nathanial arrives at the house Hannah's parents have rented in Winchester. As he waits for her to appear, he paces the sidewalk, wondering what he'll do if she doesn't turn up soon. After all, he can hardly knock on the front door and request to see her at this early hour.

He's about to give up when the squeak of the side gate shatters the silence of the deserted street. Hannah appears, dressed plainly and carrying a reticule, something she doesn't usually do. Noticing his interest in her purse, she says, 'It has one of the smaller irons from the laundry inside. You never know when you might need a bit of an advantage, especially if I encounter that brute from yesterday again.'

Nathanial wants to smile at the thought of her swinging

that iron at someone, but the tone of her voice tells him his behaviour the evening before has not been forgotten or forgiven.

To say that the air between Hannah and Nathanial is strained during their walk to the station would be an understatement. The increasing tension almost has Nathanial apologising, but he stops himself before the words leave his mouth. He hadn't been at fault. Well, not totally.

Hannah had been quiet through dinner. Then, as they left the dining room, she had said, 'I do not appreciate you paying so much attention to Miss Fielding and Miss Trelawney. It is not done for an engaged man to spend so much time with single women.'

Although she mentioned both Izzy and Basia, he was sure it was Izzy she was most concerned about. Perhaps she sensed they were more than casual acquaintances.

Hannah had always been the jealous type. Even the old Nathanial knew that. Then again, old Nathanial wouldn't have dared talk to other women when he was with her, and so this fight would have been avoided.

When he patiently explained that they only talked about the missing suffragist and that she was overreacting, Hannah had exploded. After a full dressing down, she finished with 'Your behaviour is not that of a man devoted to his fiancée but of a cad about town.'

Years of pent-up resentment broke through his thin hold on the old Nathanial facade, and he'd met her accusations head-on.

'You are turning nothing into something and blaming me for it,' he'd told her, trying to keep his voice low as they followed her parents to the drawing room. 'Your jealous nature is the problem here, not my actions.'

'Is it too much to ask for you to pay attention to me rather than courting every other young female in the room?' she'd asked haughtily.

It was her tone that did it. It told him she believed she was right and that he should apologise and do better.

'I believe you would prefer it if I were a puppy dog following at your beck and call,' he spluttered. Leaving her side, he took his own hat and coat from the stand in the hallway and let himself out, without even taking leave of her parents.

He had immediately regretted his actions but wouldn't lose face by returning. Instead he spent the next couple of hours wandering the streets of Winchester, partially to allow his temper to cool but largely because his memory of where he stayed on this particular visit was a little hazy.

Around midnight he'd stumbled upon the boarding house, and then he spent a restless couple of hours trying to sleep before giving up and reading for a while.

This morning he finds himself in a bit of a quandary. His anger hasn't abated, but he has to admit it had been fuelled by his knowledge of the future rather than the incident yesterday. He knows what Hannah would do, and he's aware he is a changed person because of her actions. Still, even without that foreknowledge, the way his fiancée treated him does not sit right with him.

Yet he's older and wiser now, and he sees how the role he was playing has allowed her to dictate the terms of their relationship. It wouldn't hurt him to smooth things over without taking the blame on himself if at all possible.

As he opens his mouth to speak, Hannah gets in first.

'Nathanial, you have changed these last two days, and you cannot be surprised that I think it is because of another woman. I mean, the only thing that has changed has been Isolde and Barbara arriving. Now, Barbara is clearly taken with the detective, so I can only assume that you have become, um, distracted by Isolde—'

'I am not—'

'Therefore, you cannot blame me for believing your relationship is more than that of casual acquaintances. The looks you share are too intimate.'

'As I was about to—'

She holds up a hand to stop him from speaking. 'No, please do not deny it. Instead, I have a question for you. Well, perhaps two. Do you still love me? And do you still want to marry me? And before you answer, let me say that I am aware that people in our position do not always marry for love. So I am quite prepared for you to say you no longer care for me but still wish for our marriage to go ahead. It would be awkward for both of us to continue on in society if we were to break our engagement now.'

Nathanial is stunned into silence. This is not the conversation he expected to be having with Hannah this morning. The cool tone of her voice is shocking, like being doused in ice water, and the way she's been speaking of their upcoming marriage as if it were a social transaction hurts. It has him wondering if Hannah ever really loved him or if it's always been a marriage of convenience for her. Had the old Nathanial been so besotted that he hadn't seen the signs?

Old Nathanial was pliable, well connected, and would

inherit the family estate when his father died. He would have made the perfect partner given her social aspirations, so he shouldn't be surprised. Then again, should any of this matter? They are where they are, and Hannah deserves an answer.

He needs to be careful, though, because he hasn't decided whether to release this body back to old Nathanial or to integrate the sleeping part of him and carry on using the body himself.

'Nathanial? Did you hear me?'

'Yes, sorry, I was thinking. There *is* a lot we need to talk about, Hannah, and as we are nearly at the station, I suggest we leave it until after we have rescued Miss Ottaway.'

His neck prickles as he feels her eyes bore into him, almost as if she's trying to search is soul. Had she expected him to apologise and reaffirm his commitment to her? Probably. He meets her gaze, making sure to keep his face neutral.

When she realises he isn't going to back down, she purses her lips and says, 'Of course, you are right. This has been an odd few days, and perhaps these questions are best left until things have settled down. But do not think you have dodged a bullet today. We *will* talk about this.'

I'm sure we will, Nathanial thinks as they approach the station. Hushed voices cut through the predawn air as they draw closer to the group assembled by the main door.

'It is hardly the done thing, Barbara. I mean, a woman wearing trousers. Well, not in Winchester, at least,' the detective is saying, at which point Nathanial realises it isn't a man talking to Alan but indeed a woman in trousers.

'I say, sir, my Doris always wears trousers when we are at my parents' farm. She says it is much easier to do some things without skirts getting in the way,' one of the young constables with them says.

'I agree, sir. If she is coming in with us, her skirts might hinder her, or us, in a confined space,' the other adds.

'If there is a possibility she will get in the way, perhaps she should not be coming with us,' Alan says under his breath, but the others appear not to have heard. 'I guess I have been outvoted,' he says a little louder and somewhat sourly.

Izzy's voice comes from behind Basia. 'If that is settled, then, now that we are all here, we should move.'

'Yes, it will soon be dawn, and we will lose the chance to hide without being seen,' Stanley adds, stepping out under the station light.

'Of course.' The detective holds out his arm to escort Basia. She ignores him and strides off, followed by the two constables.

'Leave it a couple of minutes, then head out,' Alan instructs Nathanial before rushing to catch up with the rest of his team.

'You know,' Izzy says when he's out of earshot, 'for all his planning, he has not even suggested how we might let them know when we are in place, or for them to let us know where they have hidden.' She smirks.

'And I guess you have that covered?' Hannah says tartly.

'Of course. Basia and I have sorted out some signals.' She smiles. *Good thing we can all mindspeak,* she adds for Nathanial's benefit.

He bites back his own smile, not wanting to aggravate Hannah any more than he has already.

When the first group have disappeared around the corner, Izzy asks, 'Shall we go now, Nathanial?'

'Give it a few more minutes,' he tells her. 'We want to allow them enough time to get in place before we arrive.'

Izzy taps her foot impatiently. Hannah glares at her and moves closer to Nathanial. Stanley catches his eye, grinning wickedly as he sums up the situation.

Josephine punches Stanley's arm. 'Keep your mind on the job,' she tells him.

That only makes Stanley's grin even wider.

'Time to go,' Izzy says, 'before Stanley causes a riot.' And with that she strides off into the darkness.

'It is fine, old chum. Off you go. The ladies and I will follow as the sun rises.'

'Good luck,' Nathanial says to them all as he heads off, not catching Izzy until the corner, a few houses down from Parsons's place. As he does, he spots a familiar figure. The nurse they spoke to yesterday is pushing her young charge along the footpath. For once the baby is silent.

Her eyes widen in recognition as they approach, then track from the trouser-clad Izzy and back to him. Nathanial puts a finger to his lips, hoping she understands to keep quiet.

As they walk past, she whispers, 'You're part of the group from yesterday. Have you found your lost miss?'

Nathanial nods.

'I knew there was something going on at old Parsons's place. Lulu will be quiet this morning, sir. It's me that wanted the air after feeding her. So we won't be waking no one who should be asleep at this hour.' She winks conspiratorially and walks on.

Nathanial and Izzy stop at the house before Mr Parsons's. Before they break cover, Izzy speaks to Basia. *Is it clear for us to come through?*

There's a light on in the back, so someone is up. We didn't notice any activity at the front, but check the top windows just in case. Oh, and there's a huge rhododendron to your left as you come round. That should cover the two of you.

Thanks, Izzy sends.

Nathanial leans around and checks the second- and third-storey windows. All the curtains are drawn, and there are no lights on.

All clear.

The gravel of the driveway crunches under their shoes no matter how careful they try to be. Although it sounds loud to them, it doesn't appear to disturb anyone inside as the curtains don't twitch once. They make it to the gigantic bush and crouch behind it, finding a spot with views of both the door and the street.

We're in place, Izzy sends to Basia.

The ground is damp beneath Nathanial's knees, and after a couple of minutes, the cold begins creeping through his bones. He hopes they don't have to wait for too long because if they do, he might be too stiff to move. As the sun peeks up from the horizon, he shifts a little, trying to keep the blood circulating in his legs.

'Stop fidgeting,' Izzy hisses. 'You'll give away our hiding place.'

He sends her a meaningful look, telling her to quit

216

nagging, but she ignores him. Shivering from the cold and damp, he listens for footsteps on the pavement. Nothing. Then a crunching of gravel heralds the arrival of the rest of their party. Finally. They're almost in sight at the bottom of the steps when he feels a tug on his consciousness.

Sigma, whatever you're going to do, you need to do it soon. Someone is leaking information to Jason, and he knows you know where he is.

Nathanial's heart starts pumping, and he rises to his feet to stop the others as a loud bang fills the early morning air followed by another as Hannah knocks on the door a second time. It's too late to call things off.

Rubbing his now sweaty palms down his trousers, Nathanial steps back behind the shrub, accepting that all great plans are only good until you engage the enemy. Then you have no option but to wing it. All they can do now is react to what's happening and hope Jason hasn't had too much time to prepare for them.

What is it? Izzy asks, but Nathanial is too intent on watching the door to the house to respond.

Jason answers, and he opens the door wide, a grin plastered on his face. Nathanial's stomach sinks. Jason has recognised his team and looks like a man who knows he has the upper hand.

Nathanial is about to step out and call everything off when Jason's face turns pale. He swings round and rushes inside, just as they'd planned.

Through the misty morning air, Basia makes out Hannah's and Josephine's voices as they speak with whomever opened the door. She turns to Alan, and he nods, letting her know they're ready whenever she gives the word.

Josephine's voice carries through to her. 'Sorry to disturb you so early, but we are going house to house, trying to find out if anyone has seen our friend.'

There's silence for a moment, and Basia suspects whoever answered the door is now talking. Alan had said to wait either until the others are about to be let inside or are being turned away before giving the signal to move.

'Of course the police are looking for her, but we are really worried and decided to help.' Hannah's voice holds just the right amount of anguish.

She should have been an actress, Basia muses.

The response is somewhat mumbled, but Stanley's next words are not. 'I say, old chap, that is a bit uncalled for. These two are only trying to find their friend, and language like that does not make their job any easier.'

'Look, if you are not able to help…'

As Josephine speaks, Basia turns to tell Alan their forward team has almost reached the end of their usefulness, only to find the space beside her empty.

Glancing around the yard, she finds Alan beside the back entrance, whispering fiercely to his constables. Of all the nerve! When he'd asked her to monitor what was going on at the front and let them know when to go, she believed it would help. Now she realises it was a distraction to keep her occupied so he and his men could move without her.

Leaving her hiding place and sticking to the shadows,

she reaches the three men as the two constables are shouldering the door, breaking it inwards. Alan follows the constables in, unaware that Basia is coming in behind him.

She walks through the entrance, deftly avoiding the door swinging on its hinges, and steps into a scullery or perhaps a laundry—it's difficult to tell in the early morning light. Striding forward, she makes it into the kitchen in time to see a large, thuggish man drop his teacup, stand, lift the heavy wooden table he was seated at, and launch it at the two constables.

Fortunately, they're nimble on their feet and split off in opposite directions. The table misses them. As she and Alan step back, the piece of furniture skids to a halt, blocking the doorway, wedging itself in place, and preventing them from assisting the two constables.

The kitchen's occupant is more than a match for the two younger men, and Alan struggles to move the table out of his way to go help them. Basia joins him, and they manage to swing the piece of furniture around far enough for the detective to squeeze through, leaving Basia to fend for herself.

A wave of anger threatens, and she resists the temptation to give the detective a piece of her mind. No, she won't give him the satisfaction. Taking a deep breath, she surveys the scene, wondering how she might be of use.

The thug stands in the doorway leading into the main house and is using a poker from the fire to fend off the three policemen. He doesn't seem interested in doing anything other than keeping them in the kitchen. It's a stalemate.

Searching the room, she looks for anything that might throw the man off balance and tip the scales in their favour. On the bench she spies exactly what she needs. Slipping through the gap between the table and the door, she grabs the sugar bowl and moves in behind one of the young constables.

'Hey, you,' she shouts, and all four men turn her way. As they do, she throws the contents of the sugar bowl at the thug's face before allowing the bowl to drop to the ground.

'What the—' The man stumbles forward, momentarily blinded, and the three policemen take the opportunity to close in on him.

When a gap opens behind the kidnapper, she slips past the others and runs through the doorway. If the police don't want her, she'll help with getting Maisie out of the house.

She finds herself in a dark passageway she hopes will lead to the main entrance. Tentatively moving forward, she yelps as a hand reaches out of the darkness and swings her round. Before she has a chance to react, her attacker twists her arm behind her back and pulls her in close. She shivers as cold steel presses into the soft part of her throat under her chin.

'I killed your boyfriend, so you know I'll do the same to you if you don't do exactly as I say,' says a male voice close to her ear.

Her insides turn to jelly as she recognises the voice of the man who shot her Allan in cold blood.

'What do you want?' she asks, hating the fact that she sounds as fearful as she does.

'Hold still,' Jason instructs as he forces her back towards the kitchen.

As they move through the doorway and stop, Basia is frozen in place. Her head screams for her to do something, telling her, *You'll never get back home if you don't,* but fear has robbed her of even the most basic movement.

Jason shifts the gun to her temple and takes another step into the kitchen. 'Step away, or Basia dies.'

Basia takes in the scene before them. One of the constables is standing by the sink, a bloody towel held to his forehead. The other backs away from the man lying on the floor, hands held up in surrender. Alan looks up from his position on the thug's back. Jason's accomplice appears to be out cold with his hands now behind him in cuffs.

'Come now,' Alan says as he pushes himself to his feet. 'Your friend is no help, and at best you will be up for kidnapping, which is a prison sentence. If you hurt Barbara, then you might be looking at the gallows.'

'Barbara?' Jason shifts around, dragging Basia with him. 'He doesn't have any idea who you are, does he, Basia?'

Alan's brows draw together. 'Basia? Who is Basia? Barbara, what is going on here?'

Jason's laugh rings hollow. 'What a hoot. They have no idea, do they? You've wrangled some unsuspecting local yokels into this, and they really have no idea.'

'Jason, it's over. Put the gun down, and let Sigma take you back home,' Basia says, trying to do her best to keep her voice calm.

'Sigma's here? I didn't see any animals. No, you're trying to trick me.' Jason pushes the revolver harder against her temple. 'Don't do that, or I might just kill you for fun, and won't that screw up the timeline?'

Basia freezes, silently begging Alan to calm Jason down before he loses it completely. Instead the detective stands in the middle of the kitchen, his eyes going from her to Jason and back again, as if trying to understand what's going on.

'You know this man?' he asks, the hurt in his eyes cutting through her. 'All this time you knew him, and you said nothing to me. Instead you came up with some half-cocked story about an escaped convict. Are you all in on it?'

'She's taken you for a fool, mate,' Jason crows, shuffling back towards the hallway they'd entered through.

'Whoever he is to us, don't forget he's kidnapped Maisie. The rest I can explain, will explain, after we—'

A sharp pain courses through Basia's skull. She sways and crumples to the ground. The last thing she sees before blackness overwhelms her is Alan stepping over top of her in pursuit of Jason.

As soon as Jason disappears, Josephine pushes the door open and peers inside. Izzy and Nathanial are across the lawn and climbing the five steps to the entrance in a flash, catching up with the others at the bottom of the stairs.

From the back of the house, the sounds of furniture moving and grunting suggest a fight is in progress.

Nathanial and Izzy turn almost as one to check out the stairs. There's no sight or sound of Jason that way, so he'd likely headed for the kitchen or is already upstairs with Maisie.

'Should we go and help them?' Stanley asks, an excited gleam in his eye.

'No.' Nathanial is decisive. 'Our task is to secure the release of Miss Ottaway. We should wait at the bottom of the stairs and stop anyone following the women up. They can call out if they need us.'

Stanley's shoulders slump.

Nathanial claps a hand on his shoulder. 'Do not be so glum, Stanley. The fight may end up out here yet.'

'Come on, ladies.' Izzy hooks her arms through Josephine's and Hannah's. 'Let us not waste any time getting Maisie out of here.'

At the top of the stairs, Izzy takes a moment to orient herself. She need not have bothered, as Hannah has it all figured out.

'The window we saw the woman at is along this way.' She turns to her left, pulling the others behind her.

The corridor is dark and lined with closed doors. Hannah walks past them all, stopping in front of the one at the end. A key is sticking out of the lock, and Hannah reaches for it.

As the lock clicks, Josephine turns to Izzy. 'Perhaps you should stay out here and keep watch. You might upset her, dressed like that.' She gestures down Izzy's body, indicating the male clothing.

Izzy grimaces. She'd only thought of ease of movement when she dressed, not of how Maisie would react to the appearance of another strange man. She allows Josephine to slip past her and peers into the dark room, her eyes following Hannah and Jo.

A single bed is tucked into the far corner, its occupant curled into a ball under the blankets. They've been so quiet, the person in bed doesn't even appear to know they're there. Hannah clears her throat, and the figure reacts immediately, sitting bolt upright, then cowering against the wall, blankets pulled up under her chin.

The sound of a door banging downstairs reminds Izzy she's supposed to be lookout, and she reluctantly turns her back on the room but keeps an ear out, listening to the conversation.

'Maisie, it is all right. We are here to take you home.' Hannah has pitched her tone low so as not to distress the young woman.

She's really quite good at this, Izzy thinks as she peers along the gloomy hallway. Did something move down the far end of the corridor? As her eyes adjust to the dim light, she scans back and forth, trying to pick out a potential threat. If there is anything down there, she can't find it. It must be the dawn light playing tricks on her.

Distracted by the moving shadows and lulled by the sound of the soothing words coming from the room, she jumps when Josephine's voice comes from just behind her.

'Isolde, we need your help. Maisie is terrified and unable to move. She knows you. Maybe you can gain her confidence.'

With one last glance down the hallway to reassure herself that she was probably imagining things, Izzy enters the bedroom, leaving Jo to stand guard. Someone opened one of the curtains, flooding the room with early morning light, making the figure crouched in the far corner of the bed easier to see.

Izzy gasps, then stifles the sound, realising it won't help Maisie to know how frightful she looks. She's dressed only in her undergarments, and her hair has worked its way free from the neat bun she normally keeps it in, forming a knotted halo round her face. Though it's the bruises on her arms and the swelling on one side of her face beginning to colour purple that upsets Izzy the most.

With her arms wrapped protectively around her body, Maisie has forced herself as far back into the corner of the bed as possible. The eyes that peek out through her hair are frantic, and Izzy fears their dawn raid has scared her beyond reasoning.

Spying Maisie's outer clothes on the trunk at the end of the bed, Izzy fumbles for her coat before approaching.

'Maisie, you remember me. I am Isolde, Augusta's niece. We met on the train. Mrs Trimms is worried about you and sent us to find you. Come now, put this coat on you, and we will take you to her.'

As she speaks, Izzy reaches out her hand and waits patiently for Maisie to respond. Finally, trembling fingers reach for hers, then grasp her hand with surprising firmness. Izzy pulls the other girl into an embrace, nose wrinkling at the smell, and then she drapes the coat over Maisie's shoulders.

Hannah comes to help button the garment while Izzy holds Maisie upright. They're almost done when a voice from behind echoes through the nearly empty room. 'And what do you think you are doing?'

Maisie trembles in her arms and moans softly. Izzy half turns to find an elderly man standing in the doorway. He's obviously been woken from his sleep, as his thin white hair stands out in tufts, and his spindly white stick legs poke out from under a nightshirt. She would have laughed at his challenge except for the fact that he has a shotgun pointed directly at them.

'You young women, you think you can do anything you please. Well, not in my house.'

The gun wavers a little, as if it's too heavy for the man to hold. This makes Izzy even more worried. What if the shaking causes him to tug on the trigger? He might shoot them all without meaning to.

Then she realises that the man is so focused on the three of them, he hasn't seen Josephine, who stands less than a step behind him, chamberpot raised above her head.

'I am so tired of men telling us what to do,' Josephine tells his back as she brings the porcelain pot down towards his head.

Turning, Mr Parsons sees the danger too late to move and can only watch in dismay as the pot descends.

As the old man crumples to the floor, Josephine's anger disappears. 'Oh, I did not expect that. Have I killed him?'

'Feel for a pulse,' Izzy instructs.

Josephine bends a knee and places a couple of fingers on the man's neck before looking up and grinning. 'Still strong.'

'Good. Now take that gun of his, and Hannah and I will get Maisie out of here.'

As she and Hannah walk Maisie towards the door, Josephine picks up the weapon. A country girl at heart, she's no stranger to guns. She pushes the lever to the side and breaks the gun open. With the weapon made safe, she leads the others out of the room.

As they reach the stairway, a crash reverberates through the house. They wait at the top of the stairs as Nathanial and Stanley move to block someone from coming up.

'It is over, Jason. Put down the weapon, and we will take you back home,' Nathanial says in an even voice.

Izzy peers down at the figure in front of the Time Guardian. He's shaking, and his eyes are erratically scanning the room. Finally, they return to the two men keeping him from the stairs.

'Who are you? I don't know you. Out of my way. I have to finish what I started.'

Jason sounds unhinged, and the thought turns Izzy's blood cold. Always excitable, in this state Jason might do anything.

'Does Nathanial know that man?' Hannah asks.

'Shh,' Izzy tells her without taking her eyes off the scene below. 'I want to hear what he is saying.'

'Ah, Izzy, I see you. Bring the girl down, and no one else needs to get hurt.'

No one else? Where are the detective and Basia? 'You know I will never do that, Jason.' Izzy moves so she's in front of the quivering Maisie.

'Please... do not let him have me,' she whispers between sobs.

'You know him, Isolde?' Josephine asks, stepping one stair down and in front of the group as she closes the shotgun, making it ready to fire. 'I hope you are not friends, as I would hate to shoot someone you hold an attachment for.'

Izzy cannot help but chuckle in spite of the tension in the room. 'Feel free to fire away.'

'I only want the girl,' Jason says, moving back and raising his pistol.

'And we have already said no,' Josephine responds, raising her own weapon.

Nathanial takes a step towards Jason, hands out in front. 'Put the gun away, Jason, and perhaps we can talk about this.'

'Don't take another step.' The gun moves from the women at the top of the stairs to Nathanial. 'I *will* shoot!'

'Halt and place your weapon down. You are under arrest for kidnapping and assault. Do not add murder to your charges.'

The tension in the room snaps like a rubber band. Izzy flings herself at Maisie and Hannah, forcing them to the floor as gunfire fills the room.

CHAPTER ELEVEN
FALLOUT

Jason is becoming increasingly more erratic. Sweat is beading on his brow, and the gun shakes in his hand. Nathanial is doing all he can to keep the Time Fixer's attention on him, but Jason fixates more and more on the women at the top of the stairs.

If only he were able to talk to the man as Sigma, he might be able to calm him down. Jason obviously doesn't recognise him as a Time Guardian in human form, and for the first time ever, he regrets his penchant for under-taking his missions as an animal.

A movement from the back of the house catches his eye and Jason's as well. At least it takes his attention from the women. With Jason looking elsewhere, Nathanial takes a step forward, but the man isn't as distracted as he thought.

'Don't take another step,' the rogue Time Fixer says.

Nathanial stops, not wanting to push his luck. He's now close enough that he might be able to disarm Jason if there's another distraction.

At that moment Alan chooses to stride forward and command, 'Halt and place your weapon down. You are under arrest for kidnapping and assault. Do not add murder to your charges.'

The fragile balance in the room is broken, and it's as if time slows for Nathanial.

Jason's finger begins to squeeze the trigger as he launches himself at the Time Fixer. The thunder of guns discharging blasts through the room, and Jason falls to the ground. Nathanial hits the floor beside him. Thrown onto his side, he looks up to find a tumble of women falling down the stairs.

Utter confusion follows. Stanley is bellowing for Josephine, who's leaning against the banister, a patch of red blooming on her dress. Alan is helping the other women untangle themselves as Izzy yells at him.

'What did you think you were doing?'

'Taking control of the situation as I was trained to do,' Alan responds.

'You threatened him, you idiot. You pushed him over the edge, and whatever happens now is on you.' Izzy's voice is stern and steely underlined with a touch of fear.

Nathanial pushes himself up on an elbow. He readies himself to tell Izzy it isn't Alan's fault, that Jason was so out of his mind, anything could have set him off, but something moves beside him. He turns to find Jason reaching for his gun. He drags himself across the floor towards the weapon, the wound in his leg leaving a bloody path behind him.

Nathanial pushes himself to his feet and rushes for the gun. Kicking it away, he does something he's been wanting to do since he met the Time Fixer. He pulls back his arm, leans down, and punches Jason square on the chin. It's satisfying to watch his head jerk back, and even more satisfying when it cracks on the tiled floor, and Jason's eyes lose focus.

Hannah's shocked voice comes from behind him. 'Nathanial, what are you doing?'

Unable to deal with her for the moment, he bends at the knees and hauls Jason's limp form over his shoulder in a fireman's lift.

Alan rushes forward. 'I will take him now.'

'You have done quite enough!' Izzy says as she joins them.

'I already told you, it is how we are taught to deal with such situations,' Alan protests again.

Izzy puffs out an impatient breath. 'Common sense should have told you Nathanial had it under control. How about you give him a pair of cuffs, and then you head upstairs and deal with the old man we left up there. He had a bit of an accident with a chamberpot, but he should be coming around soon.'

'Cut him some slack, Izzy. We all rely on our training when under pressure, and it is not Alan's fault his training has been inadequate,' Nathanial says as he shifts Jason's body to a more comfortable position.

He holds his hand out to Alan, and for a moment, he thinks the detective is going to protest. Perhaps it's because he sees sense, or maybe it's because Nathanial defended him, that he reaches under his coat and hands a pair of handcuffs to Nathanial.

'Thank you,' Nathanial says as the detective moves off to help Stanley.

'Go on, do what you must,' Izzy says, opening the door for him. 'I will keep the others busy in here.'

Nathanial steps outside, and before the door closes behind him, he hears Izzy's voice rise in panic as she shouts, 'Barbara? Has anyone seen Barbara?'

'Oh my god, Barbara,' Alan's voice responds just as the door slams, cutting off all noise from inside.

He drops Jason onto the steps and kneels beside him. After placing a cuff on the closest hand, he rolls Jason so he can cuff both hands behind his back. Then he pushes him none too gently back against the house and takes a couple of deep breaths before opening his mind.

Beta?

We're here, Sigma.

It's done. Maisie Ottaway is safe, and I have Jason ready for pick-up. We're outside, and no one else is around, so I can say he jumped me and took off.

Well done, Beta says.

Umm, about that pick-up, Cynthia adds. *No one here can decide exactly what to do with Jason, so I suggest you let the local authorities take him until they do.*

'Are you all right, sir?'

Nathanial looks down the steps to find one of Alan's constables staring up at him, concern written on his face. Considering the nasty gash on the constable's forehead, and the fact that Nathanial himself only has a couple of bruises, the question makes him smile.

'Thank you, yes. I brought our friend out here while everyone sorts themselves out inside.'

'Detective Barker sent me to fetch a doc and transportation for the prisoners and the wounded, but I can help you take him round to the kitchen with the others if you like.'

Sigma?

Wait a moment.

'No, thank you, I can manage. You go ahead and do what the detective asked.'

'As you wish.'

Nathanial waits until the young man disappears through the gate and has had time to walk well down the street before resuming his conversation.

Cynthia, are you sure you want to leave him here? Prisons can be quite brutal in this time.

Quite certain. In fact, it's a shame they stopped sending convicts to the penal colonies.

Nathanial chuckles.

'Wasso funny?' Jason mumbles from beside him.

Gotta go. Will give a full report later.

Nathanial closes his mind and turns to his prisoner. 'Come on. If you can speak, you can walk.' He hauls Jason to his feet.

'Where to?'

'Inside with your accomplices to await transportation to the cells.'

'Hold on, where's the extraction team?' Jason asks, now more alert.

'No extraction team for you, mate. It seems you have annoyed quite a few of the Time Fixers, and they have decided you will face local justice.'

Jason went white, his eyes wild with fear. 'No, they can't do that. Won't it screw up the timeline, or... history? The Time Guardians... they won't let that happen.'

Strangely, Nathanial finds no joy in Jason's fate. Used to being pulled out by the Time Fixers, the self-centred man had wreaked havoc in a number of time periods. Because he'd always been extracted by his organisation, he never faced the consequences of his actions. That he'd face justice now did little to make up for what he'd done, here or in the past.

Hauling the reluctant time traveller back into the house, Nathanial finds the hallway empty. Voices drift in from one of the rooms to the side, but Nathanial ignores them and heads to the kitchen.

Alan is settling an elderly man into a chair, his hands tied behind him with a silk scarf. The man is grumbling about unnatural women and the state of the world. He glares at Jason as he comes in.

'You said we would have our revenge on them, put them back in their place. And look what that got us.'

Jason turns to Nathanial. 'Take me back outside, please. If I have to spend another minute with that nasty curmudgeon, I won't be held responsible for my actions.'

Nathanial pushes him into a chair. 'He is all yours,' he says to the detective and walks away before he does something he won't be proud of.

234

On their arrival at Augusta's what seemed liked hours ago, Izzy's aunt had gone into organisation mode. She'd allocated the two guest suites on the first floor for use as an infirmary for Maisie, Basia, and Josephine.

Although still a little woozy, and with blood seeping through the makeshift bandage on her head, Basia had instructed a maid to bring hot water and towels. By the time the doctor had arrived with his nurse, she had Jo's bleeding under control.

Hannah and Nathanial, after seeing they weren't required and ensuring the patients were comfortable, had left to clean themselves up, promising to return later to give their statements to the police.

Detective Barker had taken the prisoners to the station and had agreed that everyone could give their accounts later from the comfort of home. Izzy still hadn't forgiven him for what happened to Jo. However, he'd been so distraught and so aware of how his lack of experience had almost caused a fatality that she'd at least stopped haranguing him.

Stanley had been clearly quite shaken and, after carrying Jo up to the guest room, would not move from her side. After ensuring Jensen would look after things in her absence, Augusta left to tell Mrs Trimms the good news and bring her back to see Maisie.

So, Izzy now finds herself alone in the dining room, picking listlessly at some scrambled eggs. Unable to force the food down, she pours herself some coffee and returns to the table.

Staring out the window, she attempts to calm her mind. She keeps replaying the moment the bullet hit Jo.

Any wound in the stomach area is not good news, not in this time and not in the future. Finally, she admits it's no use staying down here. She heads upstairs to the makeshift infirmary and knocks on the door.

A maid answers, poking her head through a small opening. 'Doctor says no one is to be let in, miss. Sorry.' She closes the door.

Izzy raises her fists to pound out her frustration but stops short, realising that won't help the patients. No doubt they will let her in soon, and she'll be here waiting.

Pacing along the carpeted hallway, she tries counting her steps. Then she runs through song lyrics. Nothing is working. Nothing calms her growing fear that Josephine isn't going to make it.

She had lost a lot of blood after the rescue, and when Stanley carried her up the stairs to the guest suite, she'd passed out. Although medical science has been making great strides, people here still die from things that could be easily cured in later years. Izzy is about to contact Cynthia to have Josephine moved to Time Fixer headquarters for treatment when the infirmary door opens.

She spins on her heel, hope blooming, only to be quashed when Basia, not Josephine, appears. Of course it wouldn't be Jo—she'd passed out less than an hour ago.

Still, Basia doesn't look so good either. Although her head wound has been more professionally bandaged, she's pale and a little shaky on her feet. When she turns towards her, Izzy can see the edge of a black stitch peeking out from the white cloth that mostly covers the purplish bruise above her right eye. Moving swiftly to her side, Izzy allows the girl to lean on her.

'Where are you going?' Izzy asks, alarmed she's wandering around so unsteady on her feet.

'To my room. The doctor says I have a concussion and I need to rest, and there aren't enough beds for me in there.'

'Surely you shouldn't be alone. I'll help you upstairs and stay with you.'

'Oh, Izzy, don't look at me like that.'

'Like what?'

'Like I'm about to die. The doctor couldn't find any sign of internal bleeding, and my skull appears to be intact. He gave me aspirin for the pain and told me to rest for the day. His nurse will pop up and check on me every hour or so, but I should be right as rain tomorrow.'

'Are you sure? Head injuries can be quite tricky, especially when there's no way to x-ray or monitor what's happening inside.'

Basia chuckles. 'Izzy, you forget, I've treated many such injuries myself, and I'm not showing any signs of brain trauma.'

Izzy sighs. 'The moment you do, I'm taking you to Time Fixer headquarters where you can get some more modern treatment.'

Basia says nothing and allows Izzy to lead her to her room. She even lets Izzy help her into a nightgown and pour some water into a glass on the bedside table in case she gets thirsty.

'Do you need anything else?'

'I'm hungry. I wouldn't mind some tea and toast.'

Izzy smiles. 'That's a good sign. I'll go find Jensen and have something brought up.'

When Izzy returns a few minutes later, Basia has a bit more colour in her cheeks. Izzy helps place some pillows behind her head and finds a book for her to read should she become bored.

'Is that comfortable? Breakfast shouldn't be far away.' Izzy is torn between taking a seat on the bed and flying back downstairs to wait on news of Josephine.

As if sensing her mood, Basia says, 'Sit for a minute, Izzy. They won't be finished with Jo and Maisie for some time yet.'

'But Stanley is with her. Am I destined to spend any crucial time in Jo's life relegated to the sidelines?'

Basia chuckles. 'Don't you think we've had enough drama without you adding to it?'

Izzy grimaces.

'Would it help if I tell you that even Stanley isn't allowed in with her? He's been in the room next door, waiting on the outside, just as you are.'

Izzy sinks onto the bed. 'I know it's petty, resenting his being at her side, but.... Now, tell me how Maisie is.'

'Maisie is fine. Actually the doctor spent most of his time with Jo when he arrived. It was his nurse who questioned the both of us, then had Maisie strip down and take a bath before she saw to her. The maid your aunt assigned helped her bathe in the downstairs bathroom while the nurse stitched me up.'

Izzy flinches. 'That must have been painful.'

'Yes, it still is. What I wouldn't have given for some local anaesthetic. While I recovered, I listened to the nurse and Maisie. She's battered and bruised and hasn't eaten for a couple of days, but other than that, she's physically unharmed.'

'She was lucky.'

'Yes, she was. Last I heard, the nurse was going to fix her a sleeping draught before putting her to bed. Just after, the doctor popped in, checked my head again, then ordered me to bed.'

'And I should be letting you rest.'

Izzy makes to stand, but Basia puts a hand out to stop her. 'Don't go. You're not tiring me, honest.'

'All right, but tell me if you get tired. Oh, I almost forgot. Did you find out anything about the missing papers?' Izzy asks. 'Did we find Maisie's satchel?'

'I don't think we did, but it didn't matter. The speech she took to the meeting was an old draft. The final copy was in her room at Mrs Trimms all along. She'd hidden it under her mattress to keep it from prying eyes.'

'Ah, cunning. How will they get it to Miss Fielden? She needs it for tomorrow. Will Maisie be okay to take it to her?'

'The nurse wanted Maisie on bedrest for a couple of days, which upset Maisie, as she was determined to take the speech to Haslemere. She calmed down when the maid assured her she would tell Mrs Trimms where the papers are if Maisie is asleep when she arrives, and that your aunt and Mrs Trimms will make sure the speech gets to Miss Fielden in time.'

She relaxes a little with the news that Maisie and Basia are fine, but Izzy still can't settle. Still running on adrenaline, she needs to move or take some sort of action. *What on earth is happening with Josephine?* She should be with her.

As if sensing the reason for Izzy's restlessness, Basia says, 'She'll be fine. The bleeding had stopped by the time the doctor arrived, and we both agreed the bullet didn't break any bones or go through any major organs. As soon as the doctor removes it, she should be fine.'

Izzy is so wound tight with worry, she can't let go of her fears that easily. 'She lost so much blood, though.'

'I'm not saying her injury isn't traumatic or that she won't need to be careful for a while, but there's no reason why she shouldn't make a full recovery.'

'I almost lost her once, Basia. I can't lose her again.' Izzy's voice trembles as she acknowledges her greatest fear.

'And you won't.' Basia pats her hand. 'I guess you've made up your mind, then?'

'I guess I have. I had better get used to waiting outside while Stanley is with her.' A sad smile pulls at her mouth.

Stanley appears in the doorway as if thinking of him had called the man. 'Ah, there you are. I thought I heard voices.'

Finding Basia in her nightclothes, his eyes go wide, and colour instantly stains his cheek up to the roots of his hair. His hand goes to his eyes, and he turns away, not knowing what to do with himself. 'Ah, um... I am sorry, um....'

At the sight of Stanley so awkward, Izzy bites back a laugh, something she would have thought impossible just moments ago.

'It is all right, Stanley. I am decent. What do you want?' Basia clearly does not feel the need to hide her amusement at Stanley's antics.

Turning back around, Stanley grins at the both of them. 'The nurse sent me out so Miss Ottaway can rest. She said the doctor is almost finished with Josephine and that there will be a few minutes before the sleeping draught takes hold when I might talk to her. So I came to find you, Isolde, so we can both go see her together.'

CHAPTER TWELVE
A NEW DAY

Harold isn't comfortable having guests in his new home, and in human form too. And he certainly isn't comfortable with them calling him Harold instead of Beta, regardless of Cynthia's advice that it would make him more approachable.

Cynthia enters from the kitchenette, carrying a coffee tray, and, as if sensing his discomfort, smiles at Nate and Izzy, who were still standing by the door.

'Goodness me, take a seat, both of you. Make yourselves at home. Harold, will you pour the coffee while I get the cakes?'

He fidgets while he waits for everyone to eat and drink. Harold has no idea why seeing Izzy and Nate in person has thrown him so off kilter. Over the years, he's spoken to them both so many times, they're almost family.

SUFFRAGETTE

Perhaps it's this face-to-face thing. It's going to take some getting used to. It's so much more... personal.

When everyone has finished and the small talk dies down, Harold leans forward in his seat, resting his elbows on his legs in what he hopes looked like a casual pose.

'Hem, ah, thank you for joining us this morning. Cynthia and I want to try a less formal way of closing off cases and thought meeting like this might be the trick. Well, we'll see how it goes.'

'Although, perhaps not so informal given your current dress.' Cynthia smiles at Izzy and Nate's turn-of-the-century clothing.

In spite of their efforts, the atmosphere in the room remains stilted, and Harold has to admit that changing the formal review process might be more difficult than he thought. Sighing inwardly, he says, 'All right, let's get started. Nate, where do things in Winchester stand now?'

'Well, Beta... um... Harold, Jason is being held in the local jail, pending formal charges being laid. They're still questioning him, but I understand Mr Parsons's evidence is quite damning. He claims Jason met him on the street at an anti-suffragette rally and convinced the man he needed to take positive action or he would be personally responsible for the breakdown of god's natural order.'

'Interesting,' Cynthia interrupts. 'We had wondered why history didn't eject him from the timeline. I should have guessed he was able to suggest a course of action to a local, and I'm sure there was no shortage of people prepared to go along with him.'

Nate nods. 'If it hadn't been Mr Parsons, he would easily have found someone else. Jason even provided the muscle. He met his co-conspirator in London before heading to Winchester. Barry needed to get out of town fast, as the police were looking for him. Jason facilitated his escape in return for help with his plan. Although, to be honest, I think Barry would have helped just for the fun of it.'

'What do you mean?' Harold asks.

'The police were looking for him with regards to some rather violent attacks on women. He's already on his way back to London to face those charges,' Nate expands.

Izzy shudders, perhaps imagining what a man like that could have done to Maisie had she been left there any longer.

'Izzy, where is Maisie now?' Harold asks.

'She's still at my aunt's house. When she's well enough, Augusta will take her back to London and see her safely settled back with her parents.'

'And the papers?' Cynthia prompts.

'They're being delivered to Miss Fielden as we speak, so she'll be delivering her speech today, as history recorded. Do either of you have any idea why this speech in particular was so important?' Izzy asks.

Cynthia shrugs. 'We're still not quite sure. We can't trace any particular historic movers and shakers to having heard it. We believe it may have influenced some local members of Parliament, but that's pure speculation. Or it might have some influence on a future event. We found references to it in some books, and it can easily be found on the internet, so maybe it has an impact on someone hundreds of years later. Or maybe Jason chose his victim simply because she knew you, Izzy.'

Izzy catches her bottom lip between her teeth. 'I would hate to think Maisie went through that nightmare because of me.'

'Whatever his reasons, you are not responsible for Jason's actions,' Cynthia reassures her.

'Definitely not, Harold says. 'Now, just one final thing before we're done. What about Alan? I understand Jason told him you all knew him from before?'

Nate smiles. 'It seems when Alan questioned Jason at the station, he was going on and on about time travel and that Basia was from the future. Of course, Alan wrote that off as hysterical rantings, and we didn't have to explain anything.'

Cynthia leans forward. 'What about the fact that Jason said he knew you?'

'Basia covered that. She said she might have met him when she was working with the poor up north, and he must have gotten her name wrong,' Izzy explains. 'Oh, and we told him that when I told Nate he could take Jason outside and do what he needed to do, I meant he should keep him out of Stanley's way by handcuffing him. It was a good thing there was no extraction or Alan would have really had something to be suspicious about.'

Nodding, Cynthia asks, 'So we don't have to fix a cover story or anything?'

Nate and Izzy shake their heads.

'Good, good, a most satisfactory outcome in the end,' Harold finishes off.

With the report complete, the room falls silent. No one wants to be the first to bring up the elephant in the room. As if avoiding the subject, Izzy asks, 'Do you know what will happen to Jason in the long term?'

Cynthia blows out a slow breath. 'Yes, well, that's a tricky situation. His parents are lobbying for his extraction from the timeline, but the Council is arguing that he's now too embedded in it to be removed without creating chaos. I suspect it's more that they want him to face the consequences of his actions for once.'

Nate rubs his chin thoughtfully. 'I hope his staying hasn't put your new venture at risk. I mean, you already have Alpha lobbying against you. Won't Jason's parents cause you even further problems?'

Cynthia turns and catches his eye, and he gets the message. Nate is too good to let go. However, he knows they'll have to tread gently if they want him on the team.

'It's true, they have been pretty active in trying to put up barriers for us to jump over, but we can handle them.' Harold shifts his gaze to Izzy. 'From our perspective the important thing is to keep Jason locked up for as long as possible.'

Izzy smiles. 'I second that. I hope they let him rot in prison for a long, long time. It'll save a few Time Fixer careers to have him sidelined for the time being.'

Aware she speaks from bitter experience, Harold says, 'I'm sure there are many agents who agree with you.'

'Speaking of careers, what now for you two?' Cynthia segues, finally getting to the real reason the two were invited here in person.

Izzy and Nate look at each other as though each is willing the other to speak first.

Nate is the first to break eye contact, although he can't look his old mentor in the eye. With his gaze firmly fixed on the ground, he starts.

'If I'm honest, I'm still not sure. I had thought to remain in this body, but I can't be the man who Hannah once spent the next two years with. I've changed too much, learned too much, and it wouldn't be fair to her.'

Harold doesn't want to ask the next question, but in his experience, all things are better out in the open. 'So you will choose to expire rather than return to the Time Guardians?'

Nate nods slowly. 'That's the way I'm leaning. I no longer believe what they're doing will benefit humankind. Besides, I was never really cut out for the hit-and-run lifestyle. Dropping into a time period, fixing things, then walking away doesn't suit my essentially homebody nature. So, I think it might be for the best.'

When it's clear Nate has finished speaking, Izzy takes over.

'I'm leaning towards leaving the Time Fixers and staying in my own timeline. However, I want to talk with Josephine and Stanley first and discuss whether what I have in mind will work or not.'

Cynthia raises an eyebrow. 'You would do that even though you know there's a war coming?'

'Yes, and perhaps my decision is all the more important because there *is* a war coming. We all have so little time together, and humanity seems to want to hurtle towards its own ending regardless of what I do to thwart it. If they continue ignoring warnings to change their ways, then all any of us can do is grab what happiness we can while we can.'

Perhaps we've lost her regardless of what we say next,

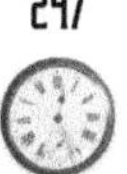

Harold sends to Cynthia.

I haven't given up on her yet.

'We have something we want the both of you to consider,' Harold says. 'You're aware we've been setting up a new joint taskforce. I'm sure you both expect to be invited to join, and we're inviting you now.'

Nate shuffles in his seat before turning to Izzy. Harold is sure that look is meaningful, but he can't decipher it.

Nate speaks for himself and Izzy. 'I'm not sure there's anything you can say to change our minds.'

'Please, hear Cynthia out before you make your final decisions. I think you will be pleasantly surprised by what we've worked so hard to get agreement on. Cynthia?'

Cynthia stands and hands out the booklets she had stashed under her seat.

'The details of what I'm about to tell you are in there. They're the operating guides for the new unit. In a nutshell, though, we won't be overseeing joint Time Fixer/Guardian missions but setting up a new team that Guardians or Fixers can apply to join.'

Seeing both Nate and Izzy about to speak, Harold holds up a hand. 'Let Cynthia finish.'

Cynthia smiles at him and continues. 'Both our organisations have always been limited by what we're able to achieve because if we interfere too much with the timeline, history will eject us. So, we want to place operatives in a time and let them live their lives as normal.'

Cynthia stops talking and waits for a reaction. Neither Nate nor Izzy speaks, and Harold once again can't read what they're thinking from their faces. This is a once-in-a-lifetime opportunity, so why aren't they more excited?

He rises to his feet and begins pacing around the room, unable to contain his enthusiasm in an inert body.

'There will be none of this dying and living outside of the world. We will no longer be limited to having to work through people living in a time period, because our agents will be a part of whatever is happening.'

'How does this change anything other than that we'll be able to act as individuals rather than through others?' Nate asks.

Finally, a reaction. Even if it is negative, it's better than being stonewalled. Harold has been expecting this criticism and is prepared for it.

'Well, that's where you're wrong. Though we'll still follow Time Guardian strictures on not removing or killing anyone critical to history—'

'And we won't fundamentally tamper with agreed key historic events,' Cynthia adds.

'What does that leave?' Izzy asks before Harold can finish the pitch.

'Ah, now this is the fun bit.' Harold is truly excited about his new team and unable to keep that feeling inside. 'We have identified key moments in history where the tide of human thinking almost changed but got stalled. We aim to place operatives in key positions to ensure those ideas gain traction.'

'Won't that change history?' Nate asks.

'Potentially, so we'll have to monitor it closely. What we're aiming for is that key events still happen, like the collapse of civilisations or the rise of leaders, no matter how much we abhor their actions. Underneath all of that, though, we want to have a groundswell of change that grows through the centuries so that after the war that leaves humanity's future in the balance, we end up with people left in key countries still working for a better future. People who want to destroy their weapons rather than turn them on one another. People who support diversity while they rebuild for the future.'

Harold turns his back to the window and faces the two agents he hopes to be the first two members of his new team. Cynthia sends him a nod of encouragement, but he's waiting on tenterhooks.

Izzy is the first to react. 'Okay, I get the big picture, but how will this work day to day?'

'Let's take you as an example, Isolde,' Cynthia says, making her pitch to win Izzy over. 'You would return to your original timeline in 1913 and continue to work as a journalist, and we would use our contacts to get you assigned to one of the less-major dailies. The idea we believe you could push forward is the rights of women. Women getting the vote and moving toward equality is a precursor for all minorities being accepted. If we can nudge the timeline even a little, we project that by the time World War Three comes along, equality will be so entrenched in human consciousness that it will simply become a part of the post-war world.'

'And a breakdown of the data shows this small shift will make it easier for the disparate communities to get along after the war,' Harold adds.

Izzy sits forward in her chair. 'So you have actual analysis that shows the acceptance of women as equals models the way for other marginalised groups in society to find their own voices?'

SUFFRAGETTE

'Yes,' Harold tells her. 'And if we also get enough resources to nudge at the edge of racism and acceptance of different sexual identities, look to find commonalities rather than differences, who knows what impact that may have on the future—we may even be able to prevent World War Three.'

'Prevent it?' Izzy asks. 'But it's an historic event.'

'Apparently not,' Harold tells them. 'There is some debate on whether it's a fixed event or not.'

'Okay. And if I'm back in my own time, I can still try and work things out with Jo and Stanley?'

Cynthia smiles. 'Yes, so long as you're able to take up the journalism job we sort out for you.'

Izzy asking questions is a good sign, and a spark of hope blossoms in Harold, but Nate is still not engaged. Time to draw him in with his own new life option.

'And you, Nate. We would like to place you into the 2010s. The rise of the Me Too Movement, along with Black Lives Matter in the United States, goes hand in hand with the rise of extreme right-wing politics and the rise of nationalism.'

Nate laughs. 'You want me to go in as a white liberal in one of the most volatile times in world history?'

'Not exactly. Well, yes, exactly that. We would like to place you in an organisation called Hope Not Hate in the United Kingdom. It has an interest in cleaning up social media to prevent the dissemination of misinformation.'

For the first time, there's a tiny spark of interest in Nate's eyes, but Harold doesn't want to celebrate yet.

'You would want me to live in that time because there would be no incarnations of me, because I officially died in 1914. Right?'

'Yes,' Cynthia says, 'but it would be a place and a time where you could set down new roots if you wished.'

Nate draws his bottom lip between his teeth. Finally, he says, 'You've given me a lot to think about.'

'Given us both a lot to think about,' Izzy says. 'Although, if I go down this path, I will miss working in other times.'

Cynthia smiles. 'Oh, we're not ruling out agents needing to help one another out from time to time if situations become volatile.'

Izzy grins. 'This is almost too good to be true. Let me talk with Stanley and Josephine. If I can get Jo to meet me halfway by moving to London, then I'll be able to be with them and also still work for you.'

I think we have her, Cynthia crows.

But not Nate. Harold is somewhat desolate that he might have lost his protégé after all these years working together.

The train is rocking back and forth, and Basia struggles to keep her eyes open. It had been an early morning start from Winchester to catch the bus to Portsmouth Harbour, then a short wait for the connecting train to Petersfield, where she and Alan will join the Pilgrimage for Women's Suffrage as they walk to Haslemere. Both trains had been packed with suffragists of both sexes and all walks of life, and it's quite a party atmosphere.

Glancing sideways at Alan, she chuckles. He's well out of his comfort zone with this group of people. In fact, Basia had been surprised when he offered to escort her when he found out she was intending to go even though Izzy couldn't accompany her.

Knowing he struggles with the idea of modern women, she had politely refused. He insisted.

'You have had a nasty bump on the head, and it is a long journey. It may not be my cup of tea, but as I feel somewhat responsible for your injury, it is a way for me to make things up to you.'

After self-consciously raising her hand to her bandage, Basia had assured him there was nothing to make up for. Then she explained that it would take more than a hit on the head and a couple of stitches to keep her from such an historic event.

Then Izzy had jumped in. 'Barbara, you really should not go alone, and Detective Barker does seem quite keen to take you.'

Too tired to argue, Basia gave in, and they agreed on a time for him to call the following morning. The detective had then taken his leave, as he wished to visit Josephine before heading home.

'I must apologise to her,' he said, 'although I have no idea what I can possibly do to make amends for causing her wounds.'

Izzy had widened her eyes as he closed the door, but Basia had forestalled any teasing.

'Don't say a word. He's doing his best to make up for his mistakes.'

'He's sweet on you,' Izzy sang.

'I need an escort, and he's offered. And that's all there is to it.'

Izzy had winked and responded, 'Of course it is,' and she'd been conspicuously absent when Alan called early this morning.

When the train stops, and they finally alight at Petersfield, he resolutely slips her hand through his arm and hangs back behind everyone else as they walk to the village square.

'Barbara, I have wanted to… that is, I feel I should formally apologise to you for my actions yesterday,' he says, nerves causing his hands to shake. 'It was my first time leading such an operation, and I did not cover myself in glory.'

A bit of an understatement. Basia is still a little annoyed at his attempt to leave her behind when they entered the house, as well as the fact that once everything was over, it had taken him a while to remember she'd been knocked unconscious and was left lying on the floor. In fact, it had been one of his constables who'd helped her up and into the sitting room. Instead of voicing all this, she tells him, 'You could have handled it better, I am sure.'

'Yes, well, I have been reflecting on my actions, and I am afraid I allowed my insecurities to get the better of me. I was uncomfortable with Nathanial taking charge, and I acted without considering all possible outcomes. I have made a list of things I need to work on for next time.'

Unsure about how she's supposed to respond to such an honest accounting of his behaviour, Basia simply says, 'We all make mistakes, Alan.'

Something in the tone of her voice, or perhaps the set

of her face, alerts Alan to the fact that she hasn't totally forgiven him.

'And I must atone for mine. I have apologised to everyone else, and now I must make amends to you in particular.'

A small smile begins to form at the edge of Basia's mouth. He's so earnest and so intent on making everything right, it's difficult to stay mad at him.

'I am pleased you have taken responsibility for your actions, and I am sure everyone has forgiven you. However, I do not think any of them will be letting you take charge of anything any time soon.' She nudges his arm and laughs, trying to lighten the moment, but Alan appears intent on vilifying himself for yesterday.

'They may have offered their forgiveness, but I am yet to forgive myself. If it were not for me, Jo would not have been injured.'

That's true, but there's no point in going over it again. Besides, they're coming up on the square, and Basia doesn't want to miss a moment of the march. As the square comes into view, it hits her that she's going to experience a bit of history first-hand. There is no way she's going to let Alan spoil this for her.

She turns back to Alan, and his face is sombre. She forces conviction into her voice and says, 'Maybe she might have, or maybe not. We have no way of knowing. I always think what is more important is learning from our mistakes, and maybe in the future, you will take time to read the room before acting.'

Basia hopes that will be the end to it, as women are spilling into the square from all sides, and someone on the back of a horse and cart is speaking through a megaphone. She steps forward, excitement racing through her, straining to hear the words and join the crowd. However, Alan stands firm, determined to get everything out in the open, and forces her to stay with him.

'If I am being totally honest, Barbara, I was already off balance when I entered the fray. You had been hurt, and I was angry at Jason for hitting you as well as at myself for not protecting you better.'

She knows she should say something placating, or even just say, *Can we talk about this later,* but history is happening around her, and she's becoming increasingly more impatient to join the march. Biting back a sigh, she makes herself speak calmly but forcefully. 'Remember what I said about reading the room—now is not a good time to discuss this. Besides, I neither wanted nor needed your protection yesterday.' The stricken look on his face causes her to pause a moment and add in a lighter tone, 'What happened to me was on my own head—excuse the pun.'

Even the attempt at a joke doesn't remove the hurt from Alan's face.

'I am sorry, Alan. I did not mean that to come out the way it did.'

'Gosh, I really have misread things. I thought we were getting along well… that perhaps we had… and I have gone and completely mucked it up.'

Guilt washes over her. Basia lets out a slow breath before turning to Alan and reaching out a hand to clasp his. 'We were… are getting on. I like you, and if I were staying in Winchester, I would probably want to get to know you better.'

He takes her other hand and raises hopeful eyes to meet hers, searching for something more—something she knows she shouldn't give.

'What I was referring to was your assumption that I would look to you for protection and to look after me. The world is changing, Alan, and although there will always be some women who look for that in their partners, I am not one of them. I intend to make my own way in the world, and anyone I choose to be with will need to understand that.'

As the words leave her lips, she realises she really means them. She's ready to go home and decide her next moves without the weight of Alan's expectations or her parents'. She isn't quite sure yet what that will look like, but she is sure she won't decide that hiding here in this make-believe existence.

'So you have made up your mind? You are heading back to London?'

It's time to be fair to them both and put an end to this... whatever it is.

'Yes, Alan, I am.'

'Are you sure I cannot tempt you to stay? Perhaps if we started over again?'

The way he looks at her with such intensity sets her heart racing. It would be so easy to say yes, to allow him to wrap his arms around her. To kiss those lips. She mentally shakes herself.

'Tempting though that offer is, this is not where I am meant to be.' Staring into his eyes she knows she could get lost in, she wills him to let her go as she's been forced to do with him. 'We can still be friends and enjoy today, can we not?'

'Ah, the friend gambit. There is no coming back from that, is there?' Alan says, doing his best to put on a brave face. 'If that is what you wish, we can try,'

As it turns out, enjoying themselves is easier than they expected. The atmosphere of the march is joyous, and the speeches are rousing—especially Miss Fielden's, although that may be because they know what Maisie had gone through to make sure the speech was perfect.

Basia sleeps on the train on the way home, allowing her head to drop onto Alan's shoulder. Something about their being together feels so right, and as he walks her back to Augusta's, her sadness grows.

This is the last time she'll be with Alan, and it would be so easy to let temptation take over logic, to rebel against what's right and let her desire take over, to at least have this one night with him.

He rings the doorbell, and as they wait for Jensen, he lowers his head and presses his lips to hers. The first touch is gentle, sweet. Then, as she responds, the kiss deepens, and a familiar fire begins to glow deep inside her.

At the sound of the locks being released, he draws back, and his green eyes meet hers. 'Goodbye, Barbara. If you ever change your mind, you know—'

'Where to find you,' she finishes, a smile hovering on her lips.

He tips his hat and jauntily walks off down the stairs, taking a piece of her heart with him.

CHAPTER THIRTEEN
EVERYONE IN THEIR PLACE

Izzy stands in the hallway, staring at the door. *I can do this!* No, she can't. Turning on her heel, she walks back towards the stairs, sucks in a breath, turns, and walks back to where she started.

It's time to face the music. Time to talk with Josephine and Stanley and find out once and for all if they could plot a way forward—together.

She takes a deep breath and knocks. When Josephine tells her to enter, she walks in, head held high, a smile on her face.

Josephine is propped up in bed, a book lying open on her lap. Stanley is sitting in his shirtsleeves in the chair by the window. A newspaper open to the finance section lies on the floor beside him, and his jacket is slung over the empty chair.

She falters at the domestic sight. 'I am sorry, you were talking. I did not mean to interrupt.'

'Nonsense,' Stanley tells her. He rises, pulls on his jacket, and brings the other chair in the room closer to the bed. 'Sit. Stay with us a while.'

Izzy perches on the edge of the chair, not quite knowing where to start. 'Ah, that is just it. I do not have much time. I have to pack, as I am going away for a couple of days, and I just wanted to check whether or not you will be here when I get back.'

Jo's brows draw together in a frown. 'Are you sure you are not running away again? Or that you are checking when we are leaving to find out when it is safe to return?

'Now, Josephine, give Isolde a chance,' Stanley says, patting Jo's hand.

Izzy sends him a grateful smile. 'I really do have to go. Barbara has to return to London, and it is only fair that I accompany her given that I dragged her all the way down here, then got her tangled in... everything.'

'Fair enough.' Jo tilts her head to one side. 'When are you planning to be back?' Her dark eyes flash a challenge, and Izzy resists the urge to look away.

She runs her sweaty palms down her dress, 'Well, that sort of depends on you.... Well, you and Stanley.' She glances from one to the other, then closes her eyes, trying to find the right words. When she opens them, the words just flow. 'I would like to attend your wedding, and I would like to stay as part of your lives, but I will not marry to make this work.'

Stanley's face breaks into a wide grin. 'You know where I stand. I always wanted you to be a part of our

family, damn convention.'

Jo sighs. 'As always, it comes down to me, and I will not fly in the face of convention. That is not in my nature.'

'I do have an idea—a way this might work for all of us,' Izzy says, 'if you will hear me out.'

'Go on,' Jo prompts.

'Aunt Augusta is going to approach my father and ask him if he will allow me to open his London house. She thinks she can convince him it is a good way to bring me back into the family fold.'

'I do not see how that helps,' Jo says, looking from Izzy to Stanley, then back to Izzy.

'Well, Lionel is due any moment now to pick up my story for his paper.'

'I thought he was meant to get it yesterday,' Stanley interrupts.

'He was, but he was late for his train and ended up staying the night in Guildford. Jensen informed me of the new arrangements this morning.'

Jo shifts in the bed. 'And how does Lionel fit into this? You have already said you will not marry him.'

'I thought to ask him if he would like to move out of the dump he is living in and move in with me.'

Jo's eyes sparkle with a flicker of amusement before she carefully schools her face again.

'That will cause a bit of a scandal with both of you being unmarried,' Stanley says, grinning as though he relishes the thought.

'So you will not marry him, but you will allow people to think you are living in sin?' Jo's voice is prim.

'Not exactly.' Izzy smiles. 'If you two move into the

master suite once you are married, you will be suitable chaperones for us. He can continue to bring his men friends home, and I can continue unmarried and still be chaperoned… and we can all be together.'

Jo cocks her head to the side, studying Izzy with an unconcealed intensity. 'Why not move into your father's house in Dorset, or into ours, for that matter?'

Izzy takes a deep breath. She knew this would be a stumbling block. However, part of her feels if she can accept Jo marrying Stanley, then Jo can meet her halfway and move to London. Besides, if she isn't in London, she can't work for a newspaper, and she can't be a part of Cynthia and Harold's new agency—and she would really like to do that.

'Oh, Josephine, you know I could not do that. You have your family's business interests to keep you occupied, but what would I do in the wilds of Dorset?'

'You could write for the local newspaper,' Jo offers.

'What, you want me to write about bake sales and fetes and the latest fashion? I would die a slow death.' Izzy shudders at the thought of it.

'Or you can be badly behaved and shock the local gentry like you used to,' Jo chuckles.

Izzy joins her. 'Still, Josephine, it is not a job.'

'London is not so bad, Josephine. There are shows and soirees, and you know you enjoy pitting your wit against Lionel's cronies,' Stanley says. 'You can run the business from anywhere, and Isolde can get on with her newspaper things. Besides, Dorset is but a train ride away. We can go back and forth anytime.'

Izzy stares at Jo, beseeching her to understand she's

shifted on letting Stanley into her life, and she now needs Jo to move a little, but she won't lose her over this. 'If you insist, then I will give up London.'

Jo's eyes widen. 'You are sure about this?' Her voice isn't particularly enthusiastic, and Izzy's stomach clenches as worry worms it way through her. She nods her answer, not trusting herself to say anything, lest she say the wrong thing.

'Well, you have given us something to think about,' Jo says, still scrutinising Izzy. 'How long—'

She's interrupted by a knock on the door.

'Come in,' Stanley says.

The upstairs maid pops her head through and searches for Izzy. 'Begging your pardon, miss, but Mr Lionel is in the morning room. He asked for you to join him immediately as he is on his way to catch a train.'

'I guess I will leave you to discuss my proposal, then,' Izzy says, relieved to leave the room.

After quickly slipping upstairs to retrieve her article, Izzy heads for the morning room. Her stomach is still churning, but she hopes she's schooled her face to hide her inner turmoil as she enters.

'My darling Izzy, whatever is the matter?' Lionel asks as he kisses both her cheeks.

Guess I'm not as good at hiding how I feel as I thought. Izzy smiles at Lionel. Then again, she has known Lionel far longer than she has Jo, and they have so much more in common, both living on the fringe of acceptable society as they do.

'Nothing... everything. Lionel, I am thinking about returning to London, and Aunt Augusta has said she will try and talk Father into allowing me to open his house.'

'Bravo. I never did like that boarding house you were in.'

'It is perfectly respectable,' Izzy responds, rising to the bait. 'Still, if Father says yes, and I can find a way to keep the gossips happy, would you like to come live with me—in your own room, of course?'

'Are you serious?'

'Yes. I mean, there is really only the Sewals to do for us, so it would be pretty basic.'

'Oh, poppet, you have seen where I am living. Tell me when you are moving in, and I will join you, gossips be damned.'

Relief rushes through her, making her light-headed. Even if Jo turns her down, Lionel will be there for her, helping her mend her broken heart.

Izzy flings her arms around him. 'Lionel, you know if I were ever to marry a man, or decided to let my mother down and marry for convenience, you would be my first choice.'

'You *are* a silly thing. Now, I must be on my way, or I will miss my train. Telegram me the details of your arrival. Oh, and in the meantime, I expect a thousand words on your adventure with Miss Maisie Ottaway. My editor says he will print it under your name, and, if it is any good, he will consider a regular column.'

Her breath catches in her chest. He can't be serious. 'Lionel, this is too cruel if you are teasing me.'

Lionel's Cheshire-cat grin splits his face. 'All totally above board, my pet. It seems your recent notoriety has made you marketable. Now, really, I must be off, or I will miss my return train.'

Izzy sees her friend out and heads back upstairs, her heart radiating such pure joy that her fear of what Jo and Stanley might say does little to dim it. She finds Jo alone in her room.

'Stanley has returned to the library to give us a moment alone.'

Izzy's stomach drops. Jo is so serious, Izzy knows what she's going to say, and she steels herself to take it without breaking down.

'You broke my trust when you ran away, and my heart as well. You will always be the love of my life, but....'

Here it goes. Be brave now, Izzy.

'...trust is everything to me. You need to earn that back before I can make a commitment to you being in our lives permanently.'

Izzy does a double-take. Is Jo turning down her offer or not?

'I am not sure what you mean,' she finally says.

'Stanley and I will move into the house in London with you—that is, if your father can be brought around—but it will only be a temporary arrangement.'

'What Josephine is saying,' Stanley says from the doorway, 'is that we will return to London after our honeymoon, and we will stay with you for six months. That is when I plan to leave for Australia to check on Josephine's father's holdings.'

'I had toyed with the idea of going with him because there was nothing keeping me in England,' Jo adds. 'If things work out, though, I may then decide to remain here while he is away.'

'Or maybe you will be so tired of the Big Smoke that

we might all set out on an adventure together,' Stanley says, unable to hide the gleam of excitement in his eyes. 'Do you not think it would be great fun to take on the New World together, just the three of us on safari in the Australian outback?' He walks towards her, rubbing his hands together like an excited child.

Izzy knows she's grinning deliriously. She hugs Stanley, then Jo, then Stanley again. 'I will not let you down, I promise.'

'All right, enough of this mush,' Jo says. 'I need my rest, and, Izzy, you have a train to catch. The sooner you go, the sooner you can get everything organised for us.'

This time she's reluctant to leave Winchester, but Izzy walks upstairs to her room on a cushion of air, safe in the knowledge that her future will be waiting for her when she returns.

Nate is about to knock on the door to Basia's room when footsteps on the stairs have him ducking into a doorway. Cook had allowed him in via the back door to say his farewells on the understanding he wouldn't compromise either lady's reputation. Actually, she made him promise on pain of death.

Now he's trapped and has nowhere to go. The door in front of him opens, and Basia's head pops out. Finding him cowering in the doorway, she sends him a "What on earth do you think you're doing?" look.

He straightens himself up and brushes down his suit.

'Are you coming in, or are you going to stand out in the hallway all day?' Basia asks.

'I … um… shouldn't….'

'If you're worried *I* will say anything about your being in a lady's bedroom, then you're mistaken,' Izzy chuckles as she joins them. 'Besides, it's almost respectable, now I'm here to chaperone you.'

'You're in a good mood,' he says, trying to hide his very Nathanial embarrassment.

'I am, aren't I?' Izzy says as she virtually pushes him into the bedroom before closing the door behind them. 'To what do we owe the pleasure of your visit without the lovely Hannah?'

'I heard on the grapevine that Barbara is returning to London, so I thought I had best come and say goodbye to Basia before you return her home,' he tells them. 'Although I'm surprised you're leaving so soon. I thought you might want to take a couple of days to enjoy Winchester before heading back.'

Basia grins. 'I think it would all be too quiet for me after the excitement of the last few days.'

'Besides, if she stays any longer, she'll be back to fighting off an amorous detective,' Izzy chuckles.

'Yes, I'm not sure I could let him down gently a second time.'

'You mean you might rip his clothes off and do something you might regret later,' Izzy teases, mischief gleaming in her eyes.

Rather than joining in the fun, Nate studies Izzy closely. She'd been but a shadow of herself the last couple of weeks, and it's heart-warming to see the old Izzy again.

'What?' Izzy says, catching him staring at her.

'Nothing. It's just, you're different. You're Izzy again.'

Her smile lights up her face. 'Yes, I am, aren't I? I'm staying in my world, and I'm going to take up Cynthia and Harold's offer. I finally feel like I'm where I want and need to be.'

'You know, with spending most of your time here rather than in headquarters, you'll start ageing again,' Nate teases.

Izzy contorts her face into one of mock fear. 'Oh no, I guess I'll have to give all this up.'

Basia laughs along with Izzy, but Nate can barely manage a smile.

'You, on the other hand, seem even more sad and detached,' Basia says, placing a hand on Nate's arm. 'You may not want to hear this, but it would be a shame for the world to lose you. I wouldn't have any life to go back to if it weren't for you—and I bet there are many other people who feel the same way.'

Izzy is nodding. 'I chose to work with you more than once, Nate, even though our organisations were at loggerheads. It would be such a shame for you to melt out of existence. You deserve better than that. Besides, I shall miss you, even if we won't see each other as often.'

He looks from one woman to the other, and a sigh escapes his lips. 'A part of me is proud of what I've achieved, I really am. It's just, I'm....' He stops, unsure of how to put his feelings into words.

'You're not happy,' Basia offers.

He considers this for a moment, then nods. 'Yes, that's

exactly it. I'm not happy, and I'm not sure I can even place a finger on when I last was.'

Now it's Izzy's turn to study him, and tears come to her eyes as they find the bleakness in his. 'You know, Nate, if I have learned anything these last few days, it's that happiness does not just happen. Life is full of chances and opportunities to be happy, but sometimes you have to be prepared to take a risk and reach for those opportunities when they present themselves.'

Nate's brows drop into a frown. 'I'm not quite sure what to say to that, Izzy.'

'Oh, Nate, you goose. I'm saying that for so long, you've bound your happiness to Hannah, and when she stopped making you happy, you didn't know where to look next. Now you've finally let her go, you should take the time to find out what truly makes you, Nate, happy. Only to do that, you have to be brave and take the first step.'

'And what would that look like, in your opinion?' he asks with a touch of curiosity.

Basia moves to stand beside Izzy. 'It doesn't look like staying here with Hannah.'

'Nor perhaps returning to the Time Guardians, where you'll more than likely run into Theta,' Izzy adds.

'Exactly,' Basia chimes in. 'You need a fresh start.'

'If you don't like the one Cynthia and Harold offered you, negotiate another.'

'But don't simply allow yourself to blink out of existence before you've even tried,' Basia finishes up.

Nate holds his hands up in front of him, but he's smiling, really smiling, for the first time in days. 'Whoa, guys, I get the picture.'

'Good,' Izzy says, 'because I, for one, cannot bear the thought of not ever seeing you again.' She wipes a tear from her eye before it has a chance to fall.

Nate finds she isn't the only tearful one. He hadn't realised how strong his bond to Izzy had grown. Somehow, throughout their adventures, they've become friends, and the thought of her not being in his life saddens him.

'All right, I'll think about it. That's all I can promise. Now, I have very little time, as an operative is being sent to restructure Nathanial's memories to integrate my takeover with his life. Then I… I mean *he*—considering I'll no longer be inside Nathanial—has a lunch with Hannah to discuss whether the new and improved Nathanial still wants to be with her.'

'And will he?' Basia asks.

Nate shrugs. 'I have no idea. The original Nathanial would have fallen at her feet and begged forgiveness. However, he'll retain some memory of what happened and his role in the rescue, sans the Time Guardian bits, and that has to have changed him. So, anything might happen.'

'And when you're released from his body?' Izzy asks.

'I'll return to Time Guardian headquarters to finish my sabbatical. Then it's decision time. And before you say it, I will take your thoughts into consideration.'

The two of them smile at each other.

'Then our job is done,' Basia says, leaning over and kissing him on the cheek. 'Thank you for saving my world, and for being… well, for being you. I'll miss you.'

'And I shall miss you too,' he tells her.

'No you shan't,' Izzy says, 'because whatever time you choose to live in, the original Barabal—or Barbara or

Bebe or Basia, whatever reincarnation is in that time—will gravitate towards you, and so will the others.'

He frowns at her, and her face takes on a belligerent set.

'Don't you look at me like that, and don't you dare say goodbye, because we *will* see each other again.'

Before he can answer, she gives him a quick kiss on the cheek and storms from the room.

Basia pushes herself through the dark, filmy gauze of the portal, fighting for her breath as the diaphanous film clings to her face, fighting her way to the future—her future. As if sensing a part of her is reluctant to return home, travelling back is more difficult than leaving had been. It's as though time is holding on to her, giving her a chance to change her mind. She stumbles, struggling to find her footing as the gateway spits her out behind a building in the Portsmouth dockyards.

'Wasn't that fun?' Izzy says, grinning. 'Well, welcome home.'

Basia's stomach roils as she surveys the dockyard, pinkish in the early morning light. 'How long have I been gone?' she asks.

'We left last night. As promised, only Johan knows where you've been, and he covered for you to make sure no one interrupted your sleep.'

'And you're certain no one can see my stitches?' Basia tugs at the headband Izzy had given her before touching the now yellowish bruise around her eye. Izzy had concealed it with make-up, popping the tube into her pocket for Basia to use until everything healed.

'You look fine. Grab a hat and keep it low, and no one will notice.'

'And Lee? Is he still here?'

'Of course. Theta will come and get him in one month. That ought to give him time to get fixing this world out of his system.'

'That'll be odd, now that I've met her as Hannah. Hey, will she remember having met me before?'

Izzy frowns. 'I have no idea. I've never been around to see how altering someone's timeline affects them in the future. You'll have to find some way to let me know.'

Basia laughs. 'No worries. I guess that will be the least of the odd things I face. I mean, I've been through so much, it seems strange coming back here where nothing has changed at all.' As she speaks her stomach churns, and she's not sure whether what she's feeling is excitement at returning home, disorientation at having been away, or trepidation over what's to come next.

'I wouldn't quite put it that way,' Izzy tells her. 'It was a busy night here in Portsmouth. The Commander and his Council have been up all night, working to find a way to defuse tensions between Portsdown and the outlying communities. Last report was that he was almost at his wits' end.'

'And what about Portsdown?' Basia asks.

'Theta is probably still there, trying to keep things calm and talking them down from using the weapons they've stockpiled in their bunker, or trying to convince the Time Guardians not to call her back until things are more settled.'

Izzy's eyes cloud over, and as she communicates with someone, Basia sighs. The gulf between the peoples seems as insurmountable as ever, and the plan she's been working on in her head will take time to implement and take hold. Would it be enough?

Izzy's gaze refocuses. 'Beta said Theta is still here. The timeline is still in the red, so it'll be some time before they can release her. Are you sure you want to stay? I can always take you back to your detective.'

Basia laughs, as she was sure Izzy intended her to. 'No, I'm where I'm meant to be, and I think it's time for this reincarnation to find a life away from Allan. Besides, I have some ideas that I think might work to help bring things out of the red.'

'Ah, so you've been inspired by the leaders of the suffrage movement as Nate thought you might be.'

Basia shakes her head. 'No, quite the contrary, and it isn't because I don't want to be a leader of a great movement. It's because I think we've put too much emphasis on leadership, and the Commander here has shown me there's another way—change by consensus. I like the way he talks, and listens, and builds a solution along with the people who follow him.'

'So, if you don't want his job, what do you want to do?'

Basia grins. 'I still want to be what I always wanted to be—a healer... a doctor.'

'What about what Allan was working for?'

Sadness seeps its way into Basia's heart. Being back home brings the raw hurt of her soulmate's loss back to the forefront of her mind. She doesn't want to let him down, but she's her own person, and she can't take on his fight. At least not in the way he would, and she has to believe he wouldn't want her to.

'Not only do I not want to lead and inspire people, but I have learned that great people and big ideas aiming for a shift in society can sometimes create fear. And that fear often alienates people who might otherwise have supported what they're working towards.

'Look at the difference between the suffragettes and the suffragists. They both worked for the same end, but suffragettes ended up polarising people, whereas suffragists worked on bringing everyone along with them.'

'So you're saying the suffragettes were wrong to aim big and push hard?' Izzy asks, frowning.

'Yes... no. I'm not sure. All I know is, here and now, in this time, we can't afford to polarise anyone—the stakes are too high. Perhaps we need to learn to walk together for a while before we start pushing for radical change.'

Izzy nods, a thoughtful look on her face. 'Funny, over the past week, I've been thinking very similar things myself.'

Emboldened by Izzy's support, Basia stands taller. 'I think if we can build some communities of interest to share ideas, then that will be a step in the right direction. Allan's growers could work with our farmers. Portsdown's medics with our healers. Even their soldiers with militia. My hope is that as we share ideas, understanding and friendships will grow, and then we might find we're more alike than we are different.'

'And with understanding maybe will come change for the better.'

'Thank you for everything, Izzy. I wouldn't be here, literally physically or emotionally, if not for you.' Basia sniffs and wipes her eyes.

Izzy's face softens with a look of quiet pride. 'You would have gotten here eventually.'

Basia throws her arms around the Time Fixer who's become her closest friend and hugs her tight. 'Who knew saying goodbye would be so hard? I will miss you, Izzy.'

'And I you.' Izzy's voice chokes.

'Not so much, I think,' Basia gives Izzy one last squeeze. 'You have a new adventure to start. You'll soon forget me.'

'Never,' Izzy swears, wiping the tears from her eyes.

'Basia, you're back.' Johan's voice cuts through the morning air, preventing the scene from getting even mushier than it already is.

Her brother pulls up when he realises Izzy is still with her, and he grins. 'You're still here. Does this mean you're staying?'

'I'm sorry, Johan, but no. I have somewhere I must be.'

The sadness in his eyes batters Basia's already tender heart.

'I thought...,' he starts, then trails off.

Izzy reaches out and takes his hand. 'Once, I may have taken you up on that offer, believing it may have been enough. But I know for sure your true love is out there somewhere, as is mine. You just need to be patient and not settle for anything less.'

Their eyes lock, and the emotion running between them is tangible enough for Basia to believe she could reach out and touch it. She turns away to give them a little privacy as fresh tears trickle down her cheeks.

'Come on, Johan. Izzy has things she has to do, and you need to help me find the Commander. I want to talk to him about something.'

Reluctantly her brother steps away but stops by Basia's side, not taking his eyes from Izzy until she's opened her portal and returned home. Reaching for Johan's hand, Basia gives him a squeeze of support.

With his other hand, Johan brushes the tears from his eyes and clears his throat. 'All right, Basia, tell me what's so urgent. I hope you're not thinking of taking off on another harebrained adventure.'

His face is back to his normal mix of bossy with a faint smile. Basia chuckles. It's good to be home.

EPILOGUE
AGENCY HEADQUARTERS
– JUST TO THE LEFT OF TIME

Harold curls his legs underneath him on the sofa and wraps an arm around Cynthia, who drops her head onto his shoulder.

He takes a sip of whiskey and sighs. 'Well, that was a trial, wasn't it?'

'One day you'll have to stop expecting Alpha to treat you with anything but disdain,' Cynthia says, giving his thigh a squeeze to take the sting out of her words.

'You're right. It'll never happen, no matter how many millennia we live for. The only consolation is that now, no matter what he says when he goes back to the Council, it will change nothing. Everything is finally signed and sealed.'

Cynthia clinks her glass to his. 'Cheers,' she says.

'As of now we're operating independently of day-to-day oversight by either Council, unless a major incident appears on either of their horizons.'

Cynthia raises her head, then swings around to face him. Has he said something to upset her? No, she isn't frowning. There's a gleam in her eye, like she's excited.

'I was going to wait until after dinner, but I just can't. I had the techies rush through the monitoring feeds on our first two recruits, and they set up a link so we can see what's happening from here.'

A frisson of excitement fills the room. He so wants to look at the feeds, but first he wants to thank Cynthia for... well... being her. He leans forward and touches his lips to hers. 'Thank you,' he says. 'This is the best present ever. Well, apart from you.' He kisses her again. 'You surprise me and challenge me, and I'm so lucky I found you.'

She returns his kiss, then pulls away. 'Yes, you are lucky to have me, and I want you to hold that thought until after we test these links.' A frown line appears between her brows. 'Is that bad? To put snooping on our agents first?'

He leans over, pecks her cheek, then picks up the vid control. 'If it is, then I'm bad too. Let's see what we have.'

He presses button one, and the picture enlarges to show Izzy sitting in a room across from a man, who has his back to them.

'Is that—'

Cynthia chuckles. 'What timing. Izzy is on one of her three monthly visits to Jason.'

'Ooh, she doesn't look happy. I guess she won't be

sending a report telling us he's taken responsibility for his actions and is ready to be extracted.'

Somehow the thought of Jason spending another three months in a turn-of-the-century British prison does nothing to bring his mood down. In fact, he would be perfectly content if Jason was never to return.

'I had hoped to see her at home,' Cynthia says. 'Josephine and Stanley should be returning from their honeymoon any time now.'

'Oh well, we get what we get,' Harold says. 'I mean, normally we'll only be watching if an anomaly occurs, once we've thoroughly tested the feeds.'

'Testing could take a little longer than expected, though,' Cynthia says. 'Not that I want to spy on anyone, and obviously, I wouldn't watch any intimate moments, but Izzy is like a daughter to me, and what mother doesn't want to make sure their child is all right?'

Harold laughs. 'Every parent, I should imagine, but you'll just have to limit yourself to watching anomalies and those times agreed on with Izzy.'

Cynthia sighs dramatically. 'I am so lucky to have you to help me follow the rules.'

'Shall we test the feed to our other operative?'

'Of course.'

Harold presses button two, and the screen opens up on a room full of people. Some are dressed in civilian clothes, and others are wearing what could only be described as hospital scrubs.

'There she is.' Cynthia points to a woman standing at the front of the room, talking as a slide is projected onto the wall. 'Is she doing a talk on medicinal plants? I can't quite see without my glasses.' Cynthia leans forward, squinting at the screen.

'You know, your glasses make you even more attractive. You should wear them more often.'

Cynthia chuckles. 'Flattery will get you nothing unless you tell me what you see.'

'Yes, she's talking about medicinal plants. And if you had your glasses on, you would be more interested in the doctor sitting to her right. He can't take his eyes off Basia, and every now and then, she catches him watching. I can't be sure, but I think she's blushing.'

'Oh, how exciting.' Cynthia says. 'Are you sure you don't want to check in on the sly a little to see how that romance might go?'

'Cynthia!'

'Just asking.' She smiles, then reaches over and takes the controller from him. 'You are a true rule follower, but I'm doing this, and I'm doing it for you. He hasn't fully agreed to join us, but I had them set up the feed just in case.'

The picture shifts to a young man sitting in an office across the desk from an older man. A file between them seems to hold their attention. A young woman enters the room, the three speak for a moment, and then the young man rises to leave. The woman appears to be encouraging him to stay, but he shakes his head.

As he opens the door, the image flickers, and a crackle of static comes from the speakers.

'Oh, how exciting. They have the sound up and running,' Cynthia says.

'Shh, we might miss something interesting.'

280

'...toy with him, Minnie. Nate is good with the kids, and I can't afford to lose another councillor. We're struggling to keep our funding as it is, and I don't want to have to go back to Dad and beg for help.'

The girl is still looking at the door, a dreamy smile on her face. 'Who's toying, Charles? I think this one might be a keeper.'

ABOUT THIS BOOK
WHAT IS FICTION AND WHAT IS REAL

Many years ago I studied Women's History in the late nineteenth and early twentieth century. Since then I've been interested in how women have been sidelined and treated as wives and daughters throughout the centuries. It was no surprise to me when many of them fought physically to be treated as individuals when they were constantly denied their rights.

Like Izzy in Suffragette I have never been comfortable with what they did, but I can understand why they did it. How frustrating must it have been to be told your voice did not matter. That frustration is being voiced again with many groups around the world today, and I can only hope we have learned from history, and that they will not need to resort to violence to be recognised and valued.

Although I drew heavily on historic records for *Suffragette,* all the main characters in this book are fictional, and most of the events described did not happen—except for in my imagination that is.

The suffragette and suffragist organisations mentioned did exist, and The Women's Pilgrimage was real. A Miss Fielden did give a speech at Haslemere, but her secretary, Maisie Ottaway, is definitely fictional.

I could find very few details about Miss Fielden and believe she may have been the daughter of a member of Parliament who supported the movement to give women the vote. If I have this wrong it is simply because Miss Fielden leaves very little trace even with all the data on the internet.

Emily Davidson was also a real figure, and was considered a martyr by suffragettes when she threw herself in front of a horse on Derby Day 1913. Recent research has questioned whether or not she may have tripped, turning her death into a tragic accident rather than a political protest. I have chosen the second version of events for the purposes of this book.

The Fielding family do exist, and I came across them when trying to track Miss Fielden when I mistyped her name into a search engine. They were part of the peerage and a politically well connected family. I hope they don't mind me inserting Izzy into their family tree for the purposes of this story.

I have attempted to make this story as historically accurate as possible, and I apologise for any glaring mistakes, or maybe they aren't mistakes but simply history correcting the timeline.

ABOUT THE AUTHOR

Vivienne has been writing books since she was fifteen years old, but only friends and family were allowed to read them. Forced to give up work because of family commitments she was encouraged by friends and family to finally put some of her writing out there for others to read.

In the real world after leaving university with a BA in History and Politics she worked as a Personnel Officer, an Office Manager, a Project Manager, a DBA and IT Manager then as a Business and Data Analyst, adding an MSC in Information Systems along the way. In her world she continued to write.

Born in Invercargill (New Zealand), she has lived in; Dunedin (New Zealand), London (England), Petersfield (England) and currently lives with her husband and son, their dog Trouble and kitten Lola in Sydney (Australia).

If you are interested in her future releases, or simply want to find out more about her books, you can find Vivienne at **www.viviennelfraser.com.au** or on Facebook at **www.facebook.com/vivienneleefraser**

ACKNOWLEDGEMENTS

Five years ago in a hospital room this series shouted at me to be written. This series of books more than any other is rooted in my family and in my early loves of writing and history. I'm sadden to be finishing the series with *Suffragette*, but I'm sure you noticed I've given myself the option of resurrecting some of the characters should the urge take me.

If you've read the previous books you know I have borrowed heavily from my family history for these stories and, indeed, from some of my actual family members. I want to thank them for allowing me to do that, and for not mentioning it at family get togethers.

I always say it takes a community to turn a story into a novel, and this time I mean it more than ever. While writing and editing this book I've been dealing with a number of health issues. Some of the time I have been on such strong painkillers I'm surprised anyone could make any sense of what I wrote.

The fact that you have read this as a cohesive story is due solely to the editing team who supported me in getting this book out. Sali Benbow-Powers from the Creating Ink Team, thank you so much for helping me find Basia's voice, and for encouraging the more romantic elements of the story.

McKinley Hellenes Krantz and Kristen Scarce from Hot Tree Editing, this time you guys went above and beyond. Not only did you have to put up with my inability to concentrate on tenses, you also helped with separating out modern dialogue from historic. I really appreciate your commitment to the details—and I'm sure everyone reading did too.

Thanks to Kim Last from KILA Designs, who has managed, once again, to produce an incredible cover and a print version of the book that I love so much.

No acknowledgement would ever go out without a thank you to Jim and Sam who always support me by feeding me, bringing me drinks, and keeping the house going so I can meet editing guidelines.

And thank you to you for reading my stories. I'm always amazed and humbled when someone enjoys what I write.

9 780645 515763